BARD TO THE BONE

LUNA RYDER

Editor: Crystal Lee Wren, COL Proofreading
Designer: S.J. Gautreaux, Night Witchery

This is a work of fiction. Names, characters, organizations, places, events, and incidents are either products of the author's imagination or are used fictitiously. Any resemblance to actual persons, living or dead, or actual events is purely coincidental.

PO Box 873543
Wasilla, AK 99687

1

We now stood at the Precipice in every sense—well, except for the *standing* part. We were actually walking quite swiftly as Dayna led our group straight to the evil necromancer's lair in pursuit of the Genesis Crest. She didn't know that I had her mission objective tucked snugly beneath my tunic, that I'd had it for ten long years.

She didn't know, and I preferred to keep it that way.

The ice-blue bundle of scales and limbs held in Calina's arms made a curious noise halfway between a squeak and a roar. I turned to look and found Frosty, our recently acquired ice dragon hatchling, with his head tilted to the side as he awaited an answer to whatever question he had just asked.

"Yeah, I know it's not as cold as you would like, but this is the Void. There's nothing I can do about it," Calina said with a sigh. This exchange reminded me so much of watching the girl with her mother that I had to hold back a chuckle. Maybe now that she had to contend with a youngling of her own, Calina would finally cut poor Brynlee some slack. Maybe... but probably not.

I raised a brow and turned to the pair. "So you can really understand him?"

I have to admit that I was impressed by this development. Back in Mystwood Keep, she'd wandered off one night and returned the next day with the sudden ability to communicate with the cluster of dragons gathered within the throne room—and not only could she talk to them, but she could also command them. She'd orchestrated the whole escape and eventual ruin of the regent and his stupid castle.

Calina shrugged as if none of it mattered much in the scheme of things. "I don't understand all his words, but I understand his intentions. It's not too hard to do, I think trying to explain is harder than actually doing it. Actually, I'm surprised it took me this long to figure out."

This modesty would've been charming if it wasn't so wildly aggravating. Just like me, the girl was overly hard on herself. Always aiming to conquer the next challenge rather than take some time to celebrate her victories.

"Well, what's he say?" I pressed with a grin.

"Skr, skr, skr, skr, skr, skr, skr, skr," Frosty responded, narrowing his serpentine eyes at me with great interest.

I shook my head at him in confusion, then turned to Calina. But before she could translate, Frosty started hacking mightily. It was as if a small bone had gotten stuck in his throat.

Calina hugged the dragonling to her chest with uncharacteristic tenderness. "He's upset because he can't make frost right now. He says that even in Myst-wood Keep, he could still make frost."

"Is making frost essential to his survival?" I craned my neck to get a better look at the distressed creature. He seemed fine to me.

"I don't know," Calina responded impatiently. "But you know who would know? *Rurik.* Rurik would know, but he's not here. We have to find him. And Tulip, too, I guess."

"Keep quiet back there," Dayna barked, not even

bothering to turn back as we struggled to waddle after her.

Well, *I* waddled. Calina kept a much more graceful gait, even with the added inconvenience of holding the baby dragon. Even as a hatchling, Frosty was already at least as big as a cat and the two hadn't developed a comfortable position for carrying him.

And despite Dayna's insistence otherwise, it was already quiet—far too quiet. This place felt more like a mausoleum—like something had once lived here, breathed here, laughed and cried and screamed here... and then just stopped.

Even our footsteps made no sound. No crunch of gravel or tap of boot on stone. Almost like the ground itself was soaking up any and all sound, not unlike water poured out on the desert. It was unsettling in the worst kind of way. No wonder the necromancer liked it so much.

"We're going with your plan," Calina bit back in a dead-on imitation of her mother's no-nonsense tone. One that was regularly used on her rather than by her. "The least you can do is let us talk. A lot's happened. We kind of need a recap here."

I smirked, happy that the kid said the hard things, so I didn't have to.

Honestly, Dayna scared me—not just a little, but a

lot. Sure, I was handy with a dagger, but she was a ruthless, bloodthirsty mercenary. And while she didn't have a dagger, that I could see, she did have swords—two of them.

She was also incredibly irritable.

"I'd much prefer you kept quiet," Dayna snapped. The battle-hardened woman never said anything; all her words were barked, spat, or otherwise spoken with extreme disgust and force. "We're almost to the lair, and we need to make a plan. It's hard for me to think with all your yammering, so shut up already."

"And I thought Tulip was mean," Calina huffed, hoisting the dragonling higher against her chest.

"Shuff-shuff-shuff," Frosty seemed to agree.

I said nothing. Instead, I took the opportunity to glance around the vast nothingness we found ourselves in. The Void was the place where magic had been ripped from the land during the Great Fae War.

The World Tree that fed Verandel had been poisoned and torn from the ground, leaving behind an ugly, horrible scar. At first, mage scholars tried to study it, but soon, they couldn't survive the depressing, desiccated landscape. They abandoned their enclave before it could destroy them. Not long after that, Maltherius moved in, claiming their old research station as his villain's lair.

His imposing fortress, known as the Precipice, loomed large before us as it hung clear over the abyss.

And when I say "hung," I mean it in every sense of the word—like some skeletal hand had reached up and grabbed the edge of the Void. At first glance, the blackened tower could've been mistaken for a minor keep or a lesser noble's castle. But most of the structure's mass lay in the very Void itself. Broken crenellations ringed the top, like a brawler that blocked hits with his face. And the structure itself seemed to give off a sickly miasma, the fractured walls bleeding with faint magic. It pulsed like the heartbeat of something ancient and not quite dead. The worst part was that if I stared at it too long, I swore it stared back... And dear sweet divinity, I simply couldn't pull my eyes away.

I'd been here before—ten years ago with Gaaron—and he was the only reason I had now willingly returned. Ever since I found out that he was still alive, part of me had spent every second worrying about his safety and wondering how I could help him regain his freedom. And still, I worried. But I also had other, even greater concerns to contend with now.

Three annoying teenagers had wormed their way into my heart. And thanks to an unfortunate turn of luck, the two biggest and loudest of them were no longer with us.

When Dayna and the other wing scouts had cast the teleportation spell from Mystwood Keep, it had gone wrong, and our party had been split. My clumsy and awkward half-orc wizard and spoiled princess centaur barbarian were lost in the great unknown.

I didn't even know if they were together, with Finnian, or all alone. Considering everything else, I wasn't sure which of the options was worse.

Whatever the case, I was scared for them. The kind of scared that settles low in your gut and simmers, slow and quiet, like a stew left too long on the fire.

I hadn't realized how much they'd meant to me until they were gone. Not just as students or companions—but as people. Tulip, with her endless rage barely masking her boundless loyalty. Rurik, brilliant and earnest and heartbreakingly fragile under his orcish bravado.

I wasn't just their mentor—I was their Tilda. And they were my kids now.

Mine to protect.

Mine to lose.

As soon as I'd realized what had happened, my instincts screamed for me to reunite our party before we did anything else, especially given that Rurik's new celestially imbued powers were too strong for him to handle.

He needed me.

I'd signed on as their mentor—reluctantly, well press-ganged into it—but now I fully embraced a role I'd never considered for myself. It was my responsibility to keep Rurik safe not just from Maltherius and Finnian Sly but also from himself.

It was my responsibility. And I wasn't there.

Still, I knew better than to go against Dayna's plan. I wouldn't be able to win a fight with her, so the best I could do was play along while secretly working toward my own ends.

That's why we were charging straight into the necromancer's lair rather than searching for the two of them first.

Our mercenary "friend" believed we were retrieving the artifact. Given that this specific artifact was still with me, I knew we'd instead be rescuing Gaaron—bard extraordinaire, my former partner, and Calina's long-lost father.

Once we located him, I would have to think quickly to keep Dayna on task and on our side. It would help if I could discuss all this with Calina. She was a good thinker, and I needed her input.

Previously, we'd written messages back and forth on an old map when we were worried that Finnian was listening through a sending stone. *Oh, the sending stone!*

I reached into my pocket and extracted the smooth obsidian, holding it to my lips as I murmured, "Hello, hello, is this thing on?" If Finnian had the receiver, we could find out where he'd landed and whether he had the other kids with him.

"Hi, Tilda," Levvy's cheerful voice greeted me. "Johan is taking me to the forest. Isn't that great?"

This was, in fact, great news. It seemed my former mentor had adopted the half-dryad child. Together, they could escape their cruel masters and live out their days in nature. I was happy for them.

The tiniest weight lifted off my chest at the sound of the young druid's voice. Just a sliver of relief, like finding a patch of shade in the middle of a heatwave. One kid safe. Two more to find and protect.

"Tell Johan I say hi and that I hope to visit soo—"

"SILENCE!" Dayna boomed at maximum volume. The two sharp syllables seemed to shake the entire Void, echoing her rage and sending it vibrating through me in a way I did not much care for. Of course the echo stopped at us. Whatever deadened the noise here, didn't allow sound to carry like it should.

"Ouch, stop being so loud." Calina held her dragonling companion half over her shoulder with one arm and swirled a finger in her ear to clear her hearing.

"I have to be loud, so that you will hear me over your own mindless yammering. Now, no more words. Only forward movement toward our goal," Dayna rasped as if that last forceful shout had caused her some lingering pain.

I smirked. Served her right.

"Do you have our map?" I whispered to Calina after a few silent moments had passed. We were moving very quickly now, and it would be challenging to scribble our notes to each other, but some communication would still be better than none.

A knowing smile lit Calina's elven features. "Oh, yeah, sure."

Then, just as quickly, the smile dimmed. "The supplies are with Rurik, I think. Or, at least, they're not with us. Ugh, even my bow and quiver are gone."

For the love of the blessed mother, this was not good. We wouldn't last long without supplies. Then again, we probably wouldn't last long heading straight into the most powerful dark magic user's lair, either.

"Okay, so what if we—" I began, but Dayna cut me off with a snarl.

"If words aren't enough to keep you quiet, I can

gag you. And if that fails, I'll have to resort to the blade."

I opened my mouth to speak but thought better of it when Calina sucked air in through her teeth and shook her head.

"I really don't like her," she whispered, using one hand to cover the front of her face so her words were less likely to reach our angry taskmaster.

Well, if we couldn't talk with words—spoken or written—maybe we could...

I stretched both arms high overhead and tried to draw the shape of a centaur.

Calina studied me with narrowed eyes, then nodded and began to motion back, creating the outline of Rurik—or so I assumed.

I nodded and began trying to relay the plan.

As much as there was one, anyway.

"Stop being so loud," Dayna snapped, this time turning to face us with a wicked glint in her eyes. Her necklace of battle trophies flopped against her chest, catching my attention. Amidst the shrunken pygmy skulls and assorted bones and feathers was one very recognizable tusk. I'd watched her rip it from the mouth of my half-orc companion in cold blood to punish him for standing up to her with his flame cantrip. I'd been so proud of him for that and then so horrified by her reaction.

I suspected Calina noticed it, too, because she shuddered and hugged Frosty tighter to her chest. "We literally weren't even saying anything."

"Your movements are loud. Stop it."

"Don't we need to discuss our plan for infiltration and retrieval of the artifact?" I asked, attempting a more affable approach.

Dayna stopped briefly and made eye contact with me as she said, "I'm working that all out. On my own. Which is why I need you to stop all of this." She puffed out her cheeks and waved her hands around like a crazy person. Apparently, this was an impression of us—and it was not flattering.

"Stop everything, except for walking," she finished with another snarl and then started forth again without leaving even a fraction of a second for our response.

"Got it," I said and grimaced, knowing she wasn't listening. She heard everything but listened to nothing.

Calina rolled her eyes and lifted Frosty closer to her face.

He whimpered softly, communicating thoughts I wasn't able to understand.

The girl whispered back, barely audible, "I don't like her, either."

Frosty moaned, and for a few minutes, the two conversed. Interesting that Dayna didn't yell at the two of them. It seemed only my voice grated enough for her to threaten violence. *For the love of the mother.*

I stared ahead, but there was nothing new to see. The emptiness of this place made my thoughts echo. It brought back things I thought I'd outrun—Gaaron's scream when they took him, the look on Rurik's face when he realized his new powers could kill, Brynlee's shining eyes when she asked me to take care of her daughter.

No, I couldn't think like this, couldn't revisit all my worst memories right before I had to relive them again. I had never felt so alone—at least, not for a very long time.

I attempted to listen to Calina and Frosty's low murmurs for a while, but soon, my thoughts drifted back to Briarhaven once more. To Brynlee. Calina's mother. Gaaron's love. My love, too, even though I knew it was unrequited.

This was all for them. The three of them.

I would never have agreed to take Calina and the other two teens on this harrowing quest if sweet Brynlee hadn't begged.

She wanted what was best for her child. For the girl to be happy. And the girl wanted adventure. She wanted her dad.

I'd wanted to say no. To slam the tavern door shut, pour another mug of mead, and pretend the world didn't need me anymore. But I looked into those violet eyes, so like Calina's, and saw the same fire I'd seen in a hundred adventurers before they marched to glory—or ruin. And I knew. I knew I was taking the kids with me, for better or worse. No, most definitely for worse.

Even though we couldn't form an exact plan as we marched boldly toward our enemy's headquarters, I had to trust that my ability to act quickly, taking each new challenge as it came, would soon deliver Gaaron to the family who needed him so desperately, who had waited so very long for this reunion.

We'd find him, save him... And then what?

I didn't know what kind of shape we'd find Gaaron in after his ten years spent in a dungeon. Would he even be able to walk? And would he be happy to see me or furious that I had let him rot so long?

I hadn't known. I thought I was doing the right thing—laying low, hanging back. And as soon as I found out I wasn't, I'd set out to fix it.

I hoped he would understand.

I hoped I would forgive myself.

"We're stopping here," Dayna announced in her deep timbre.

"Oh... kay," I said, drawing out both syllables slowly. "Does that mean we're allowed to talk again?"

"Yeah, do whatever you want. I'm going off to take a leak." She hissed before breezing away, quickly vanishing between two jagged black rocks as she muttered something under her breath in a language I didn't recognize but was probably just curses arranged alphabetically. Good riddance.

"What were you two talking about?" I asked Calina as she settled on the ground and crossed her legs.

Frosty frolicked after Dayna—a decision I assumed he would soon regret, but I didn't have the words to stop him.

"Well, he's a bit concerned about the climate," Calina said. "He says frost dragons need at least some moisture in the air, or they get very sick. And the Void doesn't have that. His concept of time is strange, but I think Frosty believes he can spend a couple of hours here at best before he starts to become ill."

"Well, that's not good," I said. "What can we do about it?"

"Honestly, I'm not sure." Calina sighed and pinched the bridge of her nose as if to stave off a headache. "Frosty uses a lot of technical words that I don't necessarily understand, and even his emotions behind them aren't always clear to me."

She paused, then added, "You know, in that way, he reminds me a lot of Rurik."

I deadpanned. "Of Rurik. Really? The silly little dragon thing reminds you of the smartest person either of us has ever met?"

Calina shrugged. "Yeah. I mean, don't you know by now that you shouldn't judge people based on appearances? You're the toughest person I've ever met, including Dayna. And you're hardly half my height."

She had a point.

I rubbed the back of my neck, pretending I wasn't blushing. Stupid kid. Always saying the exact right thing at the exact wrong time.

"Are we really going to rescue my dad right now before we even find the others?"

"I don't think we have a choice. Dayna's pretty determined."

"Can't we just, like, leave?"

I'd thought of that. But the moment Dayna entered that lair, Maltherius would know the rest of us were coming. I shook my head and attempted to explain all this in a way that would stick with the girl. "Maltherius told us to meet him here before the

Solstice, so he knows we're coming and soon. If he's got spies watching us, they would've lost us when that teleportation spell went awry. All that to say, our best shot at rescuing your dad is right now, before he figures out we're in his territory."

Calina pressed her lips into a firm line and stared out at the Precipice.

"Okay, then," she said. "As soon as Dayna gets back, let's go. It's time to end this thing once and for all."

2

This was it. The edge of... Well, nothing. And let me tell you something: *nothing is terrifying.*

I didn't know what was scarier—Maltherius's massive lair or the endless drop into nothingness below. They said if you fell here, you would never stop falling. Of course, I didn't know anyone who had done that and lived to tell the tale, but I preferred not to be the first to find out.

At the same time, confronting the Precipice itself was equally daunting. I tried to focus on the physical details, on the here and now. The massive building the necromancer had claimed as his dominion jutted out from the scarred, desiccated landscape, like it was holding on as the abyss slowly pulled it in. And it felt as if, in its last moments, it could grab me and drag me into the nothingness with it. I shuddered at the unpleasant thought. The last thing I needed was more anxiety.

The air here didn't help either. It wasn't just cold —it was wrong. Every inhale tasted stale and hollow, like it had been recycled through centuries of despair. There was no wind, no sound, no life at all. Like the area was yet another reanimated corpse in Maltherius's army.

And it didn't like us. Not one bit.

My fears kept stacking upon each other, building a thick wall that seemed to trap me in my worst nightmare. This distorted dream was all the more fearsome because I'd lived it before. I knew just how wrong everything could go for us.

I knew, and still, I marched forward despite the mounting dread, despite the many unanswered questions, despite the horrible stinging sensation that seemed to have lit my forearm on fire. The brand Maltherius's agent in Briarhaven had marked me with puckered like a fresh scar as the rest of the burn merely ached with every heartbeat. The burn had been my reminder of Gaaron's fate for these last ten years and now it felt more like a goad pushing me toward his rescue. But was he really alive or was this all a twisted trap?

For the love of all things divine, I sure hoped not.

More fears, fewer choices. *March, march, march.*

We were so close. Couldn't stop now.

Of course, given all that I had lost here before, I had vowed never to return to this place. But that was before I learned that Gaaron might still be alive, waiting for me to rescue him. How could I not attempt to save him?

He was the truest friend I had ever known. I loved him more than Durgan, Brynlee, and even the kids that comprised my current adventuring party. We had laid our lives on the line for each other several times over, and now it was time for me to offer mine up yet again—perhaps for the very last time.

I didn't let myself look back, not at Calina, Frosty, or even Dayna. If I looked back, I might see the edge behind us crumbling or the expression on Calina's face —the one that said she still believed in me, even now, when I was running entirely on fumes and vengeance. I couldn't handle seeing another reminder of something I loved and may yet lose.

My spine was already locked with tension, and my fingers curled around the hilt of my dagger like it could ground me. It didn't. But letting go might break me, so I kept holding tight.

"This place gives me the creeps," Calina muttered. From the corner of my eyes, I saw the girl wrap her arms around herself in what appeared to be a self-soothing gesture. And still, I refused to take a closer look.

"Skirr," Frosty intoned, leaping from the ground and nearly managing to flutter up to Calina's shoulder. It was the first time I'd seen the little dragon try to fly. Honestly, I would've been more impressed if he hadn't turned it into a bit of a comedy act—ascending grandly one second and then panicking the next. With a meek squeak, he lost his balance and plopped back onto the dark, dusty ground.

This caught my attention, forcing me to turn and fully take in the scene.

Of course, Calina scooped the little guy up immediately, clicking her tongue in a mix of worry and comfort. Poor Frosty looked about as majestic as a soggy wool cloak, especially with his tiny wings that seemed more decorative than functional.

"If he's going to be a liability, then he needs to stay behind," Dayna grumbled, her voice cutting through the quiet like a knife. "It's dangerous enough as it is without a baby dragon whimpering for its mama the whole time."

"You're lucky I don't have the words to translate his opinion of you," Calina shot back with a huff, giving Frosty a reassuring kiss on his forehead. The little dragon, snug in the safety of her arms, peeked out with wide, curious eyes that seemed to take in more than you'd expect. "There, there, it's okay. I'll keep you safe, buddy."

Frosty's tail twitched, wrapping weakly around Calina's wrist as if to say thanks or maybe just holding on for a bit more assurance. He might not be the fierce dragon you'd expect from the stories, but he sure knew how to tug at your heartstrings without even trying.

Something about how his little claws trembled, though—that was more than just fear. Instinct. He had that ancient dragon sense, buried under all the baby fat and bumbling. And it was on high alert. I saw the change in him before I registered the tingling at the base of my neck. That sixth sense I'd acquired from my many years of thieving, solidified by my many years of adventuring, and accentuated by my years in Briarwood.

Something wasn't right. But what?

Dayna let out an exaggerated sigh. It seemed everything any of us did upset her, and I wasn't sure that would ever change. She turned to me, eyes narrowing. "Shouldn't there be thralls or gravens or some other such monster patrolling this place? This Maltherius guy commands an undead army, does he not?"

The only thing I remembered clearly was that last moment before Gaaron was captured and I barely escaped. The image of that locked door had been seared into my mind, and I often saw it when I closed my eyes to sleep. The pieces before and after didn't matter. Because it was that single moment, that single door, that had ruined everything.

I shrugged. "Honestly? I can't remember much, but there weren't patrols last time I was here. It would draw attention if he were seen to be gathering a massive army."

Even as I spoke to Dayna now, I heard Gaaron's voice speaking to me back then. A flash of memory surged forward.

"Necromancers are a secretive bunch," Gaaron had said. "He's not about to send a missive to the Crown saying: 'My Dearest Mortal Foes, come and get me if you dare. Hugs and Kisses, Maltherius.' But between you and me, I'd like him a whole lot better if he did. We could be friends then. Do you think the old chap has any living acquaintances? Any at all? And if he does, what could they possibly talk about? Under different circumstances, I might have..."

Gaaron's bombastic chitchat had filled the emptiness of the Void, making our journey into it light and enjoyable, presenting a sharp contrast to Dayna's current displeasure and demand for silence.

"You've come here before," the mercenary pressed, thumbing the hilt of one of her swords as she yanked me away from my soothing reverie. "Don't you have any intel to share?"

"I've been trying to *not* remember for a long time," I muttered, stepping toward the edge of a rocky outcropping and glancing down into the abyss.

It stared back at me. It seemed the Void had eyes. Not literal ones, but a presence, a pressure that felt like a thousand unfocused stares trained on my soul. I didn't tell the others that. No point freaking them out when I was already so unsettled myself.

There was only one place to go from here: inside.

"A lot has changed," I admitted. "It's been a long time for me, but a drop in the bucket for a millennia-old necromancer. I suggest we just go in and see what he's got waiting for us. We'll take each new challenge as it comes."

"Good enough for me," Dayna grunted, striding toward the massive spine-like structure.

"Wait!" Calina cried, rushing after her awkwardly as she carried Frosty. "That's the whole plan? Be ready for anything? That's not even a plan at all! Shouldn't we take a little more time—"

"Enough," Dayna snapped, raising a clenched fist without looking back. "Stay quiet. That's our only chance of completing this mission without complications."

"Complications?" Calina questioned. "What do you mean by—"

"She's right," I cut in, stopping her mid-sentence. "We have to stay quiet. Make sure the dragon knows it, too."

"But I want to help, Tilda! Just tell me how, and then we can—"

"She's told you nicely," Dayna interrupted sharply. "Don't make me say it more harshly."

Calina yammered something under her breath, but I didn't catch it. We just had to trust each other now. The stakes were higher than they'd ever been. I knew Calina and I could work well together. I didn't think we could trust Dayna, but she was with us for better or worse.

And truth be told, I'd rather have a bitter sword arm beside me than no sword arm at all. Dayna might've been as warm as a dead trout, but she was lethal, focused, and not likely to scream if a skeleton popped out of a wall. That was more than I could say for most adventuring companions I'd had in the past.

Of course, I was deceiving her. She wanted to retrieve the artifact and get paid. By Finnian Sly, my former master, of all people. One of the few people who would be almost as bad as Maltherius getting his hands on it. But while that might've been Dayna's purpose, the only thing on my mind was reuniting my scattered party—first Gaaron and then the others. Right now, it was easier to work with Dayna than against her. I'd have to think quickly. Once we found Gaaron, I'd need to convince Dayna that we had also just found the artifact and that it was time for us to skedaddle.

I hoped I wouldn't have to actually give up the crest. But even if I had no choice, I felt confident it would be better in her hands than Maltherius's. I'd just have to find a way to get it back before she offered it to Finnian. I still didn't know what he wanted with it, and I hoped never to find out.

We crept closer to the fortress. Dayna craned her neck, surveying the perimeter for any entrance other than the main. I vaguely remembered a winding pathway we had taken to find a back door, but I couldn't specifically recall any of the landmarks

Gaaron and I had used to find the path to begin with. The Precipice had stood here for hundreds of years, but it seemed different now, and I couldn't quite figure out why.

The fortress was bigger than I remembered. Perhaps it had been built up more since my ill-fated mission here. But the outside still looked uniformly old and decayed. Maybe my memory had been warped by time or my vision had been affected by the sheer wrongness of the Void.

"Scree!" Frosty yelped and awkwardly scrambled from Calina's arms onto her shoulders.

"Hey, boy, it's okay. What's wrong?" she asked, startled.

"He stays quiet, or he stays outside," Dayna hissed right on cue.

"He's trying to warn us," Calina said.

"Okay, but where?" she asked the little dragon.

Her eyes went wide a moment later as her mouth fell open. She lifted a shaking arm and pointed.

I followed her line of sight but couldn't understand what she was seeing.

"Use your words," Dayna commanded—at direct odds with everything else she'd said to us up until now.

Calina stuttered, "D-Dragon..."

Dayna rolled her eyes. "Yes, yes, you have a little

dragon friend. How wonderful. Now, if we could please just focus on—"

Her words trailed off as the Precipice itself shuddered and then slithered.

"Oh, sweet divinity," I cursed, blowing a low whistle.

We all saw it now. The massive, mountain-sized dragon, Cindara, had been so perfectly camouflaged against the fortress that she seemed to be a part of it. Her scales, a mosaic of dark stone and shadow, mirrored the jagged, craggy walls of the necromancer's lair. At first glance, or even the second, you'd think she was just another part of the twisted architecture, an eerie statue carved from the Void itself.

"Cindara," I exhaled. "It's Maltherius's familiar."

"Finnian told me there would be a dragon," Dayna quipped, almost amused. "But not that it would be so large."

"She's been around a very long time," I explained. "Pretty much as long as he has. At least a thousand years, by even the most conservative estimates."

Dayna grinned, looking the happiest I'd seen her to date. "This mission just got a whole lot more dangerous. I'm going to make sure Finnian increases the bounty. What a stroke of luck."

"Luck, right," Calina muttered in disgust.

Now that Cindara had shifted, a small door was visible beneath her massive form. Right where the path was supposed to lead to the other entrance. After the last time, someone had decided to make a minor attempt to strengthen security.

Her wings unfurled slightly, rustling against the crumbling stone like thunder echoing through a distant mountain pass. Even that tiny movement sent gusts of heated wind barreling over us, stinking of brimstone and ancient decay. My cloak snapped backward with a loud *crack*, nearly yanking me off my feet. Frosty squeaked and ducked into Calina's collar. I was seriously considering joining him.

As Cindara moved, her immense body unfurled, at last making it clear how much of the fortress she had been hiding. Her movements were slow and deliberate, as if revealing herself was part of some dark ritual we had accidentally encountered.

We stood there, our mouths agape, as the dragon's true size became apparent, dwarfing our sense of reality and certainly any plan we might have had. It was one thing to know you were facing a dragon. It was entirely another to see one hiding amongst the bones of a cursed fortress, watching you with eyes like molten graves. If Maltherius was considered the Lord of Death, his dragon was death itself. She didn't just live in the shadow of death, she shaped the shadows around it.

And she was looking at me. No mistake. Her head tilted with the slow menace of a predator that knows it doesn't need to chase.

I felt it again—the heat blooming up my forearm where Maltherius's mark lived beneath my skin. The brand throbbed like a heartbeat as it recognized her. Or she recognized it. A low, guttural rumble drifted out from her chest, and every molecule in my body screamed at me to run. But my feet betrayed me by refusing to lift from the ground. And with an almost imperceptible flick of the eyes, I could feel her permission to enter the Precipice. Ice filled my veins, and a cold sweat broke out on my forehead.

"Okay, team," I said, trying to inject some confidence into my voice that I didn't feel as I pointed to the flimsy door that the dragon had revealed. "Let's not keep our host waiting any longer than necessary." And with a deep breath that did nothing to steady my nerves, we headed toward the newly revealed door into the belly of the beast, quite literally.

The moment we stepped beneath her—under that terrible shadow—everything went dark. She wasn't attempting to kill us. It was instead as if she were welcoming us inside. I definitely didn't like that.

Even still, going in felt much safer than staying out. I knew even greater dangers awaited us within the lair. But every now and then, we had to ignore our better instincts and push on against all logic and all odds. And this was most definitely one of those times.

"Here goes nothing," I mumbled, reaching for the handle and pushing.

It was warm. That's the part that struck me. The door handle—crafted from some twisted bone or blackened brass—should've been cold, dead, lifeless like everything else around us. But it wasn't. It pulsed with the faintest heat, almost like it was *alive*. I flinched. But the door creaked open, and the scent of thick and foul magic washed over me like sewage made of stars.

I swallowed hard. No turning back now.

3

The first thing I noticed was the stale stench of death.

I'd killed many a bandit or monster in my day, but those had always been fresh bodies. What I was faced with now made me gag. The air felt thick and heavy with decay. And this was new. When Gaaron and I had come through, the air had been like crypt air—dry and stagnant with a touch of embalming potions. Now it was like hundreds of bodies left to cook and rot in the sun. Perhaps part of that was the ongoing magic Maltherius needed to employ to keep his undead horde reanimated. Or maybe he'd ramped up his minion production.

"By Sylric, I've never been somewhere so disgusting," Calina cried.

Dayna immediately reached for the hilt of her sword, clearly ready to threaten the girl.

I raised my tunic over my nose to create a makeshift filter. "Keep quiet, keep moving, breathe through your mouth," I instructed, pulling ahead of the others as I navigated an eerily familiar passageway.

Calina sucked in a deep breath and then sputtered, breaking apart in a fit of coughs. "Ugh, that's worse. Now I can taste it!"

"Don't breathe at all," Dayna growled. "Or leave, for all I care. Just stay quiet and don't get in the way."

I patted Calina's lower back to reassure her, then motioned for her to stay behind me.

She clutched Frosty tighter, the dragonling giving an indignant squeak that was thankfully more a hiss than a chirp. His scales shimmered faintly in the gloom, catching the minimal light like dew on midnight leaves. I tapped a finger to my lips and shot them both a stern glance, praying they'd heed my warning.

The corridor ahead funneled forward like a tunnel carved by fear itself—narrow, damp, and claustrophobic, as if the walls were inching closer with every breath. Mildew slicked the walls, and the torches cast more chill than light, if you could even call those sickly blue wisps torches. Every few steps, the floor creaked beneath my boots in a way that made me want to strangle whoever built this place for not believing in solid craftsmanship.

Movement further down the hall caught my eye, and I instinctively pressed my small body against an alcove in the dank stone wall.

It was cold against my cheek, slimy, suggesting something had been there recently—and hadn't washed its hands. I tried not to think about who or what it might have been.

The floor shifted slightly beneath my heel, and I winced in expectation. Of course, there were traps. We'd found them last time, and I'd disarmed them. It seemed I'd just found another... except nothing happened. With no acid, blades, or poison gas descending upon us, it appeared Maltherius probably hadn't even bothered to reset his traps after my last visit.

Something was unsettling about walking through your own footprints from ten years prior, like time had rewound without asking your permission.

Calina fell back into a crouch, but she and Frosty remained too exposed to the patrolling graven. Leaning forward, I yanked them back and pointed ahead.

Her eyes grew wide as she nodded, but thankfully, she didn't speak.

Once the graven had passed, we crept forward, sticking to the shadows. Of course, within the Precipice, almost everything was shadow. This place had been touched by death and evil, worn down by time. I was thankful we were here, so close to rescuing my friend, but I still didn't know whether we could succeed.

A draft whispered past us—cold, wet, and vaguely scented with rotting citrus. It felt like a ghost breathing on the back of my neck. I clenched my fists to stop the shiver. You'd think I'd be used to death by now. I wasn't.

For his part, Frosty perked up almost immediately upon entering the Precipice. The air in this place was heavy, wet, and apparently far preferable to the nothingness outside. I just hoped he would stay quiet as we did what needed to be done.

Dayna reached beneath her armor and extracted a bit of parchment, which she quietly unfolded. She studied it for a long moment with her one good eye before tucking it away and charging ahead.

I wanted to ask where she thought she was going. After all, the treasure she was searching for remained on my person. But I knew better than to say anything about that.

We needed to focus on finding our target and

avoiding Maltherius. The moment he saw me, he would force a confrontation. And if that happened, we had no hope of rescuing my friend while continuing to keep the dangerous magical artifact out of his ne'er-do-well hands.

A gentle moaning rose from the section of the hall we'd only just left behind, and our entire group immediately moved for cover.

Glancing back, I saw a trio of thralls lumbering down the corridor. They weren't intelligent enough to keep a proper patrol but would still attack on sight. And any battle would draw attention we didn't want directed at us.

One of the thralls dragged its leg like it was throwing a tantrum with its pelvis. Another wore a jester hat—bells and all—which jingled with every awkward step. Had the corpse actually been buried like that? After all, a mime was a terrible thing to waste...

Regardless, who in this place had enough of a sense of humor to make this monstrosity happen? I knew it wasn't the boss necromancer himself.

My stomach gurgled with dread and disgust as we waited for the monsters to pass. Something wasn't sitting well with me, something beyond the obvious. But I didn't have time to puzzle it out, not when I needed to focus on the mission.

After a few moments to make sure the coast was clear, Dayna led us forward again. She consulted her crudely sketched map now and then and seemed confident about where she was headed.

It wasn't the same place Gaaron and I had gone during our last mission—the place where the artifact had actually been. But of course, I wasn't planning on telling her that.

Right now, the name of the game was to be ready for anything.

I stayed on alert, looking for any signs that might lead us to the prison cells so that we could free my old friend. When we'd come ten years ago, we hadn't happened upon the dungeon, and I had no idea where it was. I just had to hope that we would stumble upon it by accident.

It's not like Maltherius would put up road signs to help direct errant adventurers.

This place was like a maze when it had been abandoned and drastically expanded upon over the last millennium. Maltherius was meant to be the only living entity within.

Thankfully, most undead lacked basic intelligence, which would help us keep our cover longer. And they tended to rattle and clank when they walked, a side effect of reanimated corpses. Unfortunately, he had so many. It would only take one to discover us, and then they would swarm like ants.

This was one anthill we didn't want to kick over. I generally made it a point not to battle necromancers at all, but when I did, I made sure it was never within their own territory. There was no way we could defeat him while he had access to all his power and resources —not to mention that mountain of a dragon outside. Not even Dayna's scarily impressive battle skills could stand up against that, which meant we had to sneak.

We made slow progress, pausing often to conceal ourselves.

Water dripped from the ceiling and oozed slowly down the walls, eroding the dank edifice. Puddles of varying size and depth were scattered about, and we had to be careful not to splash.

At one point, Frosty merrily rolled about in one of the deeper trenches of stagnant water, waving his tail and shaking his wings as he rehydrated.

Dayna threatened him with her swords, but the little creature either didn't understand the threat, or more likely didn't care.

Calina scooped the baby up, deciding it was easier to have him confined in her arms than risk any more noisy play on the dragonling's behalf.

He let out a wet snort of disapproval and dramatically flopped over her shoulder, tail trailing behind them like a limp scarf. Honestly, I'd have admired the flair if we weren't about to die.

The little beast chirped indignantly, then flopped over dramatically, fully committing to being carried. A youngling, through and through.

Long halls wound round and round, almost as if in a spiral. It seemed the more we walked, the less distance we gained—like we were circling a singular location that we couldn't quite reach.

Dayna paused and ran her finger over an outcrop of mushrooms growing through a crack in the wall. The fungi glowed faintly—just enough to make me worry they might be carnivorous. Or sentient. Or both. I made a mental note to never touch anything that grew in Maltherius's house without poking it first, preferably with someone else's sword.

Dayna sniffed at the residue on her finger and harrumphed. I knew what she was thinking. It was the same thing that had entered my mind—that we'd seen these mushrooms before, more than once even, and that we weren't progressing toward our destination. If we didn't figure out a new way forward soon, we would undoubtedly be discovered by the patrols—or by the necromancer himself.

"What are we going to do?" Calina whispered,

bending down so that her words tickled my ear. "We're lost, right?"

She looked at me with those wide, glassy eyes, offering a glance that made me feel both responsible and very, very doomed. I hated how much she looked up to me, depended upon me. Even more than that, I hated the possibility that I could still let her down.

I swallowed down a lump in my throat and nodded. We were lost, just as she'd said.

I tried to think back to how Gaaron and I managed to navigate this dank labyrinth before but came up short on answers. Was there something important that I'd forgotten? It didn't make sense.

If Finnian Sly had given us our original quest to retrieve the artifact, and he had given Dayna the same quest, then she and I should have had the same information. She frequently referenced her map and handwritten instructions but seemed just as helpless as Calina and I were. Maybe there'd been changes to the inside of the fortress that rendered my past journey and Finnian's map useless?

Dayna took her map out again. She'd folded and refolded it so many times that the paper was beginning to wear. I poked her in the hip and motioned for her to hand it to me.

She made a noise between a sigh and a grunt but complied, nevertheless.

Once the paper was spread out between my hands, I worked quickly to soak in every detail.

The ink was smeared in places—possibly water damage. Possibly sabotage. Perhaps it was just Finnian Sly's usual organizational skills, which ranked somewhere between a feral goblin and a drunken raccoon.

Then, in the upper left corner, I spotted something I hadn't noticed before. A faint set of scratch marks that looked more like claw rakes than ink. It was almost like someone had tried to carve a message into the paper but stopped halfway. It didn't help, but it creeped me out, which seemed on-brand.

What were we missing? What were we missing?

I felt Calina move behind me as she, too, studied the map from over my head.

Frosty cooed and hopped out of her arms, hitting the ground with a thud and sprinting forward.

"Shoot," Calina spat under her breath, taking off after the dragonling.

Dayna and I exchanged a glance before we also gave chase.

Was there something this silly little creature understood that we could not?

It was as good a lead as any—and the only one we had—so we continued to follow.

Frosty brought us back to the same deep puddle he had wallowed in before. He waited for us to catch up and then fell back on his haunches, lifting his snout high and looking proud.

"What's he trying to tell us?" I whispered to my half-elf companion.

"I'm not sure. Let me ask." Calina got down on her hands and knees, having a quiet but urgent conversation with her new sidekick. After a moment, she popped back onto her feet, nodding vigorously. "He says that—"

"Quieter," Dayna practically yelled, which was pretty counterintuitive if you asked me.

But Calina listened, dropping her voice low. "He says the ground is lower here, that the puddle is deeper because of some structural detail I don't fully understand. He thinks there might be a hidden door."

"Okay, then," I said, tightening my grip on my daggers. "Let's find that door."

4

I watched as Dayna's one good eye zipped back and forth, studying the bare wall before us. I was typically pretty good at figuring out traps and puzzles, but this one had me stumped. Only the little dragon seemed to understand what needed to be done. The puddle he'd found earlier had shown us where to go to locate the door—or at least where it should be. To my surprise, Calina reached out and adjusted the unlit sconce, centering it under a leak. It began to catch the liquid dripping from above.

A noise, low and echoing like a beast waking after a long nap, ground out behind the wall. Dust shook loose from the ceiling and drifted through the air like ancient ash, and for a moment, I held my breath—

partly from anticipation, partly because the musty decay in this place had only gotten worse.

I watched in slow horror as the wall pulled away and that stupid door materialized before me. It was the exact image that haunted me every night since I'd first come face to face with it. This door had signaled the end for me and Gaaron. The smooth metal handle and lock had seemed so deceptively simple. Metal bands on a thick stone slab formed a barrier too heavy to break through with our might, but I had been confident I could pick my way through it.

I'd been wrong.

I had failed, and Gaaron had been killed. Or rather, *taken.*

This door had remained, stuck in the same exact spot, only hidden behind its protective puzzle. For years, it had haunted me from afar, and now it was here, taunting, teasing, reminding me of my inadequacies.

And the worst part? It looked exactly the same. Not even a speck of new rust, like time had passed for me but not for it. Like it had been waiting, ready to pick up exactly where we'd left off before.

Seeing it now was suddenly too much for me to handle. I wasn't ready. Not yet.

My chest felt heavy, my knees weak. I closed my

eyes tight, hoping the vision before me would be different when I opened them again. But no. That same door stared me down. What made me think this time would be any different? I reached into my pocket and retrieved my lockpicks, gripping the metal shims so tightly that my knuckles turned white, and my entire body shook.

"Tilda," Calina whispered. "You don't look so good. Are you all right?"

Her voice floated toward me like it was underwater. I was trapped in some slow-moving dream where nothing responded how it should.

I tried to shake my head but couldn't take my eyes off the obstacle before me. Not even for a moment. That's when I realized the truth of the matter.

Maltherius knew. He knew I would come for Gaaron and that I would attempt to extract him secretly. He also knew I wouldn't be able to reach him —not if he put him behind this one specific door. I had already proven I couldn't do this.

The edges of the lockpick bit into my palm. I welcomed the sting. It was the only thing tethering me to the moment. But even that wasn't enough.

My breaths turned shallow—ragged. Spots floated in my vision. My knees buckled, and I fell to the floor, landing in the rancid puddle. Water splashed up onto my face, and I let out a strangled cry.

Brynlee dropped to my side, rubbing slow circles over my back, doing her best to comfort me, but I didn't even register the sheer impossibility as I barely noticed her presence. What cruel irony that I had come all this way only to fail again. And this time, I wasn't even brave enough to try. That made it even worse. I had endangered the lives of these children. And for what?

"Tilda, Tilda, Tilda," Brynlee chanted softly, her voice a steadying presence. I must've been hallucinating since Dayna didn't try to shut her up.

"It's okay. It's okay. It's just a door. You can do this."

She stopped rubbing my back and reached for my hands, loosening my fists to reveal the small, flat metal strips that made up my lockpicks. She took them from me, stood, and extended an open palm. "We'll do it together. It's all right."

I wanted to believe her. By the blessed mother, I wanted to. But the door loomed like a memory with teeth. There was no one that could understand. She hadn't lived through enough to have this kind of regret, this shame.

I tried to reach out for her. I tried to rise—both to

my feet and to the challenge—but I wasn't enough. All of this happened in my mind while nothing occurred outside.

"It's okay, Tilda," Calina soothed, the vision of her mother melting into the younger features of the precocious youth. "It's okay. We'll find a way. I know it." Then she turned her back to me, facing the door that I wasn't strong enough to approach.

"I'll keep watch," Dayna said flatly, walking a few paces out to peer down the hallway. I didn't know whether she did that to give us some privacy or if she'd deemed it the best tactical move. Whatever the case, I appreciated it. I hated that anyone had to witness what I had become in this moment.

Calina fumbled with my tools, unsure of how to make them work. It wasn't until Dayna came rushing back, quiet but hurried, that I realized how much time had passed.

"There's a whole patrol on its way," she hissed. "We have to get through that door, and we have to do it now, or we'll be caught." She turned to me, her expression sharp. "Come on, Tilda. I know you've got this. Get on your feet and open the door."

I could feel the heat of her urgency like a torch lit behind my ribs. But I stayed on the floor, wet, useless, *small.*

I so badly wanted to obey her order. I so badly wanted to be the one who saved us. But I couldn't do it.

Frosty let out a panicked trill. Then, without warning, he climbed up the door and placed his mouth over the lock. A shrill noise emanated from him and ice spread across what could be seen around the dragon. The door shifted with an audible pop and the lock snapped.

"Good job, boy!" Calina said, bringing her elbow down to bash the frozen lock. The pieces of it fell to the stone floor, practically noiseless—at least not audible over the sound of my heart beating rapidly.

I couldn't do it, but the baby dragon had. The blast had cost him, though. I could see that immediately. His wings drooped, and even his pale blue shimmer dulled to a darker shade, and some of his luster faded. For a creature so small, it must have taken everything he had.

Calina gasped as his little body sagged in her arms. She dropped to one knee, pressing her cheek to his snout. "Frosty? Come on, please be okay. You did so well. Just hold on." For a long moment, there was no sound but her shaky breath. Then his tiny chest rose and fell—barely. Still alive. Just spent.

Calina heaved a sigh and closed her eyes in silent

thanks. Then, with the strength usually only mothers seemed to possess, she shifted him into one arm and scooped a handful of the puddle water, tossing it on the dragonling. With surprising alacrity, she returned to her feet and threw her shoulder into the door with a grunt that was part fury, part adrenaline.

Still, the cursed door didn't budge.

"Dayna, help me with this!" she called. Together, the half-elf and the mercenary slammed their shoulders into the broken, unlatched door and pushed until at last the door gave way and they tumbled through its threshold.

Farther down the hall, footsteps approached—not just one set, but many. Perhaps a dozen, perhaps more. I remained anchored to the floor, a liability to both myself and the others. But they were safe now. Calina and Dayna could get Gaaron and go.

As for me, I would remain here. It's what I deserved. That was the truth that had gnawed at my bones for years. Not that I'd failed, but that I'd let myself fail. That I'd walked away. That I'd lived while he hadn't, at least not really.

Maltherius had kept Gaaron as his prisoner for so many years, but I had been trapped too—by the memories, fear, and failure I knew I could never live down. This place was already overflowing with corpses.

Mine would make a small, perhaps unnoticeable addition. At least I would finally belong somewhere.

"Are you coming?" Dayna's voice cut through my thoughts. She stood on the other side of the newly uncovered doorway, watching me.

Strange clicking sounds floated down the hallways as Maltherius's undead guard grew closer. I shook my head, gagging on the stench that wafted ahead of the fast-approaching thralls.

"We don't have time for this," Dayna grunted. "Get up!"

But still, I didn't move.

Why didn't I care more about my own life? Had it always been this way since growing up as a parentless child on the mean streets of Mirathane? Or had I acquired this nihilism during my adventuring days?

I didn't like that this was who I had become. But I also didn't see any point in trying to change it. At least all the bad feelings would die with me.

"That does it," Dayna snapped, and in the next instant, she charged toward me, grabbed me up like a useless sack of flesh, and flung me over her shoulder.

I barely had time to react as she raced us both back to safety.

"You may not care about your life, but I do," she growled. "We need you to finish this mission. So whatever issue you've got, set it aside to deal with it later, and get with the program now."

With that, she dropped me to the ground with a heavy thud.

Pain crashed through me as I landed, jolting my senses awake. The wind left my lungs in a rush. I blinked up at Dayna and saw it—neither judgment nor pity. But expectation and frustrated, impatient belief.

There had been no reason to give up. No practical reason, anyway. And yet, I had done so readily.

Had I come all this way to not even say hello to my old friend? To not apologize for forcing him to wait so long? *Ridiculous.*

I planted both palms against the uneven stone floor and pushed myself up. Shaking out my limbs, I rose.

"Welcome back to the quest. Glad you decided to join us," Dayna scoffed, turning away from me with obvious disgust.

Calina continued rocking Frosty against her chest like a baby. He still hadn't regained consciousness, but he hadn't died either. He would be okay in time.

What about the rest of us, though?

I studied Calina, hoping it would help me understand her feelings. Was she ready to meet the father she hardly knew?

"Calina," I began, extending a hand toward her.

Dayna immediately shot forward and pushed my arm down. "We may have escaped that group of thralls, but you can bet there'll be more on this side of the door. We have to keep moving. We have to find the crest."

She marched confidently ahead, though I had no idea how she'd chosen the direction. Still, we followed her since she was the surest and most able to protect us should we collide with Maltherius's forces again.

"This place looks like a prison," she noted, speaking more freely now that we seemed alone. And she was right. Rusted bars lined one side of the hallway. Empty shackles laid just beyond.

It was enormous, this place.

Had all these cells once been occupied? The thought made my skin crawl. How many people had passed through here, forgotten? How many had screamed themselves hoarse to no reply? How many had felt the futility that not even death could save them from the necromancer?

"Tilda, look!" Calina cried. She raced ahead, her gait awkward, with Frosty weighing her down. "Someone's there!"

I picked up my pace, following, then nearly

colliding with her when she suddenly stopped outside a lonely cell.

In the far corner, a heap of rags appeared to tremble. Only the motion caught my eye since the figure blended in so well with the filth of its surroundings. As I trained my eyes in search of detail, I made out matted hair and dirty skin, confirming that this was, in fact, a living person. I could not discern any recognizable features, but still, this could be only one person.

Swallowing down the last dregs of my anxiety, I spoke. "Gaaron? Gaaron, is that you?"

5

The rancid heap shuddered, clearly alive but unaware of what was happening around the cell.

"Do you know this person?" Dayna asked, a bit more softly than usual but still seeming rather impatient. "Is this even a person?"

She gripped both swords, ready to fight.

"I think the answer to both of those questions is yes," Calina offered, still hugging the unconscious Frosty.

I stooped down, searching for any sign of recognition in him or myself. "Gaaron," I tried, slowly testing us both.

A low, rattling moan emanated from the form, but still, he did not look up to greet me.

I swallowed down the bile that threatened to surge from my belly and reached forward with trembling fingers. "It's me, Tilda." I pressed my fingertips into what I thought was his shoulder but only felt bone.

"*Tilda...*" he croaked in a dry, elongated rasp. It sounded like the man's voice hadn't been used since I'd last seen him ten years ago and had broken from a lack of practice.

Even still, I recognized my friend. A wisp of a man, a shadow of the vivacious bard he had once been, yet it was still Gaaron all the same.

Even though he was weakened, filthy, and hardly awake, I pulled him into my arms, sobbing with joy when, at last, his pale face came into view. His hazel eyes stared blankly from dark, haunted circles. There was a gleam in them still, just incredibly muted. "It is you. Thank the divine, it's you. Gaaron, it's me. Do you recognize me?"

He didn't answer, didn't give any indication he heard my words or felt my embrace. That was okay, though. I could guide us through this moment. After all, I was the one to blame for it in the first place.

"I came back," I whispered gently while squeezing the bag of bones he'd become even tighter. "I'm so sorry it took this long. I didn't know. But the moment I found out—"

"Dad!" Calina cried, the word cut off by a gasp as she fought her emotions. Her hands flexed as she approached unsurely from across the cell.

I could see her fighting the instinct to run to him, to collect him in her arms, but she held back. She could barely remember her father—he had left so long ago.

But judging from the flash of confused emotions that danced across his wan features, Gaaron couldn't even recognize the girl at all.

His dry lips puckered as if he wanted to speak, but I reached up and covered his mouth before he could release a syllable.

"*Who is that?*" That's what he had meant to ask.

But hearing those words would have broken Calina. She had spent her whole life longing to be reunited with him, waiting for this very moment. And now that she'd finally found her father, he didn't know her.

I held my friend at arm's length, studying how his features had changed over the years. He had become gaunt, sharp cheekbones jutting from his face. His sunken eyes looked hollow as if they had been trying to escape the horrific visions he had seen every day of his imprisonment.

His once lithe, lanky form was now willowy, like a

desiccated tree in a snag forest. His clothes clung to him like autumn leaves, ready to fall, break, and die.

His skin was mottled with grime, bruises the color of storm clouds blooming beneath the surface, and scars so thin and pale they could only have been made slowly. Deliberately. My stomach clenched at the thought. I knew what kind of creatures Maltherius kept for playthings. I'd heard the screams originating from this dungeon once before. I hadn't let myself think one of them might belong to someone I loved.

Gaaron had been hurt, but he'd also managed to survive.

I had not lost him as I'd so often feared.

And now that we had found him, we could get him out of here. Help him recover. Help him be the man I had always known him as. And the one that Calina had so desperately wished to know.

"How do you know this person?" Dayna asked bluntly.

I glanced at her and saw she was less than happy about this development.

"Clearly, you know him. And you knew he'd be here. *Why?*" That last word came out sharp—a challenge. Her eyebrows furrowed together as she regarded me coldly.

I had to play this very carefully to keep Dayna on

my side. Maltherius was a dastardly opponent, no doubt. But he wasn't here right now. Dayna was. And she could slit my throat before I even noticed her drawing her weapon.

"This is my former partner," I said carefully. "Ten years ago, we were sent on a quest to retrieve the Genesis Crest, just like you've been asked to do now."

I swallowed hard. "We failed. I had thought him dead when I... Well, I escaped, but Gaaron didn't. We can take him and the crest now that we're here. We can finish this at last."

I had to think fast. Now that we had Gaaron, I wanted to get him out quickly. I doubted Dayna would be much help carrying him, not if she thought there was still work to be done inside the dungeon.

Calina and I wouldn't be strong enough without her. Which meant I had to make Dayna think she had gotten her prize.

I stuck my hands beneath Gaaron's ragged cloak, maneuvering to release the clasp of the bracelet my beloved Brynlee had gifted me upon my departure.

"This," I said, withdrawing it as if just discovering it. "This is what we came for."

I held the glittering jeweled bracelet to the one-eyed mercenary, who now regarded me with open disdain.

"We've come for the Genesis *Crest.* This is not a crest."

"I don't know what to tell you," I said with a forced shrug, hoping she would buy my feigned indifference. "Sometimes, these magical artifacts have names that don't make sense. Do you want it or not?"

Dayna growled and yanked the delicate bracelet from my outstretched hand. "I'm not buying it, but maybe Finnian Sly will." One corner of her mouth quirked up in a grin, and I had to work hard not to smile myself.

"He'll get what he needs," I said as I pushed myself to my feet. "Help me get Gaaron up."

Remarkably, Dayna complied.

Gaaron was little more than a rag doll in our arms. I didn't know whether he could even support his own weight. Calina watched our clumsy maneuvering but didn't move to help us. She held back, battling a swell of tears that I could see so badly wanted to fall.

Her fingers twitched like she wanted to reach out —maybe to touch his sleeve. Just to know he was real. But her face had hardened, eyes gone glassy, only hold herself together by not moving. I knew that look. I'd worn it often enough. That was the look of someone bottling a scream.

"My previous escape is still a bit blurry, but I know

we can't return the way we came. There's got to be another exit close by. I can't imagine a guard having to go through all of that just to interrogate or feed a prisoner," I said, hobbling back to the door as I supported a disproportionate amount of the emaciated bard's weight. "Calina, can you help? You're closer to Dayna's height. It'll be easier. I can carry the dragon."

She stared at me dumbly, then nodded almost imperceptibly and took my spot at Gaaron's right side.

"I'll lead," I volunteered, shifting Frosty's weight in my arms. He wasn't very large, but sweet divinity he was heavier than he looked. Much more than my portion of Gaaron had been. Still, we could move faster with this new arrangement.

I had to stay strong for a few moments more—just until we got out of here. Then we could find the others and go home.

Home. What a cursed word. It didn't even mean a place anymore, did it? Not a cottage, not a town. Not Briarhaven or the tavern or any stretch of geography I could stab on a map. Home was a who. It was a collection of fools, fighters, and overly talkative pets who'd wormed their way into my heart when I wasn't looking. And now, all I could think about was getting back to them. To all of them.

It was strange how it had taken so long to get here,

but everything had happened at lightning speed once we'd arrived at the Precipice. Almost as if it had been too easy.

But no. I couldn't think like that. It would only be inviting trouble.

"Where are we going?" Gaaron's hoarse words rose behind me—first strong, then quickly losing volume as his energy dwindled. Hearing my otherwise lyrical friend struggle with even the simplest vocal cadences felt unnatural and unsettling.

"No talking," Dayna snapped. I had to admire her consistency.

I couldn't wait to catch up with Gaaron and offer more of my bumbling but heartfelt apologies. I wanted to talk but wasn't quite ready to listen. I didn't want to learn of the horrors he'd endured. The guilt would break me clean in half.

Speaking would only draw attention and hurt feelings.

Right now, we had to escape without notice. I flashed him one of our old hand signals to keep him quiet. Open hand, grasping air, and pocketing it. Part of it I knew was from his musical training, but we'd use it to mean, "I'll explain later." It had been one that Gaaron had to employ frequently, especially with his knack for improvising.

His eyes followed the motion with sluggish famil-
iarity. He blinked once, twice, and for a split second,
the barest whisper of a smile lifted the corner of his
mouth. The muscle twitched and collapsed almost
immediately, like it had forgotten how to function.
But it had been there. Recognition. The slightest shred
of it was buried under ruin. It nearly undid me.

I nodded and turned away from him, focusing on
the path ahead as I searched for a new way out. We
couldn't return the way we'd come—not with a swarm
of patrolling thralls waiting for us.

There had to be another exit. After all, that's how
I'd escaped last time. Back then, I'd found a small
passageway tucked into an unassuming corner. I'd
needed to lower myself to my hands and knees to fit,
but it had led straight outside. I didn't remember it
being overly tight, so I was sure we could all fit. Our
extra-large party members weren't with us now, which
gave us more flexibility.

I scanned the crumbling walls, searching.

Nothing yet.

"Be on the lookout for something low to the
ground," I told the others. " There should be a small
tunnel that leads outside. Some way for them to
dispose of waste or maybe a way to threaten prisoners
with the abyss. Something that will lead to the outside.

It's our safest bet to get around the patrols and get out of here."

Dayna grunted in confirmation.

Calina said nothing.

I couldn't tell if Gaaron was even still conscious.

Every few steps, I glanced over my shoulder to check for the rise and fall of his ribs. It was faint. Barely perceptible. Like even his body wasn't sure if it wanted to keep going. He needed food. Water. Sunlight. *Life.*

For a moment, I was reminded of Amariel, always dozing off. I had thought, then, that she had been old and tired, needing to sleep. But really, she had been visiting a special in-between place—a place that, for the briefest of times, I had existed too.

Hardly any time had passed since she had made the ultimate sacrifice, banishing herself from the mortal realm so that the rest of us had another chance to survive. Her willingness to put our needs above hers ultimately saved the day. And now, she wasn't here to witness our successful quest completion.

We had rescued my friend. So why did it feel so anticlimactic?

I was pleased to have him here with us. But somehow, it didn't feel right. Was it because Amariel, Tulip, and Rurik weren't here with us? We had started this quest together, yet I was forced to finish it without my entire party. That felt like a betrayal—like I was honoring my loyalty to one friend while hurting the others.

I hoped they were okay.

That Rurik had a better handle on his explosive new magic.

That Tulip could keep her rage in check long enough to make clear-headed decisions.

But more than anything, I hoped they weren't headed here. If I was lucky, the teleportation spell misfire could have sent them home. But I knew that even if they had inadvertently ended up in Briarhaven, that's not where they would stay.

They would come.

For me.

For Calina.

Because we were a party. A family. Not so long ago, I had cursed their very existence in my life. Now, they had somehow come to define it.

I remembered Rurik's laugh—loud, ridiculous, and always one beat later than everyone else's. I remembered Tulip's knack for staring someone down until they folded like soggy parchment. I remembered Amariel's patience, the kind that made you want to scream and cry and, weirdly, hug her in the same breath. These people were chaos incarnate, but they were *my* people.

"My friends," I murmured under my breath, hoping beyond hope that they could somewhere hear me, that they would somehow know. "We'll be together soon." We just had to get out of this place.

"Is that what you're looking for, Tilda?" Calina's voice cut through my thoughts, high and uncomfortably shrill. Not like herself. The strange reunion with her father had her rattled—poor thing.

But she was right. She had found our escape chute.

"That's it." I exhaled, relief washing over me. "Good job. Now let's get out of here."

I crouched beside the darkened hole, peering into it with cautious optimism. The stale air that puffed from within smelled of mold, ash, and old bones. Lovely. The walls were slick and damp, the stone glistening like the inside of a throat. Still, it was freedom, and I'd take throat-stone over prison walls any day.

Without hesitation, I dropped to my hands and knees, squeezed into the narrow tunnel, and left Maltherius behind me. This time, I hoped it would be for good.

6

The last time I escaped from Maltherius, I'd exited his fortress onto this same small rocky outcrop tucked away in a forgotten place.

Back then, I'd scrambled out, pushed myself back onto my feet, and ran as fast as my little legs would carry me. I'd been panicked and crying, gasping for air, pushing myself straight to the brink.

I knew that everything in my life had already changed for the worse. I hadn't known I'd be granted the chance to make it right again.

Ten years ago, I'd made this same escape alone, broken, terrified. Now, even though I felt weak, I was no longer on my own. I had retrieved both the crest and my partner and even expanded my party along the way. That gave me enough confidence to rise slowly and wait for the others as they emerged from the hidey hole after me.

I shook out my limbs, ready for whatever came next despite feeling relatively sure that whatever came, it wouldn't be pleasant. I probably should have felt relief, but only a hollow victory greeted me. My goals had been simple upon leaving Briarhaven: save Gaaron and keep the powerful artifact away from Maltherius.

And we'd done those things now. But it just didn't feel right. Nor did it feel like enough. Rurik and Tulip were missing somewhere out there, and I had to get them back.

But first, I had to wait for the others to emerge. And so I waited, even though I couldn't tell if the pounding in my head was because of the altitude, an adrenaline crash, or some kind of internal warning system yelling at me to get myself out of there.

Dayna exited next, dragging our semi-conscious bard behind her with increasingly hostile grunts and curses. I watched as he joined us on the outcropping, studying each movement, each expression. In truth, I scarcely recognized my old friend.

He didn't pop to his feet with a flourish like he would have done when I'd known him so well. Instead, he remained a heap of rancid clothing and sharp bones, laying awkwardly on the rocks as he stared blankly at the horizon. It was as if he were watching ghosts only he could see, and that chilled me more than the bitter wind scraping at my cheeks. Gaaron had always been intense, but there was a spark in him once—a fire that even darkness couldn't douse.

That spark was gone now. What was left felt... hollow. Haunted.

And I didn't know if I could fix him.

By the divine's everlasting grace, I would try. Oh, how I would try. And I knew that Calina would give him her all, too.

I didn't know what kind of help to expect from our newer companions. Dayna and Frosty had proven useful enough, but I was still figuring them out. We'd worked together to achieve my objective, but some-how, I felt more confused and emptier than when I'd started. This was supposed to be my triumphant finale, but it felt like a midpoint on the way to something much more. There was so much I still needed to figure out—not just how I could reunite with our missing party members and get back home, but also how to reconnect with Gaaron and help Calina do the same.

The wind howled around us like the fortress itself was exhaling. Loose stones clattered down the side of the cliff like bones rattling in a tin cup. The weight of everything—Gaaron's limp form, Frosty's semi-conscious bulk, the figgin' artifact tucked against my chest like a guilty secret—pressed down on me, heavier than any real burden.

I needed to figure out what the Genesis Crest could do and why Maltherius and Finnian Sly wanted it so desperately. They were both vile men, each in their own ways. But other than their basic detestable nature, the two had little in common, making me wonder about the artifact's powers. I also felt a sense of duty and loyalty to the trinket. It had saved our party more than once, and for that, I was grateful.

But I'd just as soon destroy it as surrender it. One thing was for sure—I couldn't keep hiding it. If I did, trouble would keep finding me, finding us. And I couldn't do that to the others or the small town we loved dearly. This was supposed to be the end, yet I still had so much more to do.

Nothing was ever as easy as it should have been. Not for me.

"What now?" I asked Dayna, hoping she had some actionable plan because I felt just as lost as ever.

"We find Finnian Sly," she answered right on cue. "Give him the... artifact."

She paused before saying that last word, telling me she knew the bracelet I'd offered her was a fake. But also that the lie didn't bother her as much as I might have expected.

Her eyes met mine long enough to say, "I see through you. I see how your fingers tremble when you think no one's looking, how you keep glancing at that pendant like it's some kind of timed explosive."

Maybe she didn't trust me, but she trusted the cause. That, or she just liked picking fights.

"No. Not yet," Calina interjected, her voice still quavering with emotion. "We have two injured party members. We need to set up camp and rest."

"We can't stay here," Dayna's voice rumbled. "There's an entire army within those walls. It is the worst possible place to set up camp."

She had a point. Calina dipped her head rather than arguing and assisted Dayna in carrying Gaaron across the jagged rocks and away from the wretched place that had served as his prison for more than ten years. I had an uneasy feeling in my stomach as I scampered after them, struggling with the added weight of Frosty against my frame.

Every footstep was a gamble. The narrow trail slanted steeply, littered with loose shale that threatened to dump us all into the yawning abyss below. The air reeked of old magic and scorched stone like the mountain had been burned inside out. And despite the newfound chill in the air, sweat was beading beneath my collar—that kind of sweat that knew something wicked was just out of sight, waiting.

"Did all of that feel too easy to any of you?" I asked my companions.

Dayna shrugged but didn't look back. "Everything is easy when you're excellent at your job like I am. Even the most impossible quests."

Well, that wasn't helpful. It was also not helpful that Calina had fallen silent. This reunion with her dad knocked her off-center, which worried me. I needed my strong, brash girl for whatever happened next. She was the only one in our small group I could trust until we figured out what was going on with Gaaron.

So, I decided to nudge her a little more firmly. "Calina," I asked, then huffed a breath of exertion. I tried to walk faster to keep up with the others, but my cargo was too heavy and my legs too short. "Calina," I tried again. "Did that feel too easy to you?"

"Nothing about this is easy," she said. Her voice was flat, disconcerting.

"I just really think—" I began, but Dayna cut me off.

"We've completed the mission. Stop questioning it."

"But I think—" I began again.

This time, my sentence was broken, not by Dayna, but by a low rumble behind us. The sound started deep and close to the ground but grew in volume, height, and pitch, forcing me to turn around so that I could attempt to figure out what was happening.

And the moment I did, my concerns about this having been too easy disappeared in a blink.

Cindara was still wrapped around the Precipice, waiting for our return. She'd been here the whole time, and in the excitement of finding Gaaron, we'd simply forgotten we'd have to face a figgin' dragon on our way out.

She'd stirred once more and now had her cruel, hungry glare fixed directly on our party. Some adventurers we were, forgetting to account for a mountain-sized monster in our escape plans.

Her body was made of smoke and nightmare, her wings spreading wide enough to blot out the slivered sun, each flap kicking up gusts of ash and old bone. Her eyes were molten gold, locked on us with a predator's precision—patient, calculating, hungry. She'd once been a flame dragon before her master had twisted her into something far worse. And even from this distance, I could feel her heat. It clung to my skin, wrapped around my throat, and seeped into my lungs like poisoned steam.

"See? Will you look at what you did?" Dayna shouted. "You asked for trouble. And it answered."

"Tilda!" Calina let out a pained cry as she attempted to stumble forward. Dayna remained anchored in place, and since they shared the weight of Gaaron, Calina couldn't break free without letting her dad go. And so she remained, too. That said a lot about the girl's character, about her heart.

"What do we do? We can't defeat that thing!" she screamed, hoping her words alone would bring us victory.

"We can't outrun it either," I muttered, heart pounding.

Calina's voice was desperate and also quickly losing its strength. "Can we hide?"

Hiding. Yes, that was a specialty of mine as a rogue. But the only thing here was the massive fortress; the dragon could easily knock that down and bury us under the rubble.

"Well, I'm not going down without a fight," Dayna said, pushing the bard into Calina, withdrawing her swords, and preparing to lunge at the great beast.

But there was no way she could win. I admired her tenacity and bravery but did not like the blatant stupidity. She'd said she wasn't *going down.*

And that gave me an idea.

Hiding... Going down... My freshly formed plan was lunacy, yes, but also the only chance we had. We didn't have time to talk about it. We didn't have time to figure out any other options. We had only a handful of seconds to act before Cindara completely eviscerated our entire party.

And I was so not going to let that happen. Not today. Not ever.

Keeping a tight hold of Frosty to increase my bulk, I ran forward and charged, pushing Dayna, Calina, and Gaaron over the edge and into the yawning abyss below.

Was there really no end to this great chasm? Would you never stop falling?

Well, I guess we were about to find out whether or not that was true.

7

In a flurry of wings, limbs, screams, feet, hands, and fires, we tumbled through the void-cursed nothingness before we crashed down on solid ground.

Predictably, Dayna was more than a little mad about the stunt I'd just pulled. She yelled a nearly string of breathless epithets in my direction, while sweat tricked down her reddened face. "You absolute *Fushik* idiot. You mule-kicked simpleton. You—"

"Saved our butts out there," I reminded her while struggling to sit despite the staggering amount of pain I felt in every inch of my tiny body. "That's what I did. So enough with berating me."

Dayna looked like she wanted to yell at me some more but lacked the strength to do it. She heaved great sighs as her shoulders shuddered. Her once-imposing griffin mantle now appeared tattered and thin, as if all the magic had been wrung out. It hung from her like a defeated banner; the once-golden feathers now dulled to the hue of old parchment. Frayed edges fluttered in the breeze that wasn't really there, stirred instead by the residual tremor of magic. Even the fur lining, always suspiciously pristine, looked like it had lost the will to fluff.

I wanted to feel sorry for her, but she made it difficult to summon any inkling of compassion. Yes, she had just saved all of our lives. But if it hadn't been for me, what would she have done?

The stubborn mercenary had been prepared to slash and stab at the giant dragon that had appeared out of nowhere to threaten us, even though she knew her attacks wouldn't even register as glancing blows. She had marched toward her death with a smile, and only my quick thinking had saved the day.

And what thanks did that get me? Insults. Always with the insults.

Calina lay flat on the ground with her arms splayed out to either side as she gasped for the thin, Void air, failing to take in enough to calm herself. She looked like someone had poured her out onto the cracked ground and forgotten to collect the pieces. Even her rosy hair had come loose from its ties, hanging in tangled streamers that clung to her cheeks. She didn't appear to be in pain, just complete and utter shock.

"How did you know that would work?" she moaned in my general direction.

I sat up, rubbing my lower legs in hopes of lessening the pain and restoring my preferred level of suffering. Eventually, when I chose to stand, I needed to make sure my limbs could support me and that my bones wouldn't crack in two from the stress.

"I didn't," I said with a shrug. "But I took a chance, and it paid off."

"If you ever do anything like that again, our alliance is over," Dayna said through clenched teeth. "You're lucky I even managed to retrieve you. Ever since that idiot orc of yours threw a fireball at me, my wings haven't worked quite right. If that dragon hadn't been the size of a mountain and unable to change directions quickly, that scenario would have ended very differently for all of us."

"I don't care about what might have happened— only what did." I was trying to play it cool as my heart raced and head spun. But cool was a tall order, given that my pulse was a stampede of centaur hooves running off in every possible direction but straight, and my hands were shaking like they had been dipped in ice for a day. I folded my arms over my knees, pretending I wasn't halfway to a complete existential meltdown.

It felt like we were still falling into that endless void. And truly, it must have been endless, for we fell quite a while without so much as a glimpse of the bottom. Everything that happened after the jump came to me in a jagged blur, filled with alternating darkness, light, bursts of necrotic fire, and the horrible screams that had ripped from our throats. There'd been no up, no down, just disorientation so complete it felt like losing your shape. My fingers hadn't felt like fingers. My body hadn't felt like mine. Just particles scattered in a wind that didn't care what direction it blew. That wind had been so loud, cold, and painful as we plummeted with astonishing speed.

We fell, but at the same time, it was as if we floated. Did it even count as falling if you never reached the bottom?

Whatever the case, I planned to never do *that* again —not even if my life depended on it. The worst part had been that, above the screams, beneath the fear, Maltherius's laughter echoed like a cracked bell tolling in some otherworldly temple. Had he even been there at all? Or had I just been losing my mind as I flew face-forward to my near death?

For what felt like a brief eternity, I'd simply belonged to the Void—to its cold air and the biting wind. There'd been something seductive about it. The silence between the howls. The sensation of being unmoored from everything—weight, consequence, even time. It had whispered to me, in that way, dangerous things often do.

Just stay. Let go. Be nothing.

It wouldn't hurt for long.

Eventually, Dayna grabbed me by my armpits and shot us back up until we reached land. Of course, she'd retrieved Gaaron first before coming back for me, probably because he hadn't been the one to create the problem or push her over the edge—both literally and figuratively.

The shock of the fall had roused our dragon companion, and Frosty had managed to save Calina and himself, which lessened the burden on the angry wing scout. A part of me wanted to ask if she'd considered leaving me there in a perpetual state of falling to nowhere. But I didn't think I'd like the answer, so I kept quiet. Also, I wasn't in the mood for another lecture on personal responsibility from someone who solved her problems with a sword and a death wish.

"There's no repairing this now." Dayna's words sounded as sorrowful as any I'd ever heard from her.

She shucked off her cloak and examined it with trembling hands. "Without my cloak, I don't belong with the other wing scouts. I'll have to start again, slay another griffin, make a new mantle." Her voice cracked slightly at the word "slay." I don't think she meant for me to notice, but I did. For all her bravado, I wondered how many griffins she'd truly killed and whether she remembered each one. Whether she ever woke up from dreams with feathers in her mouth.

"That shouldn't be so hard for someone like you," I said. I wanted to offer a smile that showed I believed in her, but I was still too shaken. "Think of all the experience you've gained. It should be little more than a fool's errand for you now."

"This whole quest is a fool's errand," she said, shaking her head. "And you're the fool." The insult should've stung more, but I was too tired to care. Fool or not, I was still breathing, which counted for something in my book.

"Well, I don't much like you either," I shot back. "I appreciate you deigning to save my life, but we don't have to stick together. Take your bounty to Finnian, get your coin, and slay another griffin. We can handle ourselves from here."

Dayna dropped her disheveled cloak to the ground beside her and scoffed at my words. It landed with a wet-sounding flap on the hard dirt and gravel like a fish tossed ashore, useless now that the life had gone out of it. "One moment, you admit that I saved your life, and the next, you say you'll be fine without me. Consistency is a desirable quality. You should seek to acquire it."

I stared at her with a slightly open mouth. My lips were dry and chapped, and my tongue darted out to wet them. Dayna's line of sight dropped to follow the motion, but only briefly before sneering and turning away. A flutter of something other than hatred or disdain flashed across her face, but it was gone before I could name it. Just another piece of the mystery that was Dayna: hard edges and soft shadows all mixed up in a scowl with a one-eyed glare.

"I don't trust you, Tilda Quickthatch," she said with a sniff. "But I trust Finnian Sly even less. If I return to him with this decoy artifact and he figures that out, there's no telling what he would do to punish me. I can't take the chance of inciting the wrath of one so powerful and well-connected, especially while my status as a wing scout is in flux. But I also can't leave my mission incomplete. Do you understand what I'm saying?"

I met her gaze—unblinking, unwavering—to show that she didn't scare me. In truth, though, she did. I decided it was best not to add words just then. Because if I opened my mouth now, the truth might come spilling out. That I knew Finnian better than I let on. That I had more to do with this tangled mess than she could even guess. That I wasn't just some meddlesome halfling who'd gotten in over her head. I was the reason the water was rising.

Dayna growled and rose to her feet, dusting off her pants with a disgusted look. Small stones clung to her like desperate barnacles, and she brushed them off as if they personally offended her. One of them inexplicably bounced off her knee and hit me square in the chest. I took it as a metaphor.

"In case it wasn't clear, I'm sticking with you. I suspect you know more than you're currently willing to tell me. At least, that's the best explanation I have now. But believe me, I'll be watching you. As soon as I figure out what you're hiding, I'll be ready to pounce on it and you. A wing scout always finishes her assignment."

"But as you just said," I pointed out with a slight smirk playing at my lips, "your membership to that group is in question without your mantle. Maybe this will be the one time you don't finish your mission."

Dayna narrowed her one good eye. The false one stayed wide open, creating an unsettling countenance.

I'd riled her. Good. Her lips curled, but it wasn't a smile. It was more like the beginning of a snarl she hadn't decided was worth finishing. That was fine. I could deal with barbed words and bladed glares. What she *wasn't* saying could very well keep me up at night.

I crawled across the ground on my hands and knees and nudged Calina, who was still panting heavily. "Are you okay?"

Her voice shook, but her words still came out strong. "There are some adventures, I think, that are too much even for me. Let's never do that again." She paused for a moment. "Let's not tell the others about that either. Rurik would want to try it himself, and Tulip would be jealous that we hit a high point of our adventure without her." The girl smiled to show me she was all right, and I chuckled with relief. A shaky, gasping sort of chuckle, the kind that catches in your ribs and only escapes once you're sure no more burning, deadish dragons are looming. Her violet eyes sparkled, though—tired, yes, but alive. And that was more than I could've hoped for a few minutes ago.

"Take your time. I'll check on the others," I said with a nod before finally pushing up to my feet. My knees buckled immediately, and I had to pretend it was on purpose. *Oh, Tilda. Graceful as ever.*

Gaaron lay nearby in a similar position to his

daughter's, although he was eerily calm. Asleep, I realized. Strange how much he reminded me of Amariel since we'd been reunited—sleeping, fragile, esoteric, and important, too.

I'd realized too late just how vital our celestial companion had been. I wouldn't make the same mistake with Gaaron. His breathing was slow and even, almost too still, like the air around him didn't dare disturb whatever magic stitched his soul together. I knelt beside him and brushed the dust off his shoulder, half-hoping he'd stir and offer some cryptic insight to guide the next steps of what was sure to be a fraught journey.

But it was not to be. He remained silent, a sleeping secret wrapped in mortal skin.

A happy, joyous cry trilled from above me, and I glanced up to see Frosty flying in wide looping circles overhead. The icy winds of the fall had truly reinvigorated the little dragon. His scales shimmered with residual magic, casting fractured rainbows as he spiraled like a glittery, airborne corkscrew. He dipped low once, brushing the tips of our heads with frost-laced wind, then whooshed upward again with a triumphant squeal that could've meant "I'm alive!" or possibly "That was *awesome!*" I chose to believe it was a bit of both.

And as reluctant as I'd initially been to accept him into our party, our dear dragonling was proving more and more useful by the moment. I wondered if we could convince him to keep watch when we set up camp. Assuming, of course, we didn't find ourselves hurled into another gravity-defying abyss in the next half hour. Which, at this point, seemed entirely possible.

Frosty was the easiest member of this party to deal with at the moment, and I couldn't even speak with him, which really said something about the state of things. Huh, maybe the whole not-speaking thing was why I considered him so likable in the first place. I was grateful for our easy camaraderie, knowing I wouldn't get easy from our other companions on the road ahead.

It also hadn't escaped my notice that he'd saved us twice back there—first by finding the hidden door and then by opening it when I couldn't. Feeling a deep surge of gratitude for the little guy, I looked up at his whirling form and offered a friendly wave. He answered with a sinewy spiral through the air. So, yeah, the two of us were good.

But we wouldn't stay good if we didn't put some serious distance between ourselves and Maltherius. And fast.

We also didn't know where Cindara had gone

during our group's plummet into nothingness. During her reluctant and infuriated rescue, Dayna had carried us a fair distance away to give us some clearance, but that massive creature could close the distance in a few swift strokes of her wings if she wanted to. I squinted at the Precipice but couldn't see the dragon there. She blended so well that it was impossible to tell whether she'd left or simply gone back to sleep.

Just another reason for us to get moving.

There was still so much to be done. I had to find the lost members of our party, revive my old friend, uplift his daughter, and outwit the angry mercenary who continued to stare daggers at me from a few paces out. And I had to manage this all while keeping the magical artifact out of Finnian's hands, dodging death by divine interference, and maybe—just maybe—getting a decent night's sleep before my next brush with disaster.

My journey kept becoming more and more complicated, but there was no avoiding it, either. I would just have to keep taking it one step at a time.

8

And so we walked. And walked. And walked.

Over-exhausted, over-fatigued, and over-encumbered, we trudged along, covering as much distance as possible before the sun began to set above, signaling the need for rest. Now that Frosty had regained his stamina, he didn't need to be carried, which made things a lot easier on me.

Dayna and Calina, however, struggled to aid Gaaron along our path. It was a grim little caravan trailed by footprints that dragged and swayed like the marks of sleepwalkers. Gaaron's knees buckled every so often, and the three wobbled off course, threatening to fall but never actually going through with it. The silence between us yawned larger with each step, filled only by the crunch of loose earth beneath our boots and the occasional grunt of effort.

Our bedraggled bard remained conscious most of the time but didn't seem to fully understand what was happening around him. Dayna remained angry, silently stewing over her torn-up mantle. Calina also remained quiet, intense sadness emanating from her. She moved like a ghost tethered to a fading dream—present but dimmed. I kept catching glimpses of her face, lit in fractured shadows whenever the meager sunlight angled through the clouds, and the grief etched there made my stomach twist.

If Gaaron had been more of himself, he would have recognized her heartbreak in an instant and immediately rushed to put a smile on her face. It wouldn't matter that he didn't recognize her because he was that way with everyone. He'd been the best, kindest, bravest person I'd known—until I met Brynlee and learned what courage meant to her.

She was willing to give up her needs to support those she loved. First, having encouraged Gaaron to adventure beyond a small-town family life and then allowing her daughter to do the same. What was she doing back in Briarhaven, I wondered. What did her days look like without Calina and me? During her shifts at the Mystic Mug did she glance up at the clock and, for a moment, think I was running late to join her? Was she keeping Calina's bedroom tidy, like a shrine or a promise, or had she packed everything away to avoid the ache? I pictured her sitting with Durgan and Pat, the three of them swapping tall tales and small worries while pretending our tavern wasn't far too quiet now.

Were Pat and Durgan inviting her over, keeping her company, making sure she was all right? Or was she doing that for herself? Picturing her now reminded me how much of our journey remained. It would still be days before our reunion—perhaps that would give us the time needed to bring Gaaron back to being the man she remembered.

For ten years, he'd been trapped in that wretched fortress. Did he ever give up hope? And if so, how long had that taken? I hated that I hadn't known, but I was doing what I could to make up for it now. The guilt lodged itself deep in my chest like a stone swallowed whole. I'd spent many nights wondering what I could've done differently if I'd only looked harder, asked more questions, and followed fewer orders. But wishing didn't bring him back. Only action could.

We had his body, but his mind and heart still weren't here with us. Time, once again, was proving to be my greatest enemy. Maltherius had been given ten years to destroy my friend, but could I rebuild him in less? I didn't know the answer or even know how to begin the work that needed to be done.

But I was still going to try. I owed him that. Owed Brynlee, and Calina, and even myself. Because if I couldn't save him, then what had this entire journey even been for? The pain, the fear, the cracks spreading across our little found family—it had to lead somewhere. I wouldn't let this end in tragedy. Not again.

Dayna stopped marching forward abruptly and flung Gaaron's arm from her shoulder, leaving his full weight with Calina.

"We'll sleep here," she announced, rummaging in her small rucksack. Her voice was clipped, raw at the edges. She sounded like she hadn't slept in three days, and she'd finally given up pretending it didn't matter. Her fingers dug through the bag with the same frustrated precision someone might use to cut an apple with a battle axe.

But the light was too sparse for me to see what she grabbed from her pack. Whatever it was, it held her complete focus now, which meant I was in charge of preparing the camp for myself and the others. No surprise there. At this point, I was used to filling in the gaps. It came with the territory of being the only one too stubborn to fall apart.

I scoured the area until I found a soft patch of dead, yellowed grass.

"Over here, Calina. I think this is the best place to set up your dad for the night." We had no tents or supplies—all that was with Rurik. So we'll just have to make do. "Tonight will be hard, but we should clear the Void tomorrow, and then we'll be able to find something to forage or hunt. We can start rebuilding our supplies and filling our stomachs." Even as I spoke, my belly growled in agreement. We hadn't eaten since... fig, I couldn't even remember when. Time got slippery around the Void. But my body hadn't forgotten. It cataloged every skipped meal like a petty grudge.

"Do you think you'll be okay until then?" I pressed, trying to hide my worry from the girl. I wanted her to be able to eat, but my fears ran so much deeper than that. More than her stomach, she needed something to fill her heart, to prove that the one thing she had always wanted could still be worth having, that her father would return to her. Remember. Even just smile at her.

"I have to be," she answered with so little passion it pained me.

This ghost of her father had not been what she'd expected, and now it was also draining her life force. I couldn't let this continue.

"Calina," I began, waiting for her to settle Gaaron so we could speak freely. "I know this isn't what you'd envisioned, but it's still him. He's just sick. We'll make him better. And then you'll have everything you ever wanted. You'll see."

Her shoulders stiffened, and she said nothing. My heart broke for the girl all over again. The way she bent over him—tucking his cloak tighter, brushing dust from his brow—wasn't just care. It was hope, bruised and desperate and barely hanging on. She looked younger now, stripped of her usual fire, and the sight twisted something in me.

"We're going to win," I said, recalling one of our earliest conversations. I thought of it often, and it seemed relevant now. "Whatever game we're playing, we're going to win," I repeated. "Just because it got harder, that doesn't make us any less capable, you know."

Calina shrugged, then muttered, "I don't know, Tilda. Maybe it was better when I didn't know where he was or if I'd ever see him again."

"Hey, hey, don't talk like that. I don't have all the answers either. That's what makes it an adventure— finding out as you go—testing your mettle. We'll get there. And so will he. We don't know what it will take.

So let's try everything. Do you have any ideas of where to start?"

Calina bit her lower lip as she thought.

"This is really hard," she said. "I thought I would recognize him and that at least he would know me and be happy to see us. But it's like he doesn't feel anything—like he can barely even think. Being around him isn't what I'd imagined. It's just really, really sad. And it reminds me even more of all the time we lost. Maybe we'll never get a chance to make it up. Like he's never going to be okay." Her voice trembled near the end, thick with something unspoken—grief or maybe guilt. Her knuckles were white against her thighs, clenched fists anchoring her to the moment like she might float away without them.

It seemed she might still say more, so I waited, offering her an ear and reminding her that there were adults who cared about her and wanted her to have all the things she so desperately craved.

Calina sighed before continuing, "I know that's not very helpful or hopeful or positive. And I know you've risked a lot to save him and to bring me and train me. And I should be grateful. But I'm having a hard time feeling the right way, believing all the things that I should. And I'm mad at myself. I—"

I had to stop her right there, yanking the girl's wrist to make sure I had her attention.

"That's enough. There's no right way to feel. You don't owe him or me anything. There are no shoulds here. None of us have been in this situation before. But we're in it now, together. And we'll sort it all out, together. Give yourself a break. We've got this. I know we do."

A brief smile played at Calina's lips, but not long enough to fully materialize. She hung her head and sighed. "I'm starting to not even recognize you, Tilda," she whispered.

That sent a pang straight to my chest. I wanted to ask what she meant—what I'd done wrong—but then she spoke again.

"I know I'm the one who's a kid here, but it seems like you're growing up. I like it."

Finally, a complete smile bloomed on that beautiful face of hers. And even though it was the dark of night, my world lit up. The stars above us blinked on one by one, but none of them shone quite like her smile. It was real—fragile, yes, but bright. It tethered me to something solid. Something good.

This was love. This was letting someone in, not in a romantic way, but just in a *person* way. We were connecting—half-elf to halfling. Our fates had entwined, and we'd formed something more significant than either of us on our own.

Tulip and Rurik were part of that, too. And Brynlee. And Gaaron. As our journey continued, more and more ties connected me to others—the family I'd found—both in size and in strength. We weren't just moving forward for the sake of the mission anymore. We were moving for each other, picking up pieces and sometimes people as we went. Building something that maybe—just maybe—could last.

I'd spent so much of this life alone. First as an orphan on the streets, then as a thief, stealing to make my way. I'd had a bright spot with Gaaron, adventuring, but that had been dimmed quite suddenly, snuffed out.

After that, I didn't want to let myself love again. I'd longed for Brynlee. I'd cared about Durgan and Pat, but I hadn't entirely accepted them into my life. I'd cared for them, but I'd held myself back.

I'd been so afraid to get close, knowing how much it can destroy you when that closeness is severed. And because of that, I'd led a nothing kind of life this past decade. It was as if I had just paused—with no intention of ever starting back up again.

For a decade, I'd hidden in Briarhaven. Not just from Maltherius but from everyone. From myself, even. And now, with this teenage companion that I had never wanted—and actively tried to rid myself of many times—I felt the most like myself I ever had.

I was going back to who I'd been in my happiest days on the road with Gaaron, but I was also transforming into someone new. As Calina had said, I was *growing up.*

Huh, I hadn't realized you could do that at my age. And yet here I was, learning all the lessons I'd failed to learn at the correct time.

But when had I had the chance? I'd been so young when my parents died, and that left me to focus only on survival. On making sure I stayed alive rather than actually living.

Apparently, wisdom wasn't reserved for graybeards and prophets. Sometimes, it came disguised as a smirking teen with pointy ears and an overdeveloped sense of justice.

Oh, sweet divinity, this was not the time for a deep personal revelation. We had too much to do.

I needed my heart and brain focused on mending Gaaron and finding Tulip and Rurik. I didn't have the bandwidth to look inward and think about myself, my life, and what I wanted from it.

This was really horrible timing. But maybe—just maybe—it was also precisely what I needed.

9

"Are you going to be okay?" I asked Calina as she sat beside a sleeping Gaaron and tucked her legs under herself.

"I don't know yet," she answered thoughtfully before glancing up at me with a small, knowing smile. "But that's what makes this an adventure, right?"

Her violet eyes sparkled briefly, meeting my brown ones before returning to her father. The flicker of light caught in her irises reminded me of the first time I'd seen them—sharp, defiant, full of purpose. Now, that shine was quieter. But it was still there.

"Go," she whispered after a moment. "Go and figure out what else needs figuring out. I'll keep an eye on him."

I nodded and turned back toward where we had

left Dayna. In the brief time I'd been absent, she'd managed to build a fire and poked at the flames with a gnarled branch. It hissed as she turned a chunk of damp wood, embers leaping up like startled spirits. The fire danced unevenly, casting her face in shifting shades—first monstrous, then tired, then something almost human.

I didn't speak, yet she noted my approach immediately.

"Gonna be a rough night," she informed me as if I didn't already know. "The first of many, I suspect."

She reached for something at her side and moved it closer to the blaze.

"At least I have this small bit of comfort," she said with a sigh before quickly adding in a terse tone, "But it's for me only. I'm not sharing."

She focused on the dancing flames as she reached into her pocket and extracted a fistful of petals. Sweet divinity, she was making wildflower tea. The scent hit me before the recognition did—lavender, honeysuckle, a touch of something citrusy and sharp. It smelled of comfort, of home. That blend was nearly identical to what Brynlee used to brew back home for those quiet times at the tavern when her shift was ending, and mine had yet to begin. I could almost hear the click of her teacup against the saucer, the way she'd say my name like it was a joke she hadn't decided to explain yet.

My mouth salivated as I thought of the special brew I so enjoyed whenever life tossed a quiet moment my way. It felt strange that Dayna also appreciated this ritual.

She seemed so hard, steely, cold. But maybe we had more in common than I'd first imagined. Maybe beneath the armor and that jagged jawline was a woman who still liked flowers. Who wanted warmth, even if she only allowed herself to hold it in tea form.

"If there's any left—"

"No," Dayna cut me off.

But I tried again.

"I meant to say I'd be willing to make a trade for a bit of tea. It's been a rough couple of days, and this would help."

She glanced up at me, her body crouching at the fire's side. I was only slightly taller than her at that moment, even though I was standing at full height.

She seemed far less imposing now. Not just because of our stances or because of the tea, but maybe because she'd slowly begun removing her armor to reveal the odd vulnerability here and there. Her breastplate lay beside her in the dirt, dented and scorched. Without it, she looked smaller. Not weaker—never that—but more real. I could see the faded bruises on her collar-bone, the angry red line of a healing gash across one bicep. It was strange how much softer a person looked with nothing to hide behind.

She was still the toughest person I'd ever known, but less so than I'd originally thought.

I eyed her bulky necklace of battle treasures—Rurik's tusk situated proudly among them. Dried blood clung to the ivory tooth, reminding me of just how brutal she had been in extracting it. The rest of the necklace wasn't much friendlier—pieces of horn, a shard of black glass, a rusted ring twisted into a spiral. If it were anyone else, I'd call it grotesque. But on her, it was... honest—a history worn like a threat. Or maybe a warning.

Maybe it meant she could turn on us at any moment. But hopefully, by then, I would have learned enough about her to see it coming and dodge out of the way.

This wasn't that dissimilar to how things had begun with the kids. They'd clung to me straight away, but I had tried to ditch them at every turn before finally accepting them into my party.

Dayna was different. Maybe because I knew I was outmatched. But maybe not.

"You'd make a trade," she asked with an upward lilt

in her words. "A mug of tea for the artifact? I know you have it. Or at least that you know where to find it. So, what's a small bit of comfort worth to you, I wonder?"

My breath hitched. I would not be so easily swayed. I did enjoy my wildflower tea, yes, but not quite enough to risk the fate of the entire continent. Still, part of me admired her hustle. A tea-for-world-domination trade? Bold. Utterly ridiculous. And also something I might've tried myself once upon a time.

I stared Dayna down, letting my gaze speak volumes.

"Nice try," I said at last, just to get her to stop staring at me so intently.

The one-eyed mercenary shrugged and returned to tending the flames.

"You're a hard one to figure out," she told me a moment later. "Most people wear their intentions like a uniform that can't be removed. But not you. I can't tell what you want at all—or why you'd want to keep something so important from being delivered."

"I think that last part answers your question," I said, raising my brows and waiting for her to get it.

"Finnian Sly is not a good person," she agreed with an odd hum. "But most people I work with in my line of duty are not. What difference does it make whether the necromancer or the master thief has the prize? We don't even know what it can do."

"Yes, yes, and that's what makes the biggest difference. We don't know what this thing can do and why either wants it. But changing the crest's owner can only bring about bad things. I'd prefer to keep the world as it is rather than risk a fresh calamity." I rubbed my arms against the chill settling in, not from the night air but from the weight of what we were talking about. It wasn't just some shiny bauble. It was a ticking bomb, and we were stuck deciding which villain to hand the fuse to.

"You want the world to remain as it is?" she asked with a smirk. "But the world is a terrible place. It's cold and cruel, unflinching and unforgiving."

"Funny. Those are all words I would use to describe you," I quipped.

But Dayna did not seem offended by my assessment. And then she did the most unexpected thing of all—she opened up to me.

As she finished mixing her tea and then sank back onto her rump to make herself comfortable, she confided a bit of her story.

"I used to think that if I worked hard enough, I could be something. I could... I don't know, make a difference. Help people even. All my life, I have heard that a human girl like me would never be able to complete the initiation into the wing scouts."

She huffed.

"That it was made for other races, men primarily. That I was just too weak and unimportant. And that made me angry. So instead of giving up, I decided to prove them all wrong." Her fingers twitched around the mug like she wanted to crush it. Like if she squeezed hard enough, she could wring out every sneer and scoff she'd ever endured.

She poked the cheekbone beneath her glass eye with a gentle finger and let out a sigh.

"I did rise to the top of the ranks. But it only made things worse. As one of the strongest among the scouts, I received the most difficult assignments. And more often than not, they were for bad men."

Her voice softened, but she did not look at me.

"They used me as a tool for change, but never the good kind. And by then, I'd already committed my whole life. I had nowhere else to turn. And if I said no to the wrong person, I would be executed or worse, exiled." Her gaze dropped to the fire again. The flames reflected in her eye—the real one, not the glass—and in that moment, she looked ancient, not in years, but in burdens. In how long she'd been carrying the weight of people she'd never wanted to serve.

I swallowed hard, unsure of what to say. I'd expected a villain—a threat. I wasn't prepared for a survivor. And I hated that I recognized something in her—some jagged mirror of myself, shaped by different choices but broken just the same.

"So you may be afraid of letting power fall into the wrong hands, of giving this artifact to Finnian Sly," Dayna continued. "But let me reassure you that, with or without our help, power will always fall to the wrong men. Because those are the ones that seek it. And there's nothing you or I can do to stop it. We can only hope to delay it for a little while."

"That's better than nothing," I said with a practiced shrug. It was the same gesture I turned to whenever things started to feel too real, or at least real in a way I was unequipped to handle.

"Maybe. But I don't think so. I've been at this too long. Seen too much," she scoffed as if anticipating the joke that immediately rose to my mind. "Yes, even with just one eye, I've seen it all. The world isn't going to change, Tilda. So we might as well get on with our lives."

She shook her head and then took a long swig of tea. Steam curled around her face like a veil, softening the hard lines. But it didn't reach her eye. It stayed sharp and alert like she was always scanning for betrayal. Maybe she was.

I left her there, not wanting to consider this conversation. Not wanting to admit how much of it made sense. How tempting it was, sometimes, to give up trying to be good in a world that seemed allergic to it.

As Calina had said, I was growing. And it seemed like Dayna had been cut off at the trunk. Would her deep roots ever give way to something beautiful again? Or was she beyond hope?

I now knew that I wasn't. Beyond hope, that is.

I could still light up this world and light the path for others. And I wanted to do that for my companions. Yes, even Dayna. I also couldn't force her to consider the world any way other than she saw it.

She was right about some things, but not everything. And even if my part to play was infinitesimally small—that was the halfling way, after all—I would still play it even if the game was rigged and the score would never be in our favor. I wasn't ready to fold yet.

But before I could do any of these things, I'd first need a good night's rest. Assuming the nightmares took the night off. Assuming I didn't wake to a sword in my back and Dayna gone with the crest.

Assuming hope didn't betray me the way it had betrayed her.

I yawned, feeling the full weight of the day's activities crash into me. Every night I closed my eyes to court sleep, I took another small leap of faith, trusting that the morning would come and deliver a day worth living.

I wondered if Dayna viewed it that way, too. Or if she always refused even the smallest leaps, deciding that anything less than full flight wasn't worth her effort.

I'd been like that. Recently, too.

But tonight, I would sleep with both eyes shut. It had been a long time coming, and I was so, so tired. Not only did I need this rest, but I'd also earned it.

Dayna had, too.

But I would have to let her figure that out for herself.

10

My stomach grumbled unhappily beneath my tunic, but there was nothing I could offer it. Our rations—the so-called tanuki cookies—had been on Rurik when we teleported, which meant they were now lost along with the rest of our supplies. It was a cruel twist of fate, considering those awful little bricks had only started growing on me. I used to call them "crumble-and-cry biscuits," but now I'd have happily eaten a whole bag of them, sobbing included.

Dayna was unwilling to share what she had, which was fair given that I wasn't even willing to share my information, either. Let alone the artifact. Adventuring was hard. Some nights, you went to bed hungry, tired, defeated. That's just how this life was. I knew what I'd signed up for, even if I had reluctantly done so the second time.

Still, we'd achieved a significant victory today. One I still didn't fully understand and definitely didn't trust. But progress was progress. The kind of progress that left bruises on your ribs and a splinter in your soul, but still. A win. I had to believe that, or the exhaustion might catch up and bury me right here in the Void-dusted grass.

I got up and paced around the makeshift camp briefly to soothe my worried mind into a state that might allow for sleep. Dayna remained at the fire. Calina at her father's side. Occasionally, I would hear the soft notes of a lullaby weaving their way through our destitute camp. The song drifted like mist, barely there, just enough to make your chest ache without knowing why. Her voice was raw, the notes catching now and then, but she kept going. Braver than I'd ever been in grief.

Calina so badly wanted to connect with her father. I wondered if the song she was singing to him was one he had once written for her and if he would recognize it.

It seemed there would be no answers tonight, seeing as Gaaron remained stuck in slumber. He didn't even twitch. Just breathed in that eerie, too-even rhythm. I kept telling myself it meant he was healing, not vanishing. That he was still in there. Just out of reach.

Where was my vivacious friend who loved life and the people who filled it even more? If Gaaron could see the pain he was causing his daughter, he would be so unhappy with himself. My friend still had to be in there somewhere, inside the skin and bones we had rescued.

And when we finally escaped the Void and made our way to more fertile lands, we'd have a much easier time reviving him. This was a problem, but still not the biggest one we'd faced.

Tulip and Rurik could be anywhere within Verandel, and with a misfired spell of that size, they could be anywhere beyond Verandel as well. And I had no doubts they were searching for us, too. The chances of us randomly finding each other were slim, especially if both parties remained on the move. It felt like trying to hit an arrow with another arrow while blindfolded during a hurricane. But we had one advantage: our bonds. That annoying, powerful, maddening force that made people chase each other across impossible distances. Found family wasn't just a theme—it was a compass. And I had to trust it would point us toward each other eventually.

Whatever the case, we couldn't stay here. We had to get Gaaron to someplace where he could recover. And Dayna, too; she needed to check in with the other scouts and begin the process of reclaiming her title.

The biggest question was where Finnian Sly had gotten off to. Was he with my missing party members, or had he refused to teleport, instead remaining at the battle-torn Mystwood Keep? Had he watched us vanish with that smug little smirk of his, already calculating the next ten moves on his game board? Or had we thrown him off, forced him to adjust? I hoped it was the latter. Sly hated improvising despite often being forced to do just that.

I still didn't understand his motives or how the Genesis Crest would help him achieve them. He'd always been a schemer, but this was bigger than schemes. This was myth-stuff, and Sly had never been content with mortal legend. He wanted his name etched into the foundations of the world. I just didn't know whether he planned to rule it—or burn it down.

I knew the tanuki well, having spent many years under his tutelage. But whatever this was felt different and difficult to predict, making it dangerous.

Maybe Dayna was right. Perhaps we couldn't make a difference. But if that were true, that meant there was no point in trying—or even to life at all.

And while I might have once been able to accept that for myself, I refused to believe it for the kids. This all had to mean something, even if I couldn't yet figure out what.

Otherwise, Sylric and the other gods were cruel tyrants, tormenting us for nothing more than a simple amusement. Everything... Dayna's pain and cynicism. Gaaron's frailty and imprisonment. My shame and years spent hiding from the world. No, I couldn't believe it was for nothing.

And I wouldn't wait for meaning to find me—I would go out and secure it. Corrupt and powerful men weren't the only ones who could make things happen. Even a tiny, middle-aged halfling had the power to change the world. In fact, I'd already done it.

We didn't know what the crest could do but had no doubts of its immense power. And for ten years, I had wielded that power responsibly. I had kept it from destroying our world. Not through might or magic but by being really, really stubborn. Sometimes, that's all it took—just refusing to let the bad guys win.

I'd already done something that mattered, even if it wasn't exactly on purpose. I could surely do more if I kept trying and kept showing up. We'd gotten Gaaron back. And with time, we would see him recover, too.

Of course, I would eventually need to find a more

permanent solution to dealing with the Genesis Crest's power. I couldn't hope to keep it hidden with me forever.

But I didn't yet know another way. That was the whole point of journeys: to find your way to what mattered. I didn't always end up where I meant to go, but I usually wound up where I needed to be. Over the years, I'd become a master of taking each trail one step —or sometimes, one wild leap—at a time.

I could do this. I could save us all, even though we didn't know what the threat entailed. I could still prevent it from coming to pass.

Dayna was wrong. Perhaps I could show her that. After all, I'd already come this far. What was venturing a little bit more?

With that last thought, I finally allowed myself to grab some rest. The ground was hard, the air cold, my belly empty. But my heart? That was full. Just enough to dream.

A bright sun and cold feet woke me. No, I hadn't lessened in my resolve. My toes were literally freezing.

I shot up into a sitting position and spied our dragonling companion, huffing little ice breaths against my bare feet with glee. Tiny, frosty swirls clung to my toes like glittering snowflakes—cute, if they hadn't also felt like daggers made of winter.

"Frosty, no!" I cried and yanked my knees toward my chest to gain some distance.

The little whitish-blue creature howled with what I suspected was laughter and fell onto his side, rolling back and forth as he tittered. His little wings flapped uselessly as he wriggled in the dirt, his icy breath puffing out in rhythmic bursts that instantly melted in the pale sun. He looked far too pleased with himself.

"Calina, your dragon is being naughty!" I shouted, searching our meager campsite for the girl.

"Frosty isn't mine," she responded, strolling over. "He's his own creature. He makes his own decisions."

"Well, can you ask him to decide not to bother me while I'm sleeping?" I huffed. "And while he's at it, to not bother me at all. I'm ticklish."

Calina rolled her eyes. "Yeesh. Other than the ticklish part, you're beginning to sound like Dayna." The accusation landed like a slap. A very cold, very pointy slap.

"Take that back," I challenged.

The girl shook her head and joined Frosty in laughter. "I only speak the truth. If you don't want me to compare you to her, don't act like her."

Dayna was seated at the fire, enjoying a morning cup of tea that made me terribly jealous. I knew better than to ask her to share.

I certainly didn't want to replace my morning pep with Dayna's jaded cynicism. Whatever blend she was sipping, I suspected it tasted like bitterness and long-simmered rage, possibly with a hint of lemon.

No, I needed to keep my spirits high. Because today would be long. We had much to accomplish and no idea where to even begin. I at least knew our most pressing objective.

"We need to find the others," I said, stretching my arms overhead and adjusting my neck and shoulders with audible cracks.

"But we don't have any idea where they are," Calina argued back immediately. Her brows knit tightly together, worry pooling in the corners of her eyes. She was trying not to panic, but the cracks were starting to show.

"Well, let's think about this," I said, motioning for the girl to follow me to the fire so that Dayna could also be part of the conversation. "You know Rurik better than anyone. And you know how his mind works. I'm pretty sure that between him and Tulip, he would be the one taking the lead. So where would he have chosen to go?"

"It's hard to say since we don't know where the teleportation landed them." She kicked a rock, which bounced off a tree root and nailed Frosty in the tail. He yelped dramatically and flopped over as if mortally wounded.

"That's a fair point," I conceded. "But we only have what we have, and that's what we need to work with. So how about—"

Dayna raised her hand as she continued to slurp at her tea. We waited for her to finish since she obviously wanted to say something.

"You don't know where the spell spit them out," she revealed with a slight, self-satisfied nod. "But as one of its casters, I do."

And now I was back to wanting to enact physical violence against members of my own figgin' party. But as much as I wanted to, I would not clobber the mercenary. Mostly because I knew she would hit back—and that she would hit much harder than I could. Also, she'd probably enjoy it a little too much, and I wasn't emotionally prepared to unpack that.

"You knew this whole time and didn't say anything?" Calina's nostrils flared. She didn't even try to hide her irritation.

"No, I didn't," Dayna said simply and directly. "We had another, more pressing mission first. And after that, well... Nobody asked me, now did they?" She took another long, smug sip of tea, pinky slightly raised in the most passive-aggressive toast I'd ever seen.

"I hate you," Calina spat. "Like really, truly hate you. You are the worst person I have ever met. And I've met Finnian Sly. I've met Eldrin Grimlock. I've—"

"Calina," I said, tugging at her hand to get her attention. "You need to calm down. Dayna probably should have told us earlier. True. But at least she's willing to tell us now. And insulting her isn't the best way to get her to share the information. So, chill."

Hearing this word, Frosty waddled over on all fours, then switched to his hind legs and pawed at Calina's hip, begging to be picked up. His tail left a little icy trail behind him, a curlicue of frost on the already-dead grass.

Of course, the word "chill" would appeal to a frost dragon.

She hefted him into her arms and hugged him to her chest. He gave a delighted trill and started licking her cheek, probably freezing off a few layers of skin.

"Dayna, please continue." Given the circumstances, I addressed her as nicely as possible. "You know where the others are?"

Dayna tilted her head in thought. "I know where they landed—not where they've gone since then."

"Still, that's the best information we've got. So tell me—where *were* they?"

Dayna sighed and reached for the pack at her side. "Let me show you on the map." She rummaged for a while, muttering to herself until she pulled out a crumpled, slightly singed map that looked like it had been through at least one minor apocalypse. She smoothed it flat with a sigh, then jabbed her finger into a patch of forest surrounded by jagged mountain symbols.

Good. Now, we were getting somewhere. I just hoped it was a place we could reach with one day's walking. Because if not, I would have to choose between starvation, frostbite, or voluntarily conversing with Dayna. And frankly, I wasn't sure which possibility irked me the most.

11

Dayna unfurled her map on the ground before us, then pointed to the upper right corner. "The three of us landed—"

"Shkow!" Frosty protested and nipped at the parchment with his teeth.

"Fine. The four of us," Dayna grumbled. "But touch this map again, and I'll turn you into nice pair of new gloves for myself." She gave him a slow, dangerous blink—the kind that suggested she wasn't bluffing.

Frosty snorted a puff of frost into the air and did an exaggerated bow, tail wagging like a misbehaving dog trying to charm its way out of punishment.

I held back a laugh, not at Frosty but at Dayna. She sounded so much like Tulip, threatening anyone who dared take what was hers.

Dayna caught me with her one good eye, threatening me to let out another giggle.

I immediately fell silent, not wanting to risk her sudden willingness to help us.

Once she appeared confident I was done acting out, Dayna continued, "The four of us landed up here on the edge of the Void, toward Quartz Lake," she said. "Your friends didn't make it past Mystwood Forest. They wound up closer to our starting point than the actual destination." Her finger tapped the worn parchment twice, then trailed downward. The map lay half-curled on the ground, edges lifting in the wind like it wanted to escape our planning session entirely. A smear of soot near the Lazul River mark made the waterway look more like a scar than a salvation, and somehow, that felt appropriate.

Dayna jabbed her index finger at another spot on the map. "And based on how we've been walking so far, we're here. We're approaching the river on the northern edge of the forest but are still at least a full day out. We'll smell it before we see it," she muttered, squinting at the terrain. "The Lazul's always had a way of announcing itself. Cold, metallic. Like rain on old swords."

"Meanwhile, Finnian Sly and the other wing scout

are here," she added, pointing up and to the left. *"Sandsibar."*

As she named that last place, a shudder seemed to overtake her. The word dropped like a stone in a pond —still but heavy. Even Frosty stopped his incessant wriggling to pay closer attention.

"So Finnian is not with Tulip and Rurik?" Calina asked, either not caring about the tension or missing it entirely. "I'm not sure whether that's good or bad."

"I don't know what to tell you," Dayna replied in her signature snarl. "Finnian's probably already found a way back to Mirathane, which is why we're heading south toward the city. As for your friends, I have no idea."

I looked at Calina. She set Frosty back on the ground and approached Dayna and me at the fire.

"Rurik is coming to us," she said. "He knew that our goal was to get to Maltherius. So that's what he would have done."

"You don't think he's planning to sneak in there himself, do you?" I asked, raising an eyebrow in concern.

"Well, he's got Tulip with him," Calina answered slowly as if her words were struggling to keep up with her thoughts. "So no, he's probably going to set up camp and wait for us. Assuming we'll be doing the same."

"But we're headed in the opposite direction," I said with a slow exhale. "And the distance between the forest and the Void is huge. The chances of running into them aren't so hot." Frosty whimpered again, this time curling into a little puffball of disappointment. I didn't have the heart to mention we were all feeling the same way.

"So what do we do?" Calina wanted to know.

"We do our best to intercept them," I said. "Either way, we have to get to lusher terrain to start helping your dad feel better."

As one, our group glanced toward Gaaron, who still slept upon a bed of dead grass. His skin appeared waxen and moist like he'd been struggling with something through the night. It looked like he'd fought a dozen battles in his sleep and lost every one. He was sweating without heat, pale under the sun. He looked so fragile. Like one more wrong move might undo everything we'd worked for.

I knew basic adventure treatment—how to treat the typical scrapes and bangs, how to stitch up a stab wound, how to cauterize an arrow wound after pulling the arrow out, and even how to splint a broken bone—

but treating Gaaron required healing skills far beyond anything I possessed.

"I have to get back to Nexara," Dayna said. "That's where the wing scout headquarters are situated. And I'll need to report about the damage to my mantle so that I can officially begin a new hunt."

"So, are you going your own way?" I asked, feeling a pang of disappointment that surprised me. Not that I liked Dayna. But I was... *used to* her by now. She was a skilled fighter and navigator. We'd be better with her than without.

"I'll need to get there eventually," she clarified. "But first, I have to deliver on this quest. And as I said, Finnian will have found his way back to Mirathane by now."

Calina studied the map carefully. "So we walk down the map. That will take us through the forest and to Mirathane. And as we walk, we'll do our best to find Rurik and Tulip on the way."

"I think that's our best bet," I agreed. "Unless Dayna or Frosty have other ideas."

Frosty perked up at this, the fins on his head expanding, making him look like half a flower as he unleashed a series of clicks and hisses in response.

Calina laughed. "He says since we're going south,

we should hit Coldrift Vale. That's where his home is, and he misses it." Her voice cracked a little on that last word, quickly taking all her previous mirth with it. The thought of someone having a real home again—especially someone so small and loyal—was more emotional than she'd expected.

"Coldrift Vale is out of the way," Dayna said with no sympathy.

"Why did you laugh just then?" I asked, wanting to understand the girl.

"It wasn't what he said," Calina explained. "It was the way he said it. It just made me feel happy. Like I was part of his memories." She gave Frosty a nuzzle, and he licked her chin with a tongue that left a little patch of frost behind.

"Okay," I said slowly, trying to concentrate on the task at hand. "So we proceed south toward Mirathane by way of Mystwood Forest. Dayna, how long will it take before we reach forageable lands?"

"If we can keep a good clip, we should manage by nightfall," she replied. "Though we'll find huntable prey before then. I'll keep an eye out and secure whatever wanders our way. But the deal hasn't changed. I'm not sharing unless you share. And you know what I want."

Dayna stopped speaking and dropped her gaze to my chest with a slight tilt of her lips.

The crest felt warm against my breastbone, and I couldn't tell what that meant. Was it reminding me that it wanted to stay with me rather than go with Dayna? Or was it... *excited?*

I still wasn't used to dealing with semi-sentient jewelry, so I didn't understand how to read its various mystic cues. I knew better than to draw attention to it or myself.

So I remained still, trying to maintain a placid, almost bored expression.

Calina spoke up next. "I know you don't want to share with me or Tilda, but if you could give my dad some water, I think you'd make it easier for all of us today, including yourself. He's weak, and even a little bit would help."

Dayna nodded and handed over her canteen—another surprise.

"Not too much, though," she warned, reaching for the hilt of one sword for emphasis. "I won't be able to refill it until we hit the river. And I need to be hydrated to remain at my best," she added, nodding toward the snaking blue thread on the map. "If we veer a little west, we may be able to catch it before nightfall."

"This is your best?" I teased. "I'd hate to see you at your worst."

Dayna growled as if to say, *keep poking at me, and soon you will.* Frosty growled too, but his sounded more like a squeaky yawn. I was pretty sure he just liked participating.

Calina had been right. Getting some fluids in Gaaron helped bring him back to himself a bit. He still needed Dayna and Calina's help to walk, but he remained awake and semi-aware of his surroundings for much of the day.

Sometimes, he even mumbled something—a word, a name, half a prayer. None of it ever made sense, not to me. But Calina clung to each syllable like it was a thread she could use to pull him home.

I wanted to talk to him, but everything that needed to be said needed to be said *in private.* So, instead, I focused on putting one foot in front of the other, letting the monotony keep my thoughts at bay. The ache in my calves, the burning in my feet, the way my boots rubbed raw at my heels—all of it kept me grounded in the present. And right now, the present demanded my full attention.

The chances of us accidentally bumping into Tulip and Rurik were slight, but they weren't nonexistent. I worried about those kids—lost, probably terrified. Sure, Rurik had a level head, but he was still a teenager. He was also dealing with the overwhelming amount of magic fused into the fiber of his being through Amariel's sacrifice. Who even knew what kind of issues he faced now? And Tulip... well, at least she was with Rurik. I could only hope they hadn't stumbled into something worse than what we were already dealing with.

Knowing that our supplies had ended up with them, that they would be fed, and if nothing else, they were resilient, was a small comfort.

My stomach was now spitting acid like an angry poison-barb dragon. I needed to fill it soon. And to do that, I needed to keep moving at the fastest pace I could manage. Every step sent a small protest up my spine. My head pulsed like a drumbeat. And the corners of my vision had started doing this odd shimmering thing I didn't love.

Hunger had long since stopped growling and started whispering—an eerie, distant whine behind my ears. The longer we went without food or drink, the harder it would be to continue. So I had to give it my all and then some.

My eyes grew weary with fatigue, and the scenery seemed to dance around me. I was asking way too much of myself without offering anything in return. The trees shifted when I wasn't looking. The wind hummed like a lullaby. For a terrifying second, I was convinced the sun was blinking at me.

At least we'd made it out of the Void. Our surroundings were alive again, if still a little anemic. The farther we walked, the more the grays turned green, and the more the sun shone like it meant it. The increased vitality of the landscape only reminded me of my dwindling stamina.

Even still, I kept walking. It was the only thing to do...

Sometime in the late afternoon, we spotted a herd of hoofed creatures. I couldn't tell what species they belonged to, but Dayna made quick work of picking off one of the weaker members of the herd.

She sliced its throat with her sword—much as she had done with the regent back at Mystwood Keep— then made us wait while she butchered a few haunches and used some cord from her pack to tie them to her person. Blood streaked up her arms like paint, but her face remained calm. Clinical. The efficiency of a predator with no illusions left.

"We'll rest when we reach the river," she reminded

us, pressing forward when I had hoped we might take a break.

I needed that meat. But would it require giving up the crest to obtain it?

If I died of hunger, I did not doubt that Dayna would loot my corpse and find it anyway. The thought alone gave me enough strength to keep walking. But I knew I wouldn't last much longer without a reprieve.

12

I felt the river long before it came into sight. The way the air grew moist and heavy felt like a blessing I had started to worry I would never receive. Soon, I could taste the dampness on my tongue and hear its rushing ripples.

My vision had grown hazy from hunger and thirst, but seeing that beautiful, rushing river put everything into focus again. I somehow found renewed vitality, breaking into a sprint so I wouldn't have to wait a second longer to secure a drink. Reaching its edge, I fell to my knees, sliding forward and thrusting my cupped palms into its chilly surface to bring a small pool to my mouth.

Oh, sweet divinity, nothing had ever tasted finer than this!

I greedily consumed the entire well in my palms and then dipped my hands for another blessed gulp. I drank that and dipped my hands again.

But Dayna, who had caught up now, yanked me from behind, causing me to fall back. "You're going to make yourself sick," she barked.

Who cared? I was already sick from thirst, hunger, and plain old exhaustion. Now that my thirst had finally been sated, my stomach was beginning to fill, the discomfort disappearing with each glorious new swallow. I attempted to crawl back to the river, but Dayna grabbed my ankle and held tight.

"If you keep drinking like that, you're going to vomit," she warned. "And that's going to make me lose my appetite. And that will make me angry, so you should stop. Come help me prepare the fire."

I kicked at her, and she let go. But I knew she'd find another, more aggressive way to stop me if I made for the river again. So I followed as she collected wood and sticks from the surrounding area.

Calina and Gaaron arrived at the river just as Dayna and I moved off to find kindling. Calina immediately crouched beside the bank and took a measured sip, then another—careful, controlled, like someone who'd actually listened to past lectures about rehydration after starvation. She dipped her hands again, this time cupping the water and offering it to Gaaron, who looked dazed but grateful. He drank slowly, lips cracked and voice too hoarse to speak.

"I'm so hungry," I moaned, turning my attention back to the cruel mercenary who'd deprived me of those sweet additional sips I so desperately craved. "I really need to get some food in me, and I know you require a trade, but I can't give you what you want. Mostly because I don't have it." I flashed her an expression halfway between a grimace and a smile; it was the best I could muster in my extremely weakened state. Even still, it was the kind of glance that had, in the past, gotten me out of at least two death sentences and countless unwanted flirtations with Bramble Thistledown back home in Briarhaven. But would it work on a mercenary with cheekbones that could slice a melon? Would it convince her to help me even though I couldn't return the favor anytime in the foreseeable future?

Dayna huffed, tilted her head, and regarded me as if I were a naughty child. I tried to hold her stare, but it was like locking eyes with a wildcat—beautiful, sharp, and very possibly seconds from mauling you just for breathing wrong.

"We both know that's not true," she said with a smile playing on her lips. "But I'll feed you anyway.

It's easier than carrying this with us. And now that we've reached the forest edge, it will be easy to find more."

She turned away, so I couldn't tell whether she was being serious or simply trying to get a rise out of me. Then—because apparently being half-starved wasn't enough of a humbling experience—she knelt over a butchered haunch with theatrical precision. She slowly unsheathed her curved skinning knife, never breaking my gaze. *...slice...slice.*

I watched, half-horrified, half-hypnotized, as she began slicing the meat into perfect, deliberate strips. The knife moved like an extension of her will: smooth, efficient, merciless. I felt like I should be taking notes or genuflecting. *...slice...slice.*

"So...is that my portion?" I asked, hoping to sound casual and not like I was two seconds from licking the air. *...slice...slice.*

Dayna didn't answer. She kept slicing, slower now, as if the meat offended her. As if deciding to feed me was a punishment. *...slice.*

I tried a new tactic. I leaned in and dropped my voice. "Look, if this is about earlier—when I maybe implied you were emotionally constipated—I only meant it in the most respectful way."

No reaction. *...slice.*

"Okay, fine," I snapped, standing back up. "I'm sorry, okay? Also, thank you for all your help so far."

Her lips squeezed into a tight line...*slice.* She nodded at me—her way of saying I was welcome. I'd take it.

Dayna was ruthless, yes, but we were on the same side for the time being. It was good to know she wouldn't let me starve to death.

She was many things—and even if charming wasn't one of them—she wasn't cruel like I'd originally thought. Not the kind that lets someone waste away slowly when a clean strike would do.

Even knowing all this, I hated how much our group had come to depend on her. We couldn't carry Gaaron without her. I might be able to catch a rabbit or other small creature, but I wasn't strong enough to bring down something that could feed the whole party. Calina could hunt—if she wasn't juggling the needs of a dragonling and a semi-comatose dad—but she didn't have her bow. Dayna was also the only one with any supplies—the canteen, mug, and who knew what else.

We'd be able to restock once we hit the city, but I hoped that we would find Tulip and Rurik first, that they still had our group's original rations with them. That small bit of luck would make everything else much easier.

Another day had come and gone without them at our sides, which meant I was failing at this whole mentor thing. Calina was an emotional wreck, and the other two were still missing. They were clever, they were survivors, but they were still kids.

I honestly didn't know what was worse—watching the elf girl suffer before my eyes or losing sight of our orc and centaur. Okay, definitely the latter. The idea of Rurik and Tulip lost and alone made my chest feel like it was caving in.

No, I couldn't think about this now. It was not until morning that I could resume the search. I needed to fill my stomach, rest my limbs, and get myself back into fighting shape tonight.

I helped Dayna assemble the fire, but she paid me little attention as she focused on the work that needed to be done. Once the flame had grown to an adequate size, she situated her neatly sliced stripes of meat over its top. She then rummaged in her bag and extracted the mug I'd seen her using earlier for her tea.

"Fill it halfway with water from the river," she instructed. "Then bring it back."

And so I did. I didn't usually fall in line so easily, but I was exhausted and grateful that she had changed her stance on feeding us. When I returned the mug, she dropped several small hunks of meat into the cup and set it near the blaze.

"Your friend is weak," she said. "He probably won't be able to chew very well, but this broth should help him regain some of his strength. Give it time to cook, and then you can take it to him."

"That's kind of you. Thank you," I said, too tired and shocked to come up with a wittier response.

"As your pinkish companion said this morning, strengthening him will aid us all," Dayna muttered. "We'll journey much faster if he can support himself."

I nodded and sat watching as Frosty splashed and played in the river. The little guy looked so happy, and that had a way of lifting my spirits, too. He chased his reflection like it owed him money, then blew tiny jets of frost onto the rocks to make them slippery, sliding across them on his belly and giggling. Actual giggling. I didn't even know dragons could giggle.

Calina fussed over Gaaron as she helped him get comfortable on a bed of soft sand.

"You should probably bring him close to the fire," Dayna said, following my line of sight. "Warmth can do wonders for a tired body."

She was right. Calina had no experience tending to the sick or injured. And I'd been so caught up with the logistics of what came next that I hadn't thought about how to help my friend.

Calina had made herself his designated nursemaid early on, and Dayna had all the resources. It hadn't felt like there was a need for me, but I was the only one who truly knew the man. I could offer him comfort of spirit.

So I got up, crossed over to Calina, and motioned for her to help me resituate her father near the fire. It was difficult supporting even a small amount of his weight, but we didn't have far to take him, so I gritted my teeth and endured it.

We let him fall a bit too heavily to the ground, and he let out a soft "oof" when he made an impact with the beach. He remained sitting, though, which I took as a good sign.

At some point, Calina had finger-combed the worst tangles from his hair and looked a bit less disheveled now. His eyes remained sunken, but they burned with new awareness as they became entranced by the flames dancing before him.

He reached out a hand and leaned forward, almost letting the flames lap at his skin before Calina pulled him back.

"I remember this," he said, his voice regaining some of its previous lyricism. It was softer than before, fragile like parchment that had spent too long in the rain. But it had melody, and that alone brought tears to my eyes.

He turned his face slowly, scanning us—one by one—as if seeing us all anew. His eyes lingered on Calina, and something passed between them that I could never interpret. Grief, maybe. Curiosity. Wonder. *Recognition?* Gods, I hoped it was that.

When his eyes landed on me, his lips parted like he would speak my name, but no sound came. Still, I nodded back, a promise in the gesture. I'm here. I've got you.

And then came the most shocking part of all—he smiled. Just a little. Just enough to be real.

Dayna noticed, too. Her hands stilled where they had been prodding the meat, and she gave him the briefest once-over before returning to her work. Not impressed. Not interested. Maybe she just didn't trust him. Perhaps she didn't trust anyone. I wasn't sure. But her disinterest stood out—especially to a man like Gaaron.

Frosty returned and curled around Gaaron's back; he made a happy cooing noise, and the bard responded with a tiny, grateful hum.

Dayna handed me the mug of broth, and I held it out toward Calina, but the girl shook her head and motioned for me to take the lead. "He knows you," she whispered. "He remembers."

So I helped Gaaron hold the mug and guided it to his lips. He took a slow sip, then another, his trembling hands eventually steadying around the cup. With each swallow, color began to creep back into his cheeks, and the vacant look behind his eyes retreated just a little further. It wasn't a miracle. But it was something.

"This is good," he murmured after a moment. "You cooked?"

I laughed softly. "No, that was Dayna." I tilted my head toward her.

He followed the motion, and something wavered to life in his expression—mischief, charm, that spark he'd always wielded so carelessly. "A woman who knows how to cook and wield a sword? Be still, my heart."

Dayna didn't even blink. She threw another stick on the fire and kept chewing.

"You'll need more than flattery to impress me," she said flatly. "Like a pulse."

I snorted. Calina giggled. Gaaron just looked faintly embarrassed and went back to sipping. And me? I studied Dayna's profile in the firelight: that sharp jaw, stoic mouth, and the one good eye that gave nothing away.

And suddenly, I wondered—what if Dayna was the one person Gaaron couldn't charm? What if she saw something the rest of us couldn't? Or maybe... what if I liked that she couldn't be swayed? That she wasn't falling under the same nostalgic spell I was spinning around myself like armor?

I tucked that thought away. I wasn't ready for it.

We sat there for a while, sharing the meat Dayna had cooked, passing it hand to hand, and letting the fire warm more than just our skin. The Lazul River whispered beside us, its soft, steady current sounding a little like hope.

And for once, I didn't argue with it.

13

Night settled over our camp like an old blanket someone forgot to shake the sand out of—technically warm, but not exactly comforting. The Lazul River murmured beside us; it was almost as if the stream knew we were barely holding it together and wanted to help in its own babbling way.

Cross-legged and fog-brained, I sat by the fire, gnawing my strip of meat like it held the answer to life's big questions. And for that brief moment in time, perhaps it did. My stomach was filled past bursting, but still, I ate, so relieved to no longer be starving.

Gaaron sat across from me, back straight, legs folded, fingers twitching like they were searching for a long-lost instrument. He looked... better. Not exactly lively, but less like a corpse someone had forgotten to bury. Calina stuck to him like a hopeful shadow. Dayna was off to the side, sharpening her blades on an endless loop. The constant *shhhk-shhhk-shhhk* reminded me of the sounds Frosty made, but I knew better than to point that out.

The little dragon himself had passed out in a tangled heap of tail and wing, tucked happily behind Calina to avoid taking in too much heat from the fire.

"Can you remember anything else from the time before... well, you know?" I asked my old friend casually, tearing another bite with my teeth.

He hesitated, then smiled. "I remember that you always claimed the burnt pieces for yourself. And it seems you still do."

I blinked at the charred hunk of flesh in my hands; it was extra-crispy but still perfectly edible. "No use in letting good food go to waste."

He chuckled, deep and warm, glancing up to study the stars overhead before leveling his gaze back at the others. "Is there a chance any of you good folk have a pan flute on hand? I'd also settle for any well-strung instrument, but this evening simply requires a bit of song," he asked suddenly.

"A flute?" I blinked. "Unless Dayna's hiding one in her boot, I'm going to go with no."

"Hmm." He scanned our surroundings, eyes settling on a cluster of reeds near the riverbank. "Give me a moment."

He stood—wobbly but upright—and shuffled toward the water. Calina made a noise like she might follow, but I waved her off. "Let him try."

A few minutes later, he returned with a stick and a small bottle gourd he must've found near the riverbank. He sat down with a determined air and began tinkering.

Dayna snorted. "What are you doing?"

"Making something worthwhile," he answered.

She scoffed. "Music is a waste of time."

"So are most beautiful things," he said without missing a beat, twirling the stick into the gourd with elegant fingers.

Dayna rolled her eyes and returned to her sharpening, the metal scraping on stone growing louder.

Ten minutes later, Gaaron lifted his creation—a sort of gourd flute—and blew a cautious breath through it. "It's not a gabblewonky, but this should do in a pinch."

He spent the next few minutes testing the notes, adjusting the force of his breath and position of his fingers, and then, all at once, he began to play. The melody that filled the camp was soft, haunting, and far more beautiful than it had any right to be.

My jaw dropped. Calina gasped. Even Frosty lifted his head, blinking in sleepy admiration. It was beautiful. Ethereal.

But Gaaron winced.

"That bad, huh?" he asked, grimacing.

I blinked. "No! That was... amazing. Are you kidding?"

Calina clapped her hands together, beaming. "It was perfect. Like river light turned into sound. I wonder if that's what it's always like for Amariel now that she's in the celestial realm again."

Gaaron gave a crooked smile. "I'm glad you like my clumsy attempt at music, but it's not right. Not to my ear. No, in fact, I'd say it sounds most like a bag of cats being slammed against a stone wall."

Calina giggled, and Gaaron paused briefly to smile at her. He looked sad, though.

After a few moments of silence, he played again. This time, the tune was gentler, something vaguely familiar. My chest tightened. It had to be something he'd written once, long ago. Back when music poured out of him like breath. But how could he remember it now? How could someone who'd been barely coherent hours ago create something so moving, so precise? Unless...

Unless something wasn't adding up.

"You always had a talent for that," I murmured.

He hooked an eyebrow. "Making instruments out of garbage?"

"No. Making things feel less broken."

Calina scooted closer to him, eyes wide. "Can you teach me? I want to try."

He blinked at her like she was a distant figure behind the fog. His attention lingered, searching her face for recognition he didn't find. But then he smiled and passed the improvised music-maker into her slim hands.

He guided her gently, showing her how to hold and blow, correcting her with patience and softness. And when she giggled at a squeaky note, he laughed too—a quiet, broken sound. Not real. Not the way a father laughs at his daughter.

I watched them, heart twisting in grueling knots.

She called him Dad. But he hadn't said her name. Hadn't even stumbled over it.

How old had she been the last time he saw her? Four? Five? Young enough that her face had changed. Grown into angles he didn't recognize. Was that why he seemed unsure? Or was it something worse? Had

Maltherius taken not just control of his mind, but pieces of his memory, too?

Dayna threw another stick on the fire with more force than necessary. "If you're done serenading the wilderness, we could use a lookout. I'll take the first shift," she muttered.

Right on cue, Gaaron gave her that grin—the legendary one with a body count made up almost entirely of swooning barmaids. It was reflex more than interest, like his charm was running on muscle memory. "You don't like music? I thought every hardened mercenary needed a soft underbelly."

"Mine's plated in steel," she said flatly. "And I don't respond to charm."

"Pity," he said, then shot me a wink.

I rolled my eyes. "She's serious. Don't test her."

Dayna didn't even flinch. "You're not as charming as you think you are."

The fire popped. Gaaron chuckled and leaned back, looking vaguely pleased with himself —but not like he understood what he'd just done. Not fully.

Calina kept trying to make the instrument sing, and Gaaron kept helping. But something about it felt off, like he was only going through the motions. Like he was playing a role someone had whispered in his ear —but the meaning behind it hadn't sunk in.

He didn't see her. Not yet. But she saw him. And that was the part that hurt.

I tore my gaze away and looked toward the trees, the river, the stars. Tulip and Rurik were still out there somewhere. Cold. Possibly scared. Possibly worse.

I missed their noise. Their chaos. Even Tulip's incessant complaints and Rurik's endless lectures.

Would they be safe? Would they forgive me for getting separated? And when we finally met again, what kind of reunion would we have?

And Brynlee... What would she say when she saw Gaaron like this? Would her heart soar or break? Would she even recognize the man he'd become? And perhaps more frightening—would he recognize her?

I didn't want to know the answer. Not yet.

We sat around the fire a while longer, Gaaron's strange tune drifting into the air like mist. He smiled and laughed and played, and Calina glowed with every note.

But I watched his hands. His eyes. His distance. And I kept that whisper in my chest locked tight.

Because the truth was, I wanted this moment. I wanted it so badly that I was willing to pretend, even if it meant ignoring the feeling that the man I loved, like family, might not be the same man we had saved.

Later that night, after the fire had burned low and even Dayna's knife sharpening had quieted into silence, I finally drifted off. My back rested against a log, and Frosty had crawled into my lap at some point, his belly cool against my legs, his wings twitching like he was chasing dreams.

It wasn't a restful sleep. I kept jolting awake just long enough to remember where I was—campfire smoke in my hair, the damp hush of the river nearby, the sound of Calina's soft breathing curled next to Gaaron. I would drift again, but unease sat heavy in my gut, a knot I couldn't quite rub loose.

The next time I woke, it wasn't the usual suspects that stirred me. Not the cold, not a snapping twig, not even the gentle plop of Frosty repositioning himself on top of me. No—

It was Gaaron.

He was crouched right in front of me—close—too close. His eyes shimmered, reflecting the faintest shimmer of dying embers, but something about them was... wrong. He was not frightened, not confused, just *urgent*.

"Tilda." His voice was clear, and it hit like a slap. I

hadn't heard this voice in over ten years but recognized it instantly. "I don't have long."

I blinked blearily and sat up straighter, nearly unseating Frosty. "Wh—what do you mean?"

The bard leaned closer, his face inches from mine. "There's something... something I have to tell you. About *him*."

I sucked in a breath. "Maltherius?"

He didn't nod. He didn't blink. He just stared. "He's not hunting you. He's waiting for you to activate the trap."

My blood ran cold. "What does that mean?"

His hands were trembling now—not like earlier, with frailty—but like a man fighting something unseen. Some force yanking his strings. His whole body quivered like a poorly tuned harp.

"I tried... to keep it... but I think—" He clenched his fists at his temples, eyes squeezed shut. "I think he's *still in here*, somewhere."

That hit me like a falling boulder. "In where? In *you*?"

"No." He snapped his eyes open and locked them onto mine. "*Behind me.* Always behind. Always watching. Like a shadow that doesn't leave, even when the sun's gone."

I felt my throat dry out. "You're not making sense—"

"He needed me alive," Gaaron whispered, the words barely audible over the river. "It was the best way. The only way."

I grabbed his arm. "Gaaron, what are you saying?"

He flinched like I'd burned him and yanked away, stumbling to his feet. "You have to listen, Tilda. There isn't much time. You have to end it, Tilda. Before he does. Before—"

He gasped and dropped to his knees. His hands scrabbled at the earth like he was digging for something, for *anything* that could anchor him. And then, just as suddenly, he stilled.

The fire popped behind me. A low, ghostly whistle floated from the gourd flute where Calina had left it lying in the sand—just a single note, like breath catching in a throat.

Gaaron slumped sideways. Breathing. Alive. But his eyes had glazed again, the fire gone out behind them.

"Gaaron?" I crawled to his side and rolled him gently. "Gaaron, hey—come on."

He blinked at me, slow and sluggish. "Tilda?"

My chest cinched tight. "Yeah. You were just—"

But he didn't seem to know what I meant. His

head lolled slightly. "Sorry. Must've wandered off in a dream."

"You don't... remember?"

He gave me a crooked, sheepish smile. "What, was I sleep-fluting again?"

It should've been funny. It *was* the kind of thing he'd say if things were normal. But nothing about this was normal.

I stared at him for a long moment, pulled him to his feet, and guided him back to Calina, who hadn't stirred. Not once.

Once he was settled, I backed away, firelight licking at the edges of my fear.

The words kept echoing in my head.

He's waiting for you.

Always watching.

You have to end it.

I glanced toward the trees. The darkness between them felt deeper than it should. Somewhere, something was watching and waiting.

Whatever had just happened... it wasn't over.

Not by a long shot.

14

I stayed up for a while after that. Watching the stars. Watching the shadows. Watching Gaaron sleep like nothing had happened—like he hadn't just crawled out of a nightmare to whisper doomsday riddles into my face.

Eventually, my body gave out before my brain did. I must've passed out right there by the fire because the next thing I knew, it was morning.

Not just a sliver of dawn peeking in like a nosy villager, but full-on daylight crashing down. The birds were too chipper, the river had ramped up its gurgling commentary, and my back ached in seventeen very specific places. I sat up with a groan, sand in my hair, and regret in my bones.

And just like that, it hit me: I'd actually slept. Not

fitfully. Not with one eye open like usual. Like... *slept slept.*

Which raised a whole new concern.

What had I missed while I was out cold?

What if Gaaron had gotten up again? What if he'd tried to finish what he started, and the warning got lost somewhere between my unconscious snoring and a gust of wind?

I glanced around, trying to read the scene. Remarkably, the others still slept despite the late hour.

Only Dayna sat on a flat stone near the fire, steam curling from the tin cup in her hand. Her armor was already strapped on, dark leathers laced tight, hair scraped back into its usual unforgiving knot. She looked like she hadn't slept at all, which was true for all I knew. The woman probably powered herself on raw determination and spite.

I groaned as I sat up, brushing damp moss from my cheek. "Morning, sunshine."

She didn't turn. "You're late."

"Late for what?" I squinted toward the sun. "Is there some kind of travel itinerary I wasn't informed about?"

She raised an eyebrow at me. Then, unexpectedly, she held out her cup. "Last sip."

I blinked. "You're offering me tea?"

"I said *last sip*. Don't make me regret it."

I took the cup, a little stunned. The tea was still warm—sharp and herbal, with a faint sweetness that lingered after I swallowed. I passed it back slowly, fingers brushing hers for a second too long. Her hand was warm. Rough.

"Generous of you, Commander," I murmured.

Dayna snorted. "Don't get used to it."

Too late.

Behind us, soft footsteps approached. Calina. Her cloak dragged leaves behind her as she walked, already half-slipping as she tried to prop Gaaron up with one arm under his. He was upright, barely, but the strain showed in his face.

"Easy," Calina said gently, adjusting her grip. "You're still healing."

"I'm fine," he muttered, voice rough. "Just... stiff."

He wasn't. He was barely standing, and even with Calina's help, every step looked like a calculated risk. But his chin was high, his shoulders back. The man had too much pride to admit he needed more time. Typical.

Calina looked proud anyway. The girl beamed up at him the way only daughters who still believed in their fathers could. It was a sharp, golden kind of look. The kind that hurt a little to watch.

When she wandered off to refill Dayna's canteen for her, I slipped in beside Gaaron, settling down on the mossy patch next to him. He didn't flinch, but he also didn't look at me. His eyes were fixed on something in the distance—or maybe nothing at all.

"Hey," I said softly, trying not to spook him. "You okay?"

He blinked, slow and heavy, like his eyelids weighed more than they should. "Just tired," he muttered.

"Right. Sure. But, um... last night." I leaned in, dropping my voice. "You came to me. You said something about not having much time. About *him*. Do you remember?"

Gaaron frowned, brow furrowing like he was trying to dig through molasses-thick thoughts. "Last night?"

"Yeah. You said he's waiting for me to activate a trap. That I have to end it."

He turned toward me then, and for a second—just a second—I thought I saw it. Recognition. Fear. Some remnant of the sharpness he'd had by the fire.

But it passed. Gone like smoke.

"I don't... I think I dreamed something weird," he said slowly. "But it's all... jumbled. Was there a tree on fire? Or a fox playing a flute?"

"No," I said, barely holding back my frustration. "Just you. Being all cryptic and ominous. Like usual."

He gave a weak laugh. "Sounds like me."

But it didn't. Not anymore.

"You really don't remember?"

He shook his head, slow and heavy, like it took real effort. "Sorry, Tilda."

I nodded, forcing a smile that didn't quite reach my eyes. "It's okay. Doesn't matter."

But it did. It mattered a lot.

I watched him for a beat longer, noting the sag in his shoulders and how his hands trembled slightly in his lap. Whatever spark he'd conjured around the fire last night was gone. And the worst part? I didn't know if it had ever been real to begin with.

Calina returned then, smiling like the sun had peeked out just for her, and I made room, letting her resume her post beside her father. Gaaron smiled faintly at her but didn't say a word.

I stood and wandered a few steps away, trying to settle the swarm of thoughts buzzing behind my eyes. My stomach churned, and it wasn't from the extra helpings of dinner I'd had last night or the looming dread of another ambush. It was the slow, quiet unraveling of something I hadn't realized I was still holding together.

I didn't get far.

Dayna was leaning against a tree just beyond the edge of camp, arms crossed, eyes narrowed, watching me like a hawk who hadn't decided yet whether I was prey or problem.

"That looked like fun," she said dryly as I approached.

"If by fun you mean soul-crushing, then yeah. A real party." I dropped down on a log and clutched my head in my hands.

"He didn't remember."

It wasn't a question, but I answered anyway. "Nope. Not a thing."

She was quiet for a second, then pushed off the tree and walked over, sitting on the opposite end of the log. She leaned forward, elbows on knees, eye fixed on the ground. "You believe him?"

I blinked. "Which version?"

"Exactly."

I didn't answer right away. Because I didn't know. The Gaaron who woke me in the night had been lucid. Scared. Desperate. But the one I'd just spoken to? He might as well have been carved from driftwood. Polite. Hollow. Smiling because someone told him that's what real people do.

"I believe he wants to be better than he is right now," I said finally. "I believe he's trying."

Dayna tilted her head. "Trying what? To fool us? Or to fool himself?"

That one hit a little too close to home.

"I'm not having this conversation with you," I said, turning away with a huff.

"You already are."

I gave her a long look. "You think he's a threat."

She didn't flinch. "I think we don't know what he is. That's enough."

"He's not a monster."

"No? Then why are you watching him like you expect him to bite?"

I bristled. "Because I care, Dayna. Because he was my friend before he was Calina's dad or your 'strategic burden.' Because the last time I let my guard down, I found out he'd been alive this whole time, and I'd done nothing to help him."

Dayna was quiet for a long beat. "That's not the same as knowing who he is now."

I sighed, the air going out of me like a deflating wineskin. "I don't know who he is now. That's the problem."

She looked at me then—really looked. Not with

suspicion. Not with judgment. Just something search-ing. Curious.

"You're scared," she said softly. "That he's broken. Or worse—that he's been rewritten."

The words settled in my gut like wet ash. I didn't answer. I didn't have to.

She leaned back again, arms crossed once more, but her voice was quieter now. "You should tell the others what he said. About the trap."

"Not yet."

"Why not?"

"Because if I say it out loud, it becomes real. And if it's real, then maybe I didn't get him back at all."

Dayna didn't press. She just nodded, like she understood more than I wanted her to. Then stood. "We need to get moving again."

She left me on the log with my fear, the shadow of Gaaron's midnight voice still rattling around in my head.

He's waiting for you.

I didn't know who *he* was anymore. But I was starting to worry that Gaaron didn't either.

We didn't wait the full hour. Dayna reappeared, barked a sharp "Let's move," and that was that. She stood like a blade being drawn—fluid, silent, deadly.

"The longer we linger, the more likely something finds us."

Calina nodded and adjusted Gaaron's arm over her shoulders as she helped him forward. He was stronger than yesterday, which meant the girl's help was enough. That left Dayna free to lead, just how she liked it best. Frosty dipped and darted, dancing circles around us but keeping pace. I trailed after the others, keeping to the back of the group—my usual post.

The air felt heavier today. Maybe it was the mist. Perhaps it was the way the shadows under the trees didn't seem to match their shapes. Once, I could've sworn something blinked at me from a crack in the rocks. But when I turned, there was only moss.

We followed the curve of the Lazul, winding deeper into the gnarled landscape. Trees grew at odd angles, leaning too far forward as if eavesdropping on our passing. The ground pulsed with a low hum—magical residue, probably—or the aftertaste of whatever had carved this place from the world.

Gaaron limped but kept moving along. Calina never left his side.

A few miles in, she began to sing.

It started soft, barely more than a hum. Her voice was smooth and clear, threading through the stillness like silver wire. The melody rose and fell with practiced ease—familiar, comforting.

I recognized the tune after a moment. One of Gaaron's old lullabies. He used to sing it to me at camp when I couldn't sleep, back when the nights felt longer and lonelier than I ever let on. I'd always assumed he'd written it for me. For the sleepless halfling curled up in a bedroll three feet too short, pretending not to be afraid of the dark.

But now Calina was singing it.

And, of course, she was. Of course, it had been hers all along.

He hadn't written it for me. He'd written it for his daughter—a little girl I hadn't even known existed, one he'd left behind in favor of glory, songs, and all the wrong kinds of legends.

"The stars above are watching you," she sang tenderly, "so sleep, my child, be brave and true…"

The words felt different now. Not gentler. Just… heavier. Like they'd been wearing someone else's name this whole time.

Gaaron's steps faltered.

Calina steadied him quickly. "Sorry. I thought—it used to help."

He said nothing.

The silence that followed wasn't just quiet. It was hollow. Like he hadn't just forgotten the song—like it meant nothing to him. Like she was a stranger.

Calina's face didn't crumple, but something behind her eyes shuttered. She didn't stop walking; she just clenched her jaw and kept going, eyes fixed on the path ahead.

I kept my distance, letting the moment pass without comment. I wanted to comfort her, maybe even confront him—but I knew better. Some things you had to let play out.

Gaaron looked at her after a while. "That was... pretty," he said stiffly as if he'd never heard it before. As if it wasn't his words, his music, his love carved into melody.

"Thanks," Calina said quietly.

I exhaled, the breath catching on something too sharp.

We trudged on.

We stopped once midday-ish—not that we could tell time exactly, but Frosty flopped dramatically into the moss and let out a long, wheezing snort that I took as a demand for a break. Dayna gave a stiff nod. That was our version of a picnic invitation.

Calina helped Gaaron lower himself onto a patch of lichen-soft earth, her movements so careful you'd think she was handling glass. He groaned but didn't protest, which was its own kind of warning sign. She stayed close, hovering like she could hold him together just by being nearby.

I tore off a piece of travel jerky—dense, dry, the kind that could double as a throwing weapon—and gnawed at it while pretending I wasn't eavesdropping or watching or feeling that same old guilt twist behind my ribs.

Calina dipped a cloth in water, then gently dabbed it against Gaaron's forehead. "I thought maybe it would help if I told you a little about home," she said softly. "About... Briarhaven."

He didn't respond but didn't pull away either—a win, by our new pitiful standards.

"I'm not sure if you remember it," she continued, her voice steady but light. "You've been to so many places and seen so many things. But Briarhaven is the only home I've ever known. I was raised there. By my mom." Her mouth twitched into a smile. "You would've hated the local bard. Always off-key. Loved to hear himself rhyme. But Bramble Thistledown's Shortbread Bakery? That would've won you over."

Still no reaction, not even a flicker of amusement. Just that same vacant, tired gaze.

Calina kept going.

"She used to bring me there every other market day. Said the smell of warm sugar was good for the soul. I always ordered the berry tarts. She always got something savory and tried to trade halfway through. She said sweet things gave her headaches." A pause. "I never believed her. I think she just liked stealing mine."

Gaaron's eyes tracked her lips but didn't seem to follow the words.

"I used to imagine you were somewhere far off, doing something noble. That maybe you were writing songs about us—about her. About me. Honestly, until very recently, I thought you were a wizard, vanquishing monsters and saving the world." She smiled again, but this time it didn't quite reach her eyes. "She never spoke badly about you, you know. Even when I asked."

Still nothing.

"I don't know if you left because of adventure, fear, or something else entirely." Her voice cracked just a little, but she kept talking. "But if you're still in there, even a little, I want you to know—she's never stopped loving you. Not even for a second."

That got something. His brow pinched, subtle but real. Calina noticed, too—her breath caught, and she leaned in.

"Do you remember her? Brynlee?" she asked, voice barely more than a whisper.

Gaaron blinked. Slowly. He reached up and touched her hand. Not a firm grip—more like a reflex. But she clutched it like it meant something.

I stood quietly and wandered toward the river, giving them space—or maybe giving myself space. It was hard to tell anymore.

The water shimmered strangely, the light warping on the surface like it couldn't agree with itself. I squinted. For a moment, I swore I saw something dart just beneath—long, pale, fast. Gone in a blink.

Frosty padded up beside me, sniffing the air, then staring at the river with the kind of fixed intensity that made me deeply uncomfortable. His tail flicked. A low, almost imperceptible rumble vibrated from his throat.

"What?" I whispered. "What do you see?"

He didn't answer because he couldn't. But he didn't look away either.

Dayna appeared on my other side, arms crossed, eye already sweeping the tree line like it might bite her if she blinked. "We need to pick up the pace."

"He's still able to walk," I said, nodding toward

Gaaron, who sat propped up awkwardly between Calina and a whole lot of stubbornness.

"Barely. And at this rate, we won't make the forest edge before dark."

"Mystwood isn't going anywhere," I said. "And neither are Tulip and Rurik. They're clever. If we don't find them, they'll surely find us."

Dayna didn't argue—but she didn't relax either. Her jaw tightened, sharp enough to crack stone.

"It's not just pace," she said, voice low. "We need to be somewhere *safe* before nightfall. Somewhere we can hold position if that 'trap' Gaaron mentioned turns out to be more than fever-dream poetry."

"You think he might reach out again?"

"I think he tried once, and if it was real, he might try again. But if it wasn't?" She looked toward the shadows pressing in from the edges of the clearing. "Then we're already behind."

I felt my stomach tighten. Not hunger this time. Just dread.

"Please," I said. "Give him one hour. Let him rest. Then we move and don't stop until we're under the trees."

Dayna hesitated just long enough to make it a power move, then gave a sharp nod and turned on her heel. "One hour. Then we move fast to make up for all this lost time."

She stalked off, muttering something under her breath that sounded suspiciously like, "Sentimental halflings and their stupid soft hearts."

I chose to take it as a compliment.

<h1 style="text-align:center">15</h1>

We finished our brief rest, but Gaaron looked no better for it. Still, Dayna wasn't willing to allow even a second longer than was promised, so we hurried to catch up with the steadily flowing river and continue our progress toward Mirathane.

Danya remained in the lead, unwilling to help carry Gaaron any longer, but Calina didn't seem to mind that the burden had fallen entirely to her. Now and then, Frosty assisted by grabbing the bard's cloak with his claws and tugging him upward. Calina's eerily soft voice was a constant as she shifted between speaking to her father and chatting with the little dragon. Frosty at least spoke back, even though I couldn't understand what he said. I hoped he was offering comfort.

I kept a quiet eye on everything, knowing my words offered less than my vigilance. Calina needed support, but not from me. I worried that by trying to talk to either her or Gaaron, I would just make the situation worse. So I watched silently, hoping our group dynamic would take a turn for the better, but knowing it was probably too soon.

We'd been shuffling through the forest at a brisk pace for another couple of hours before anything of note happened. Suddenly, things went from a predictable struggle to a new difficulty level.

The air shifted—crackled, thickened—like someone had flipped the dial from "ominous" to "extremely cursed." And then yanked it extra hard for no good reason.

A shimmer of nearly invisible magic sliced through our group, and with a sharp snap, Dayna staggered. Her battle necklace—the one strung with cracked bones, feathers, and Rurik's stolen tusk—ripped itself clean off her neck and sailed into the woods.

She froze mid-step, every line in her body going taut.

"What the fig?" I blurted, instinctively reaching for a dagger to defend my ally. "Dayna, what just—"

But she was gone before I could even finish my question. No explanation, no glance back at me. Just a flurry of boots and bad intentions disappearing into the trees.

Frosty gave an excited trill and immediately launched after her, his stubby wings flapping like a moth on a sugar high. I grabbed for him but missed by a mile, nearly faceplanting into a patch of roots.

"Frosty, wait—don't—oh, you impulsive little sparkle-bomb—"

Calina steadied Gaaron as he stumbled at the sudden movement, her expression turning from exhausted to alarmed in an instant. "What was that?"

"I don't know for sure," I said, heart still thumping. "But I do know Dayna's upset many powerful people in her line of work. Maybe one of them wants revenge. Or maybe Finnian got tired of waiting for her to bring the crest back to him. Perhaps this is his way of trying to take it for himself."

I waved vaguely toward the trail of crushed underbrush and fury, mind already racing through worst-case scenarios. "You stay with your dad. I'll go make sure she doesn't hurt herself."

The girl nodded solemnly, and Gaaron, to his credit, looked vaguely alert—like he might contribute something other than dead weight to this encounter. I loved it when our group made progress like this.

I plunged into the woods after them, heart thudding like a war drum. Every crunch of leaves underfoot, every flicker of shadow in the branches, made my pulse spike. We were supposed to be laying low, maybe bonding over half-burnt stew. Instead, we were being magically mugged, and Dayna was sprinting toward it like someone had insulted her sword's edge.

Because, of course, she was.

That's just what my life is now—chaos with a side of cryptic.

Somewhere ahead, Frosty let out a warbling squeak that was either a battle cry or a dramatic sneeze. Either way, I ducked under a branch and leaped over a fallen log, boots skidding as I reached a small clearing.

Dayna stood ramrod straight, shoulders square, glaring at something suspended midair.

Frosty hovered nearby, wings buzzing as he chirped encouragement—or possibly threats—in her direction. She didn't flinch. Didn't even blink.

And I saw why.

Her necklace floated in the center of the clearing like a possessed windchime, spinning slowly. Each grim little charm gleamed with pale light. But the orcish tusk—Rurik's tusk hovered at the center like a jewel on display.

Dayna's whole body vibrated with poorly restrained fury.

"That doesn't look like a naturally occurring wind gust," I muttered, inching closer. "Just how cursed are your accessories, exactly?"

She didn't respond.

The necklace began to hum—a layered, sour note that settled between your teeth and made your skull ache. Even Frosty backed up a few flaps, hissing softly.

And then it dropped. Just like that, the necklace snapped out of the air and clattered to the mossy ground. The tusk hit last, bouncing once with a dull thunk.

Dayna lunged, snatching it up like someone had just tried to steal her soul.

And that's when I heard it—footsteps. Light, fast, and very familiar.

I spun.

Rurik and Tulip charged through the trees.

Alive. In one piece. And clearly, having not murdered each other, which, given the odds, was almost too good to believe.

"You're—wait—you're here?" I said, blinking like I'd conjured them from sheer desperation.

"We've been tracking you," Rurik said, panting slightly, his voice tinged with drumbeats. He held up a softly glowing stone, and his eyes gleamed with the same magic—warm gold laced with silver threads. "It worked."

"Tracking us how?" I asked.

"Healing magic," he said, grinning, his voice turning to a soft double flute. "I used my new casting signature—part of Amariel's gift—to tune this focus stone, then calibrated it to respond to lingering restorative energy."

He gestured toward the necklace—specifically, his stolen tusk. "When the magic spiked, we followed it."

Tulip gave a short laugh and rolled her eyes. "I told him we didn't need to wait around running calculations. We had a lead, and it was probably the best one we would get, so we acted."

She carried a full supply pack across her broad equine back, bedrolls and satchels strapped neatly down. Her long blonde hair had been plaited back with thin braids laced in silver string, and her bronze-toned skin practically glowed in the filtered light. She was still the most breathtaking creature I'd ever seen— and somehow, someway, she was now entirely and unapologetically tethered to the shy half-orc wizard beside her.

"You lose a game of arm wrestling?" I asked, gesturing at the pack.

"No," she said smugly. "I volunteered to carry it so Rurik could cast while we walked."

I turned back to the half-orc kid and did a double-take.

He looked... good. Different. Sure, his robes were scorched at the hem, and his mohawk had leaves tangled in it, but he stood taller. Balanced. Grounded in himself.

Tulip didn't hover. She stood at his side like a silent sentinel—present, ready, *his*.

Dayna's jaw ticked. "That explains the magic. Doesn't explain why you stole from me."

"We didn't steal anything," Tulip snapped with an irritated snort. "The magic didn't take the tusk—it called to it. And the tusk answered."

Rurik nodded. "It was never yours to begin with, and now I'm reclaiming it."

Dayna growled low in her throat, rolling the tusk in her palm like she meant to crush it. "It's still mine."

She reminded me so much of Tulip in that moment, right from the beginning, how she'd always been. What was hers was hers, and what was yours was also hers. I hadn't realized Dayna was like that, too. But it made sense. She only had what she could carry on her person, roaming from contract to contract. Not even her time was her own, not really. So, of course, she didn't want to give up one of the few things she'd come to value. That tusk represented her battle prowess, but it was also how we'd initially come together. Did that make it extra special to her?

I felt heat flush my cheeks and tore my eyes away from the unsettled mercenary, looking once more toward the kids.

Rurik stepped forward with a steely expression he must have recently learned from Tulip. "It was never yours. Not then, and certainly not now."

The air crackled again.

And then, with a snap of magic and a gust of wind, the tusk shot from her grip.

Dayna yelped, recoiling as the ivory projectile zipped across the clearing.

It flew like it *knew* where it belonged—straight into Rurik's open mouth.

Light exploded from his skin. Gold and silver magic lit the clearing, crawling over his jaw like vines. The tusk turned translucent, melted into him, and sealed with a whisper of divine hum.

Rurik gasped, stumbled, then threw his head back —not in pain, but in *release*.

Power pulsed outward like a breath finally exhaled, rustling leaves and kicking up dust.

When the light faded, he stood tall. His mouth was whole, and his face was complete once more.

Calina, having finally caught up to the rest of us, shrieked and sprinted across the moss, throwing her arms around him so hard he almost toppled over.

"You did it! You're healed!" she cried. "I thought you didn't *want* that!"

"I didn't," Rurik said amiably, hugging her back. "Until I did."

She wiped her face and pointed back to where she had left Gaaron. "You have to meet my dad! He's awake—sort of! But you'll like him. You'll really like him."

Before anyone could respond, Tulip's eyes widened, and she gasped. "Oh my me, is that my baby ice dragon?"

Frosty, still hovering uncertainly, chirped at her.

Tulip surged forward and scooped him into her arms like a favorite stuffed toy, peppering him with kisses. "Oh, you precious little thing! You're alive, and you're here! You're adorable! Who's a little chaos comet? You are!"

Frosty blinked, let out a satisfied squeak, and

tucked himself against her chest like he *absolutely deserved this level of worship.*

I just... watched. Watched as a girl who once thought feelings were for losers babbled in baby talk to the dragonling. I watched as Calina dragged Rurik toward Gaaron with a death grip. I watched as Dayna stared at her empty hand and silently seethed.

We were together again.

But the storm wasn't over.

Not even close.

Dayna didn't speak.

Didn't sit. Didn't eat.

She just paced.

Back and forth across the edge of the camp, fists clenching and unclenching at her sides like she was holding onto invisible weapons—or trying not to reach for real ones. Her boots tore fresh grooves in the moss, her steps sharp enough to make the nearby ferns flinch.

She was the only one not talking and not joining our delighted camp reunion.

And I couldn't tell if that was by choice or by design.

Calina, meanwhile, had all but taken charge. She stood proudly between Gaaron—who was seated now, head held higher than it had been in days—and her friends like a noble presenting her court.

"Dad," she said with a grin, "this is Rurik. He's awkward and brilliant and has a thing for complicated metaphors. And this—" she gestured grandly, "is Tulip."

Tulip bowed slightly, the movement a strange but elegant blend of equine grace and social elitism. "Sir."

Gaaron blinked at her, clearly trying to decipher whether he was hallucinating a centaur or if we'd just hit that part of the adventure arc.

"She's very tall," he said hoarsely.

"I get that a lot," Tulip said without missing a beat.

Rurik stepped forward, his head slightly bowed. "It's an honor to meet you, sir. I've, uh... heard a lot about you."

"All of it's hopefully profoundly exaggerated," Gaaron murmured, voice scratchy but dry. "Especially the good parts."

Calina beamed like a torchlight. "He's talking again," she whispered as I walked past. "He made a joke. He's *back*."

I nodded but didn't stop.

Because Dayna hadn't stopped.

She was still pacing.

Still spiraling.

The firelight cast flickering shadows over her face, making her scowl look more like a scar than an expression. I could practically hear the gears grinding behind her temple.

She didn't yell. She didn't cry.

But she was unraveling all the same.

So I followed.

I kept my steps quiet. Kept my distance.

She veered toward the edge of the trees, then past them. Toward the sound of the Lazul River's soft current whispering through the rocks just out of view.

I followed her down the slope, letting the laughter and warmth of the others fade behind me.

The river shimmered in the dying light, lazy and golden, like someone had spilled melted coins across the stones.

And that's when I saw her pause.

She stood at the water's edge, feet planted wide, shoulders taut.

Her hand slid into her pocket.

Slow. Deliberate.

She drew something out.

The bracelet.

The one I'd given her as a decoy. A glittering trinket to keep her from sniffing out the real Genesis Crest.

She stared at it, turning it between her fingers as the last rays of sunlight danced across the gem-encrusted surface. Her scowl softened—just a little. The sharp lines of her jaw eased.

And then, to my surprise, she smiled.

A real one.

Small. Subtle.

But real.

And without hesitation, she slid the bracelet onto her wrist.

Let it settle there like it belonged.

I stayed frozen halfway down the slope, caught between curiosity and dread.

She hadn't worn it since I passed it off.

Had barely acknowledged it.

So why now?

Why here?

And that smile... was it satisfaction? Nostalgia? Something else entirely?

I didn't know what it meant.

But I knew enough to feel the shift.

The bracelet had been a tool—a ruse.

Now, it was something else.

And Dayna?

She had plans.

I just didn't know if I was part of them.

The bracelet caught the last rays of the sun like it had been waiting for this exact moment. All that glimmer and gold danced across Dayna's weatherworn knuckles, softening the edges that battle and betrayal had carved into her. She didn't move for a long time— just stood there, listening to the water and spinning the thing slowly on her wrist.

The smile didn't leave her face.

And I didn't trust it for a second.

My fingers itched near my belt. Not for a weapon. Not yet. But the urge to *do something*—to say something, demand something—burned under my skin like acid.

But I stayed still.

Because I needed to see what she did next.

Because trust, when it came to Dayna, was never a luxury—it was a gamble. And I'd lost too many hands already.

Eventually, she tucked her hands behind her back and turned. She didn't look at me. She just walked past —casual as anything—and started back up the hill toward camp.

Like nothing had happened.

Like she hadn't just made a decision I wasn't privy to.

I stared at the river's rippling surface and tried not to imagine how this would go sideways because it was. Of course, it was. Happy reunions didn't mean the danger was over—they just meant the stakes had gone up.

I had the kids now.

They were alive.

Whole. Together. Moving as a team.

I had Gaaron, too. Breathing. Aware. He was trying, even if he wasn't all the way back yet.

I had them.

But I still had the crest.

And that meant I wasn't done.

Not while Dayna wore a decoy like it was a promise.

Not while Finnian stalked through the shadows, still waiting for his prize.

Not while Maltherius had even a single hand left to stretch through the Void.

And not while every step between here and home was lined with enemies I couldn't see, choices I wasn't ready to make, and memories I hadn't finished bleeding out.

We weren't safe.

Not yet.

And I didn't know if we ever would be again.

I turned toward the fading light and whispered into the hush behind her, "It's not over."

And somewhere, deep in the trees beyond the river, the shadows whispered back.

16

We were finally all together again—minus Dayna, who was still sulking like a sullen teenager, as if I hadn't had enough of those. She hovered just outside our loose circle, close enough to listen in but far enough to make a point. Her expression was locked in that unreadable scowl she wore when pretending not to care, which, of course, meant she cared a lot.

I watched her settle, her back to a tree, as I wrestled internally from witnessing her unsettling actions by the river. That bracelet had started as a simple ruse, but now it felt more like an unspoken secret between us. She'd always known it was fake, so why did it suddenly feel so real?

And why did it make something twist in my

stomach every time I saw it against her wrist? Why did my traitor of a brain whisper ridiculous things like maybe she wanted it to mean something, too?

I forced myself to stop thinking about it and focus on the music, the company, and the night.

Gaaron drummed lightly on his newest improvised instrument, a collection of hollowed reeds he'd deemed too porous for a proper pan flute, producing a steady rhythm that filled the awkward silences our group hadn't yet figured out how to handle. His hands moved gracefully, confidently, the sound rich and resonant, each note echoing slightly through the trees. It was absolutely perfect to everyone except, apparently, himself. His brow furrowed slightly with every beat, like a chef dissatisfied with a dish everyone else adored.

"It sounds wonderful, Dad," Calina said with a reassuring grin. She was now fiddling with Gaaron's gourdian flute from last night, and while the girl possessed no talent, I admired her commitment to connecting with her father in the ways that were important to him.

The bard's smile was strained. "I appreciate that. But I can't help feeling there's something off about it. It's like... like there's a missing note, one I can't quite find."

Tulip, the majority of her form lying down

between Rurik and the others, tossed her braided hair over one shoulder with a casual shrug. "Well, it's certainly better than anything Rurik or I could manage."

Rurik replied without missing a beat, his tone dry as ever, "Considering my musical abilities are purely hypothetical, I'll take that as a compliment."

Then his voice dipped into something quieter—steadier, too. "And you? Whenever I look at you, a full orchestra rises in my heart. Honestly, that's the best music there is. My favorite song."

Tulip's laugh spilled out, bright and unguarded, a warm sound that loosened something knotted in my chest. I saw a flick of her tail, playfully swatting Rurik. But as the moment passed, her smile faded, and her gaze settled across the fire on Calina and Gaaron. Her expression shifted—still soft, but more contemplative now.

"You know, I always used to wonder what it was like," Tulip murmured, picking a bit of moss by her hoof. "Having family bonds like that. I mean, my parents... we weren't exactly the hugging type. Or even the talking type. Actually, we weren't much of a family type at all. I guess that's why I had Amariel. They literally had to pay someone to care."

Something in her usually proud stance turned

inward, vulnerable. She tossed the offending moss aside. Her attention briefly darted toward Rurik, almost shyly. "But watching you two makes me realize... I might have missed out on something important that I needed from someone other than my hired caretaker."

Its honesty silenced us for all of two heartbeats.

"Well," Calina said with a friendly shake of her head, "you're certainly making up for lost time with all the hugging you've subjected Frosty to. At this rate, he might not survive your family bonding."

Tulip sputtered, blue eyes wide, " I-I don't hug him that much."

Frosty raised his head from where he snuggled in Tulip's arms and gave a skeptical snort, a slight icy mist trailing from his nostrils as if to say otherwise.

Then, before I could stop it, a bark of laughter escaped me—loud, sudden, startling in the relative quiet—and it broke the lingering tension.

Even Dayna's lips twitched into something suspiciously close to a smile before she caught herself, refolding her arms and looking back toward the forest. But the mood around the fire was brighter now, lighter.

Gaaron's drumming slowed, growing thoughtful. He looked up, catching Calina's eye, and something softer passed between them, something beyond words. For the first time, the connection didn't seem strained. It seemed... hopeful.

"I'd say you're doing just fine at figuring family out, Tulip," Rurik said, breaking their quiet moment. "Family isn't always something you start with—it can be something you build."

Tulip smiled shyly again, her fingers finding their way into the half-orc's hand and threading through his with a quiet certainty that left no doubt about their bond. "Yeah, I'm starting to understand that."

"Speaking of figuring things out," Calina interjected with wide eyes, pointing directly at her half-orc best friend. "You really seem to have your new magic under control, Rurik. But the last time we saw you, you could hardly even speak without vomiting some kind of powerful spell. What happened?"

His eyes shimmered in the firelight as he leaned slightly forward, the flames casting warm hues across his tusks and cheeks. "I think... I think she's still with me. Amariel."

Calina tilted her head. "Like a ghost?"

"No. More like..." He glanced at the stars, searching for the words. "Like a thread of music that never stops playing. She taught me discipline and how to trust myself. That doesn't vanish just because she's gone."

Then he closed his eyes and exhaled slowly, and magic spilled from his hands like glowing ribbons of light, weaving through the air in soft, geometric patterns. The sigils twisted and turned, painting shimmering spirals of energy, until a faint melody began to play—not from any instrument but from the magic itself. It was beautiful in the truest, most haunting sense of the word, both ancient and familiar. Dayna's eye widened, a soft gasp escaping before she caught herself. Even she hadn't expected something so refined from our stumbling scholar. Rurik opened his eyes and grinned sheepishly. "It's called tonal evocation. I invented it. Sort of."

Before the words had even settled, Gaaron lifted his makeshift drum and began to tap out a rhythm—soft, steady, and grounding. The beat stitched itself into the melody Rurik had conjured, the two sounds braiding together like they'd been waiting for each other all along.

Calina hesitated for half a second, then raised her gourd flute with a determined little huff. Her first note came out sharp enough to make Frosty snort in protest, but she didn't stop. She adjusted her grip and tried again, squeaking out a second note that was, if nothing else, enthusiastic.

"Sorry," she muttered. "I swear it sounded better in my head."

I leaned in with a warm smile. "It's supposed to be a little chaotic, isn't it? That's what makes it ours."

Calina nodded and tried again—off-key, but proud of it—and the music around us shifted to make room. The magic didn't care about precision. It just responded to the intention, to the feeling behind it. And we had feeling in spades.

A comfortable peace—well, comfortable enough—settled over us, punctuated by the rhythmic drumming, screeching flute, and Frosty's sleepy snuffling. For a few moments, things felt okay again. But my mind never fully quieted. Even as I smiled and relaxed into the camaraderie, the memory of Dayna and that bracelet nagged at me. Gaaron's strange episode from the night before lingered, too, unresolved and unsettling.

I found my gaze again drifting to the one-eyed mercenary who'd been taking up far too much space in my thoughts lately. She stood now with her back to us, her silhouette tense against the firelight. I knew I should leave it alone, give her space, but my feet had other ideas.

"I'll check the perimeter," I announced, rising and brushing dirt from my leggings.

Dayna turned at my approach, her expression unreadable. "You shouldn't wander alone."

"I'm not wandering," I said evenly, stopping a few feet from her. "I'm checking on you."

Her eye narrowed, sharp and calculating. "I'm fine."

"I believe you," I lied. "But humor me. You're clenching your fists so hard I'm worried you'll sprain something."

She flexed her fingers deliberately, then sighed, releasing some tension from her shoulders. "It's not important."

"Whatever it is, it's important enough to keep you sulking all evening. This can't be all about losing that gross tusk, so what is it, really?"

Dayna hesitated, her eye shifting toward the fire and then back at me. Finally, she lowered her voice, leaning slightly closer. "I just didn't expect to find myself invested in all... this." She waved vaguely toward the group, who were now laughing at something Tulip had said, probably another humble brag or backhanded compliment.

"You're starting to care about them," I said softly. "And that's terrifying."

"Something like that." Her voice was rougher now, frustration coloring her words. "Caring is dangerous. In decisive moments, it can make you hesitate. Makes you weak, and where I come from, weak is dead."

"No," I corrected gently. "It makes you strong. It gives you something to fight for."

Her eye drifted down to the bracelet on her wrist, glinting softly in the firelight. For a moment, she almost looked vulnerable.

Almost.

"And what happens when you fail?" she wanted to know.

"You don't let yourself fail," I told her simply. "You get back up and keep fighting because they're worth it. Because you're worth it."

Dayna squinted at me for a long moment—too long, really—and something in her gaze made my chest go tight. There was a rawness behind that single eye, a wound left long unattended. Not the kind that bleeds. The type that scars. And still hurts anyway.

"You're not what I expected," she muttered.

"Good," I said, forcing a smile. "I'd hate to be predictable."

Dayna looked away sharply, her jaw working silently. Finally, she nodded once, decisively. "We should get some rest. It'll be another long day tomorrow."

I recognized the dismissal, but I didn't push further. She'd opened up more than she intended, which was enough. At least, for now.

We rejoined the others around the fire, each finding our place in the circle. Tulip had finally released Rurik's hand but shifted slightly, her side pressing against his back in easy companionship. Calina settled against her father, eyes heavy with exhaustion but finally at peace. Frosty, snoring lightly, sprawled across her legs like an oddly shaped ice-blue pillow.

Gaaron's drumming picked up again, more confident now, finding its rhythm at last. But even as the mood grew easy, Dayna's words lingered, a shadow beneath the warmth.

I knew the truth of what she'd said: caring was dangerous. It made you vulnerable, but it was also the very thing that kept us alive and gave us purpose.

I'd spent so long living like a shadow, hiding behind tankards and tavern gossip, thinking that keeping my distance would keep them safe. But all it had done was keep me lonely. That was the part they hadn't told me in the rogue's handbook—how isolation didn't just protect you. It starved you. Slowly, quietly, until you forgot what it felt like to be seen. To be known.

My eyes drifted slowly across the circle, absorbing the warmth of the fire, the laughter, the quiet hum of conversation, the calm before the storm we all knew was coming in fast.

The kids—no, my companions—had grown into heroes in their own right. I could see it now, illuminated in firelight and shadow. It was a truth that was impossible to deny.

A memory tugged at me, sudden and sharp. I heard my own voice again, filled with bitterness and false bravado, echoing through the years. *"You're teenagers! You have no idea what you want."*

And all at once the past rose vividly, pressing into the present, and I saw myself as I had been—broken, fearful, utterly convinced that the only way to keep them safe was to push them away. How wrong I'd been. The kids had understood something then that I had refused to accept, something Rurik had shouted in a voice unburdened by stutter or fear.

"You're nothing more than a mean, old coward. You've been hiding for more than half our lives, and at the first sign of trouble, you're running away. We thought we wanted to be like you, but no. We're not going to be like you. We're going to be better than you."

It had gutted me then. Still did, in the quiet moments when no one was looking. But gods help me, they'd been right. And the fact that they hadn't given up on me anyway—that they'd fought to drag me out of my self-imposed exile? That was the part that undid me now.

My throat tightened. They had become better, stronger, wiser, kinder. They hadn't listened when I'd told them to abandon their dreams; they'd fought instead, both for their futures and mine. They'd understood what I hadn't: attachments weren't weaknesses. They were strengths.

I had taught them how to fight, but they'd taught me how to live.

The fire cracked again, and I drew in a deep, steadying breath. Dayna was right. Caring was dangerous. But it was also beautiful, necessary, and the best thing I had ever done for myself. I'd spent years running from bonds, terrified that connections would be my undoing. Yet here I was, surrounded by people who'd chosen to fight alongside me, not because they had to, but because they wanted to. Because they cared.

Maybe I still didn't fully trust the world to be kind or fate to be gentle. But I trusted these people, *my people.*

A small, satisfied smile touched my lips. "You were

right all along," I whispered, glancing toward Rurik and Calina.

They were too absorbed in conversation to hear me, but that was all right. I'd tell them someday, when the time was right. Until then, it was enough to know they had helped me find my way back, even if it took me longer than I'd care to admit.

Tonight, in the glow of the fire and the laughter of friends, I finally understood. I'd thought this quest was mine alone to bear...

But it had always been ours.

17

Sleep was starting to sound like a pretty decent plan.

Dayna had been right—we needed rest. My muscles ached, my brain felt like half-melted cheese, and I couldn't remember the last time I'd blinked without seeing sigils or sorrow behind my eyelids. One night without a crisis seemed almost too much to ask... but sweet divinity, I wanted it.

I was just about to make up my bedroll for the night when I noticed her.

Tulip.

She stood apart from the rest of the group, just far enough to make it clear it was on purpose. The firelight didn't reach her fully, but even in shadow, I could see the tension in her posture. She wasn't cleaning her weapons or admiring her reflection—two of her favorite pre-bed rituals. She was just... standing there quietly.

And that was the part that made the hairs on the back of my neck stand up.

Normally, she'd be trotting around making demands or flinging thinly veiled insults with the casual elegance of someone who considered tact an optional skill. But now, she held her silence with the delicate tension that suggested it was about to snap.

And that wouldn't be good for any of us.

I paused before heading over to her. It was weird having her and Rurik back. In a way, their return felt like a signal that it was time to end our adventure, to head home, and to... what?

Pretend like none of this had ever happened?

Pretend we could go back to living our lives exactly as they'd been before?

No, of course not. I knew we hadn't finished our journey yet, but I also had no idea how to bring it to a close. I still held the artifact, and Gaaron was still not quite right. Maltherius and Finnian Sly were both still out there, and they would come looking for me, too. It seemed I had forged these intense, new bonds only to break my heart. I couldn't go home with them, not when I knew danger would come looking for me at the very first opportunity. Not when I understood that Maltherius now knew precisely where to find me.

I supposed I'd just have to take it one day at a time. To cherish whatever time I had left with the little family we'd made.

And right now, it seemed like Tulip needed me.

Her gaze lingered on Calina and Gaaron, who'd settled into a quiet conversation punctuated by soft, awkward laughter. Each small chuckle was a tiny victory, pulling a little more life into Gaaron's pale cheeks, a little more hope into Calina's violet eyes. It should've been heartwarming. Instead, Tulip watched them rigidly with her shoulders and jaw set like she was trying to grind down something bitter between her teeth.

"You all right?" I asked, at last sidling up to her and trying to look casual. My voice came out softer than usual, almost gentle—probably a mistake, but too late now.

Tulip snapped her attention toward me, then swiftly away, her chin tilting upward just a fraction. "Obviously. And why wouldn't I be?"

"Oh, I don't know," I said dryly. "Because you're staring at them like they stole that fancy axe of yours. Or worse, your self-confidence."

The centaur scowled at me, but then softened

almost immediately. She let out a frustrated huff and folded her arms across her chest. Even slumped in frustration, she had the kind of presence most generals could only dream of.

"It's not that," she muttered, half to me and half to herself. "It's just, well... I just don't get it, all right? Are you satisfied now?"

"What don't you get?"

Tulip shook her head, her bright blue eyes narrowing slightly as she watched Calina fuss over Gaaron, adjusting his makeshift blanket and checking his temperature with a palm against his forehead. "I mean, look at her. She's bending over backward just to make him comfortable. Treating him like a precious, delicate thing. And he's hardly said more than three coherent sentences in return."

"She's his daughter, Tulip," I said quietly, resisting the urge to roll my eyes. "He's been gone most of her life. She wants to make up for lost time."

"That's my point," Tulip snapped, voice brittle with frustration. Her front hoof stamped down as if to punctuate this declaration. "I have family—lots of it. Enough cousins to fill a colosseum. But they wouldn't do any of that for me. Not if I was lost, not if I was dying, and especially not for no reason at all. They'd probably just scold me for embarrassing the Thunderhoof name. You know what my mother said to me while we were gathering supplies and the rest of you were waiting for us at the Stable?"

I shook my head, observing her.

"She told me to make her proud. Not in a supportive way, but, like, in an ominous way," she continued bitterly. "She said she wouldn't even remember my name unless it was written in glory."

Her voice cracked a little at the end, and I quickly looked away, pretending not to notice. If Tulip saw even a hint of pity, she'd kick me into the river and never look back.

"So no, Tilda, I don't get it," Tulip repeated, a little softer now. "Why does Calina get a father who loves her even when he can barely remember his own name? Why does she get a mother who'd cross half the world just to make sure she's safe? Why does she deserve all of this, when—"

She stopped abruptly, her throat struggling to swallow whatever words had almost slipped out.

"When you don't?" I finished gently, feeling the question settle heavy in the space between us.

She turned pointedly, eyes bright and fierce. "I didn't say that."

"You didn't have to." Lifting one shoulder in a

half-hearted shrug. "But for what it's worth, I think you do."

Tulip blinked at me in surprise, her eyes wide with disbelief. "You think I *what?*"

"You deserve that kind of family. You deserve to be cared for. I know you pretend you don't need it—trust me, I completely get where you're coming from on this—but that doesn't mean you don't deserve it. I guess I'm here to tell you that you do."

She studied my face, searching for the joke or the lie, but I stared back, stubborn and unyielding. Slowly, some of the tension left her shoulders, and she let out a short, bitter laugh. "It's really annoying when you try telling me what to do, especially when you're so nice about it."

"It's a gift," I said with a smirk. "Someone's got to balance out your boundless ego."

"Cute," she muttered, rolling her eyes. But I saw the tiny smile tugging at the corner of her mouth. Progress.

"And besides," I continued, nudging her foreleg gently since it was one of the only parts of her I could easily reach, "you do have family. Right here."

She scoffed, but it was weaker than usual. "You're not my family. You're just a bunch of misfits that I happen to tolerate."

"Same thing," I retorted smoothly, nudging her again. "Misfits, troublemakers, family—they're all interchangeable terms around here. You remember back in Briarhaven when you demanded to join this little party? Well, you're stuck with us now."

Tulip shook her head, but I saw warmth creep into her expression as her focus shifted back toward Calina. She sighed, a soft, resigned sound. "I suppose there are worse fates."

"There you go," I grinned. "Acceptance is the first step."

She chuckled softly, kicking a bit of dirt in my direction. "Don't get cocky, Quickthatch."

"It's far too late for that," I said, offering a playful wink.

She watched Calina and Gaaron again, but the edge of jealousy seemed dulled this time. When her gaze drifted slightly to the left, landing on Rurik sitting quietly across from Gaaron, the tension crept back into her posture.

"Did something happen between you two out there?" I asked carefully, noticing how her eyes lingered on Rurik with an intensity she usually reserved for highly valuable loot.

Her otherwise pale face reddened slightly, and she immediately looked away. "No. What? Of course not."

"Oh, c'mon," I prodded lightly. "You haven't made a single joke at his expense since you returned. Not even one."

She scowled at me. "Maybe I'm just out of material."

"You? Never. Besides, we all saw you flirting and holding his hand earlier tonight."

Tulip shifted uncomfortably, scraping at the ground with one hoof. "Maybe it's just...well, it's d-different now. Seeing how Calina and her father are. Seeing what she'd do for him. Maybe it m-makes me think—"

"About how you feel toward Rurik?" I finished softly.

She shot me a glare, but it melted away quickly. Again, her attention drifted back toward the half-orc, whose brow was furrowed as he carefully sketched something onto a patch of dirt, murmuring calculations to himself.

"It's not like that," she said, too quickly.

I said nothing, waiting, giving the girl the space to say what she really meant.

She made a noise halfway between a snort and a grumble. "Okay, maybe it is like that. I don't know. I didn't think about him like that until suddenly... I did.

And now I can't stop thinking about him like that, and it's driving me insane."

"Oh, sweet divinity," I said dramatically, touching my chest. "Tulip Thunderhoof, smitten?"

"Stop," she hissed, looking panicked. "I am not smitten."

"Of course not. That dreamy look in your eyes is definitely just bloodlust."

"Tilda..." she warned.

"Look," I said seriously, "it's okay to have feelings. Even confusing ones. Even ones you wish you didn't have. You don't have to be embarrassed. We're misfits, remember? We're supposed to be confused and messy. That's part of our charm."

"Speak for yourself. I am *not* a misfit." She continued to stare at Rurik, her voice dropping to a whisper so quiet I almost missed it. "But I know that he is. And, well, he's been my best friend out here. My best friend *ever*. He listens. Really listens. Not just to the parts I want everyone to hear, but the parts I don't say out loud. He sees through all my bravado. He... Well, he gets me, okay?"

I smiled gently, watching her with warmth blooming in my chest. "Then maybe you should let him know that."

"Easier said than done," she muttered, kicking at the dirt.

"Everything worth it usually is," I replied, giving her one last reassuring nudge. "And besides, I'm pretty sure he already knows."

She exhaled slowly, then squared her shoulders with a familiar resolve. "Fine. Maybe later."

"I'll hold you to that," I warned.

She grinned faintly. "I have no doubt you will."

Tulip straightened, her spine regaining its typical imperious curve. She turned back toward our companions with fresh determination.

Rurik looked up at that exact moment, meeting her eyes. His cheeks darkened, and he looked away—but not before I saw him smile.

Beside me, Tulip smiled, too—small and shy and completely unlike herself.

Maybe, just maybe, everything wouldn't go terribly wrong for once.

Of course, this was us, so something terrible was bound to be lurking just around the corner.

I smiled to myself as my gaze roamed across the campfire, inevitably landing on Dayna. She stood apart, silhouetted by firelight, her features painted in stark shades of gold and shadow. My heart did a strange, traitorous little flutter, the same one it had been doing lately.

When had that started, exactly? Probably around the time I handed her a fake bracelet and inadvertently handed over a piece of my trust along with it.

Dayna had always been a question mark—dangerous, intriguing, and infuriating all at once—but now that question mark had morphed into something else entirely. Something I couldn't quite put a name to, even if I wanted to. And gods, did I want to. She'd somehow slipped past my defenses, past the carefully guarded walls I'd spent years fortifying, and now she was there, settled comfortably inside my thoughts and stubbornly refusing to leave.

It wasn't just that she was beautiful, though obviously, it was the kind of beauty a master-crafted dagger held. It was the way her one-eyed stare could slice right through me, the way she spoke in clipped, confident tones that somehow made my pulse race and calm simultaneously. It was the little moments—the way her hand rested just a heartbeat longer than necessary on my shoulder, or the way her rare, fleeting smiles felt like secrets shared just between the two of us.

And yet, despite it all, I still wasn't sure what any of it meant. Did she feel this too? Or was this yet another one-sided thing, another cruel twist of fate in my long, complicated history with matters of the heart? More importantly, could I afford to find out?

As if sensing my attention, Dayna's gaze swung over to mine. She raised an eyebrow in silent challenge, her expression guarded—but not entirely. There was a softness there, hidden just beneath the surface. I felt a blush rise to my cheeks, grateful for the darkness hiding most of it, and quickly looked away.

Tulip had squared her shoulders, ready to face whatever lay ahead. Maybe it was time I did the same. Maybe, just maybe, feelings—confusing, terrifying, exhilarating—were worth the risk.

Because if there was one thing I'd learned from these misfit kids who'd somehow transformed into heroes, it was that some risks were worth taking, no matter how messy the outcome.

And Dayna? She just might be the biggest one of all.

18

I woke to the sound of footsteps.

Not thunderous, not hurried—just soft, deliberate, and very, very wrong. The fire had died down to a sullen ring of embers, pulsing like an open wound in the dark.

Calina lay curled up in her bedroll near where Gaaron also slept, and Frosty—who usually snored like a bubbling soup pot—was stock-still, hackles raised, his breath fogging in the chill as he nestled up against Tulip's side.

Rurik must have been off reading by the light of his magical flame as he often did during the nights. But it wasn't his footsteps I had heard. They were too swift and determined, not stumbling and awkward in how the half-orc moved.

My gut clenched. I glanced around the camp again. Calina was there. Frosty was there. Tulip, too. And Gaaron—

His bedroll was empty.

A chill crawled down my spine as I sat up, fast and breathless. My fingers went straight to my chest, fumbling beneath my tunic.

No. *No.*

The crest was gone.

My blood turned to ice. It was like taking a step and not finding the ground where it was supposed to be. I scrambled to my feet, already sweating despite the night chill, my hands clawing uselessly at the space where it should have been.

Someone had taken it from me while I slept, while I was completely vulnerable and unaware.

I gagged on the realization. The idea that someone —Gaaron, probably—had knelt over me in the dark, reached beneath my clothes, unclasped the chain around my neck...

It wasn't just theft. It was a violation. A betrayal that made my skin crawl and heart pound as if demanding answers.

The crest had hung there for years, humming against my sternum like a second heartbeat. A danger I tolerated only because I didn't know what else to do with it.

But now? Now there was nothing. Just absence. Just a yawning, hollow pit where something powerful and cursed had been.

"Sweet figgin' divinity," I swore, snatching up my daggers and scanning for tracks. The damp ground by the Lazul's edge glistened faintly in the moonlight, just enough to catch a set of footprints leading away from the firelight. Two sets. One heavy with a sure stride, the other airy, practically weightless.

That meant Dayna was out there, too. I didn't know whether that was more comforting or terrifying. Would she defend me? Would she recover what was stolen? Or would she just take it for herself? Would she hurt my friend in the process?

Oh, no.

I took off like a bolt, my boots barely making a sound as I slipped into the trees. The shadows welcomed me. Old instincts kicked in. My breath quieted. My heartbeat slowed. The rogue in me took over my entire consciousness.

I followed the sound of the river, letting it guide me. Around a bend and through a thicket—and then I saw them.

Gaaron stood at the edge of the Lazul, barefoot and soaked to the knees. His tattered clothes clung to him like seaweed, and the crest glowed faintly in his hands. Dayna was across from him, swords drawn but lowered, tension wrapped around her like wire.

Neither of them moved.

"Dayna," I said quietly.

She didn't turn. "I saw him take it." The words landed like stones.

Gaaron didn't even flinch. He just stood there, mumbling something as he stared over the water.

I inched closer, the air buzzing with the artifact's magic that held so much power over us, even though we still barely understood what it could do.

"Gaaron?" I said, careful not to startle him.

His head jerked in my direction, and then he crumbled to his knees.

"Kill me," he rasped, *begged*. "Please—before I—before he—"

Dayna didn't move. Her attention shifted to me, hard and unreadable. Any other time, she would have welcomed the invitation to violence, but now she watched me, awaiting my decision. Of course, I wasn't going to kill my old friend; we both knew that.

But still he pleaded. "I can't sleep. I can't think. He's always there." Gaaron's hands shook around the crest, knuckles bone-white. "I don't know what's me anymore."

The words didn't make sense at first. Not until they did.

"Maltherius," I said the moment I figured it out.

Gaaron whimpered—a horrible, broken sound from somewhere deeper than his lungs. "He made me take it," he gasped. "I didn't want to, Tilda, I swear—I tried not to. I resisted as long as I could, but then... then it got easier. Like letting go of the rope before it burns your palms off. I betrayed you, and I'll do it again. I'll do it as many times as it takes, not because I want to, but... Tilda, you have to stop me before I hurt you."

His shoulders shook. He let go of the artifact—it clattered to the pebbles—and pressed his forehead to the ground like he was trying to melt into it.

The Genesis Crest lay in the moonlight, and it pulsed, not like a heartbeat. No, that would have been too human. Too kind. It pulsed like a parasite. Like it knew it had been dropped and was searching for a new host.

It wasn't beautiful, exactly, but it was mesmerizing.

An oblong diamond made of shimmering gold that didn't seem to reflect light so much as consume it. Strange runes crawled across its surface like frost etching across glass, rearranging themselves when no one looked.

It whispered. I swear it whispered. Nothing audible—just a pressure in the skull. A suggestion. A promise. A temptation.

Dayna's hands tightened around her swords. Her eye locked on it. Her weight shifted unconsciously toward the crest.

Everyone wanted it. Even now. Even after everything.

Everyone except me.

The closer I got to that thing, the more wrong it felt. My skin itched. My molars ached. Every instinct I'd ever honed as a thief and a liar screamed at me to put distance between myself and that gods-forsaken artifact.

But I couldn't—not until I knew what came next. Not until I pulled my friend back from the edge. I reached a hand toward Gaaron to show him that it was all right, that we were all right.

He flinched and recoiled from my touch, refusing to look at me as he mumbled, "I marked you."

I froze at this revelation, unwilling to let it sink in. "What?"

"In Briarhaven. That night at the tavern." His voice was muffled, full of grief. "It was me."

I staggered back like he'd struck me. The ground pitched under my feet.

"That sigil—" I said.

"He made me. Said if I could do it—if I could break the one thing that kept me human—he'd give me silence." Gaaron's words tumbled out, slurred and cracked. "I fought him. I did. But you don't understand how hard it is to resist, Tilda. How painful. I just wanted it to stop, but he's never going to free me, not as long as a heart still beats in my chest."

My stomach roiled. I could still feel the cold fingers wrapped tightly around my wrist, grabbing and refusing to let go. They still hadn't let go.

Of course, he'd found me. Of course, he knew. Maltherius didn't need to tear through towns or send armies—he just needed Gaaron. He'd sent him into Briarhaven like a guided blade, counting on our bond to do the work for him. I'd been so focused on hiding, on blending in, that I hadn't seen the trap even once it had been fully sprung.

Gaaron hadn't been the hunter. He'd been the hound. And I... I was the scent trail.

I knelt again, this time more carefully. "Why didn't you tell me this earlier? Why are you telling me now?"

"Because I still hoped I could undo it. That I'd find a way to rip him out of my head. That I wasn't already..." He broke off, face crumpling. "But I am. I'm his thrall, Tilda. I'm alive still, awake sometimes. It shouldn't be possible, but he found a way. I'm an abomination. I cannot be allowed to survive. So, please, you need to kill me. I really must insist."

The sob that followed cracked down the middle as he worked so hard to hang on to the things that made him the man he'd once been, while simultaneously being willing to let them all go.

Dayna stepped forward and crouched beside us. She hesitated, watching the crest. It pulsed, then dimmed as she reached out. Her fingers closed around it. For a second, it resisted.

Then it relented.

Dayna raised it to dangle in the air between us. "Next time," she said softly, eyes locked on mine, "don't wait for him to fall apart."

I didn't argue. I couldn't. She placed the crest in my hand and closed my fingers around it.

Gaaron sagged against me, his breath hitching as he mumbled words I half-recognized—a tune we used to play on the road, when coin was low and hope was lower. I remembered it. Every note. Every harmony. He murmured the melody like a prayer until he slipped unconscious against my shoulder.

We carried him back together—me supporting his legs, Dayna cradling his shoulders. Frosty met us at the edge of camp, silent but alert. Calina stirred, but didn't wake.

We laid Gaaron down and covered him in blankets that Rurik and Tulip had brought with them. Then I took the crest and sat with it in my lap.

I didn't sleep. How could I? How do you forgive someone for what they were forced to do? And if you can't... who does that make you?

The crest pulsed in my lap, low and slow like a heartbeat I couldn't quite match. I held it in both hands, fingers splayed over its jagged grooves and cruel elegance, watching the moonlight play tricks on its surface.

It didn't speak. Not aloud. But I could feel it watching me. Judging.

I wanted to throw it into the river. Let the Lazul carry it to whatever gods were left and let them deal with it.

But I didn't. Because Gaaron was still breathing, and I didn't trust the river to understand mercy.

The longer I held it, the more aware I became of the absence it left behind when it wasn't near. The way it pulled on people, tugged at their minds like loose threads begging to unravel. It was quiet now, but I knew better. It was never really quiet.

Just waiting.

Not unlike Maltherius himself.

I looked over at Gaaron, pale and curled in on himself, and felt the bitter twist of helplessness rise again. I could fight a thousand necromancers with my daggers drawn, but I didn't know how to fight this, the rot from the inside. This infection of the soul.

I sat for hours, legs numb, back aching, and heart just a little bit hollowed out. The fire hissed and crackled, embers popping like tiny bones. Every noise made me twitch.

He'd marked me.

Not just scarred me—marked me. Maltherius had seen to it that my body carried his message, worn under my clothes like a secret I didn't know I was telling.

And Gaaron... Gaaron had done it.

My friend. My partner. The man who once told me I was the sharpest mind he'd ever met—and meant it.

I pressed a fist against my sternum. The pain there had nothing to do with magic.

He hadn't looked like himself, down by the river. Hadn't sounded like it either. But the brokenness? That was Gaaron. That was all him.

I didn't know whether to weep or scream.

"You should sleep," Dayna said, stepping out of the trees like she'd been watching the whole time.

Of course, she had.

I didn't look at her. "Can't."

She moved closer but didn't sit. "I meant what I said."

"I know."

Silence stretched between us, taut and unyielding.

"I've seen a lot of broken things," she said finally. "Most of them don't ask to be killed."

I glanced up. Her face was unreadable, all sharp lines and shadow.

"He wasn't asking for death," I said. "He was asking for release."

"Same thing."

"Not always."

She didn't argue. Just crossed her arms and looked at the crest. "What are you going to do with it?"

I stared down at it. "I don't know. Can't destroy it. Can't use it. Can't give it up."

"So we're babysitting a magical death wish?"

I snorted, but there wasn't any humor in it. "Basically."

Dayna crouched beside me, one hand braced on her knee. "You looked like you were going to shatter when he said it."

"The mark?"

She nodded.

I swallowed hard. "It's not just that he did it. It's that he didn't tell me. He was right there. All that time. I hate this thing," I said, holding up the crest. "It ruins everything it touches."

Dayna raised an eyebrow. "And yet…"

"And yet I keep carrying it."

She watched me a moment longer. Then, slowly, she sat beside me. Not close, not far. Just enough that our fingers brushed. We sat like that for a long time. Not talking and not moving. Just two tired women staring at a relic of everything we'd lost and everything we might still lose.

It hit me then, quietly and without warning—how strange it was to sit like this with her. This woman, who once ripped out Rurik's tusk in cold blood, fueled by revenge for a petty slight—this woman who'd watched me like prey and mocked every soft part of me from a distance.

We were nothing alike on the outside. She, all jagged edges and brutal calm. Me, all sharp quips and scarred nerves. And yet…

I understood her in a way I hadn't expected. Understood what it meant to push people away so you didn't have to feel the cost of losing them. Understood what it meant to survive instead of live.

But the two of us were the same in all the ways that counted most. We were both tired of being alone.

And so that night, we sat and kept watch together.

Eventually, the first threads of dawn wove into the sky.

Calina stirred.

Rurik, who'd returned to camp at some point to grab some sleep, mumbled something from the place of dreams.

Tulip muttered in her sleep, legs and hooves twitching, "Tell the stablehands to polish my hooves, peasants," before settling again.

Dayna stood.

I expected her to walk away. Instead, she paused, reached into her satchel, and pulled something out. She didn't look at me as she set it down beside me. The bracelet. The one I'd given her as a decoy.

She'd worn it all last night, then tucked it away again like it didn't matter. Now she was giving it back.

No. Not giving it back. *Sharing it.*

"I'll go get the fire started, make some breakfast for the group," she said. "I'll save you the last sip of tea, if you want."

I wanted to thank her. Wanted to say something clever. But all I managed was a nod.

19

I didn't pick up the bracelet—not right away. Instead, I stared at it as it lay in the grass beside me like it had always belonged.

It had started as a lie, a misdirect to buy me some time.

And now? Now the silly thing felt like a lifeline. A thread back to something almost like trust. Almost like care.

I slid the gem-encrusted band on slowly, feeling the familiar ring of gems hug my wrist. No pulse. No hum. No hidden powers behind its gleam. Just a simple thing given back by someone who'd once sworn she owed me nothing.

Then my hand drifted to the pendant that hung around my neck. Still cold. Still quiet. Once again pressed against the hollow of my chest like it owned me. This bracelet was a symbol. The Genesis Crest was a portent. Both were mine to protect.

The weight of it all settled in my core... only to be interrupted by a loud, gurgling protest from within. The scent of roasting meat drifted from the fire pit—smoky, savory, and impossible to ignore. I glanced toward Dayna, already crouched near the flames, turning a hunk of meat with the same ruthless efficiency she'd used to butcher the animal in the first place.

The firelight danced across her features, catching on the angular lines of her cheekbones and the scar just beneath her false eye. Her expression was carefully, deliberately blank, and I knew her well enough by now to recognize just how much effort that took.

This wasn't apathy. It was armor. That was the look of someone holding back a flood with a single thread of willpower, someone who had built walls so high, even the light had trouble getting in.

She wasn't fine. Not even close. And the worst part? I could tell she was still trying to protect me. Somehow, I'd gotten through to her—to *Dayna*. The one-eyed, sword-swinging, emotion-avoidant mercenary who had spent most of this journey pretending not to care about anyone or anything.

And now she was softening b*ecause of me*.

The realization lit something warm and quiet in my chest—a fragile joy, unexpected and bright. But right behind it came the fear, because I knew what it meant to care and to be cared for.

It meant risk. It meant weakness someone else could exploit.

Just another person to lose. Just another way for Maltherius or Finnian Sly to twist the knife.

That connection should've grounded me. It should've made me stronger. Should've reminded me why we were fighting at all. But it didn't. Not this time.

Instead of going to her, of enjoying our newfound connection, I silently stood, then walked to the river... And I broke.

"Is this what you wanted?" I shouted, ripping the Genesis Crest from beneath my collar and holding it up like an accusation. The cool metal glinted in the dawning morning light, still pulsing faintly with its unreadable power.

"You picked *me*, didn't you?" My voice cracked, loud enough to send a few birds fluttering from the trees. "You saw something in me—some spark or prophecy or divine whatever—and you thought, 'Yes, *that one*!' That emotionally stunted halfling with too many knives and twice as many regrets! Let's make *her* the key to all of this!'"

My fingers clenched around the pendant until it dug into my palm. I paced harder, boots squelching in the soft dirt beside the riverbank. The others were still focused on breakfast, either that or pretending to be. I hadn't checked. Didn't want to. I already had more than my share of worries for so early in the day.

"You want a Chosen?" I shouted at the stupid, divine necklace. "Great. Pick the bloodthirsty mercenary. Pick the half-orc genius who will do anything to prove himself. Pick literally anyone else. You've even got a dragon now! Did I miss the memo where that's not enough?"

The crest didn't respond, so I hurled it in frustration. It bounced from tree to tree, then landed with a sulky little thud... alarmingly close to the campfire.

Still, it did nothing, so I limped after it and gave it a solid kick.

Instead of flying deeper into the woods like I'd intended, the figgin' thing pinged off a root and skidded even closer to the firepit, settling in the grass a few feet from Gaaron's boots. This time, it glowed a little brighter, the way a cat twitches its tail when it's about to bite your face off.

"Oh, so you do respond to violence," I muttered, wincing and limping backward. "Good to know."

And then—because the universe has a cruel sense of timing—I heard the unmistakable *shhhhink* of swords leaving their sheaths.

"You're yelling at an inanimate object," Dayna said flatly. "And disturbing my morning peace."

I turned, ready with a quip, but she was already moving—eyes fixed on the crest, blades drawn. "Whoa," I said, backing up. "Let's not stab things we don't understand."

"I understand plenty," she snapped. "It ruins everything it touches."

Before I could move to stop her, Dayna grabbed the pendant and placed it on top of the large flat stone we'd been using as makeshift seating, then brought both swords down in a clean, simultaneous arc.

The crest flared, a sudden burst of searing light. Energy cracked through the air like a whip.

Dayna staggered back with a sharp grunt, her blades slipping from her hands and clattering to the ground. Sparks of magic hissed off the steel where it struck, searing tiny scorch marks into the stone. She stood still, chest heaving, her face suddenly drained of color. Then her gaze found mine—steady, resolute.

"If we can't destroy it," she said, voice low and firm, "then give it to me."

This, of course, was a request I refused even to consider. "No."

"Didn't you just ask it to pick someone else? Well, here I am." She gestured at herself with both hands. "Congratulations, it's me. Let me carry the stupid thing."

"No," I said louder this time, even more sure. I stepped between her and the crest. "Every time someone else touches it, bad things happen. Giant rocks attack us. People lose memories. Get dragged into other realms. Or worse."

Her expression narrowed. "And you think you're exempt?"

"No," I said, casting my eyes toward the ground so I wouldn't have to see the look on her face when I said the next part. "I think I'm already ruined."

That shut her up.

For about three seconds.

"You're becoming reckless," she said, voice low and dangerous. "Obsessed. You haven't slept. You're yelling at artifacts. You won't let anyone else near it."

"Look what it did to Gaaron last night," I snapped, the words coming out sharper than I intended. "You think I'm being reckless? He *begged* us to kill him,

Dayna. He couldn't even tell where he ended and Maltherius began. So no—I'm not handing this thing off just because I look a little worn around the edges."

"You're not invincible," she bit back, with a tight grimace. "Stop pretending you are."

We locked eyes, unmoving. The sunrise lit the space between us, casting her in a soft halo that made her hair look like it was burning. Her expression stayed hard, but her hands were still trembling.

She didn't make another move for the crest. Just bent down, retrieved her blades, and sheathed them with crisp, familiar ease.

"Just... you don't have to do this alone," Dayna said, quieter now, the fire fading from her voice. "You have your party. You have m—" She stopped, jaw tightening. A half-confession buried mid-sentence. She shook her head like it didn't matter, like she hadn't almost said something that would've changed everything.

I opened my mouth to respond—honestly, I don't know what I would've said—but then a rasp of a voice cut through the dawn air behind us.

"She never acted invincible."

We turned.

Gaaron was propped against the makeshift pack the kids had assembled for him, half-slumped but upright. His hair was a mess, his skin sallow, and he looked like he'd lost a duel with a boulder... but his eyes.

His *eyes* were clear.

"The fact that she kept going anyway," he said, his voice rough but steady, "that's what scared me the most."

I didn't move. Couldn't. I was ten years younger for one frozen heartbeat, watching the man I trusted most fade into something I couldn't reach. But this time... he'd come back.

Calina moved first. She bolted across the campsite and dropped to her knees beside him, her hands hovering for a moment before gently touching his arm, like she was afraid he'd vanish if she touched him too suddenly.

"You're awake," she whispered, voice breaking. "Like really, all the way awake. Dad... you're *here*."

Gaaron's expression softened, creased with exhaustion, but also something warm. Real. Present.

"I am," he said quietly. "I don't know how long it will last, but... I'm me. Right now, I'm me."

He looked up at me then, his expression unwavering.

"Tilda, I'm sorry. For last night. For... for all of it. I

didn't want to be a weapon. I *never* wanted to be the reason you got hurt."

And just like that, the tight knot in my chest unraveled a little.

He was back.

Finally, *truly* back.

Calina looked like she might cry. Or throw up. Or both. Her hands hovered uncertainly in the air, like she couldn't decide whether to reach for him or shove him away. When it came, her voice was small and shaking, raw with something that had festered too long.

"Why did you leave me and Mom?" she asked. "Why wasn't I—why weren't *we*—enough?"

The words landed like a dagger in our quiet, broken camp. No one moved. Even the fire seemed to still.

And Gaaron—gods, he didn't even flinch. He looked at her like she was the only thing in the world still worth answering. His voice, when it came, was soft. Tired. Honest.

"The moment I'm myself—truly myself again— that's the question you throw at me," he said. But there was no anger in it. No defense. Just the heavy weight of someone who knew she had every right to ask. And that he might never have a good enough answer.

Calina's lips parted, but no words followed. Her breath hitched. She winced and stepped back, hugging her arms tight to her chest like she needed to hold herself together. Then, quieter but steadier, she tried again.

"Tell me. Please. I need to hear your answer. Why weren't we enough?"

Gaaron closed his eyes. His whole body trembled with the breath he pulled in, like it scraped against his ribs on the way down.

"You were," he said. "By the essence of the divine, you were. That's why I left."

Calina blinked, fast and fierce, like she was trying to wash the truth from her eyes. Her jaw clenched, but she didn't interrupt. She let him speak, even as her heart appeared to crack a little more with each word.

The silence that followed wasn't quiet at all. It was full of the Lazul, rushing steadily behind us. The creak of leather. The faint hiss of embers. The whisper of Frosty's breath, slower now, even he knew not to interrupt. And beneath it all, the echo of everything Calina had waited her whole life to ask.

"I needed to make sure Tilda was set up," Gaaron said. His voice faltered but didn't fail. "Just a few more bounties. One last haul. I thought if I could get her someplace safe, I could finally come home. For good."

He looked at her then, really looked. And in his eyes, there was no fog, distance, or performance. Just a man who had made the wrong choice for the right reasons, and knew it too late.

"Your mother... she understood," he said. "She knew I had to walk away from that life on my own terms. She didn't want it to break me before I could let it go."

Calina stared at him, her expression unreadable—but her voice was clear, confident.

"You loved Mom." A statement. Not a question.

"I did," Gaaron said. His words were reverent, sacred. "I do. With everything in me, I do."

A pause.

"But you chose Tilda."

A pin-drop moment. The kind that freezes even the wind.

Gaaron didn't look away.

"I chose to protect you. All of you. I thought I had time to come back and explain. I thought I could have it both ways."

My breath caught. I opened my mouth, but nothing came out. Because what could I possibly say to that?

I hadn't known. Not the whole shape of it. Not

the full cost of what he'd given me. What he'd taken from her.

And if I had...

If I had known he was walking away from a family —from *her*—I would've stopped him. Gods help me, I would've told him to stay. I would've packed my bags, disappeared again, vanished into the shadows where I belonged. I would've done anything to make sure that little girl didn't grow up wondering if she'd been worth staying for.

Because I knew that feeling too well. Knew what it was like to carry that ache in your chest, the gnawing question no one ever answers—not really. Not in a way that makes the doubt go away.

And maybe that's what hurt most of all. That I couldn't fix it for her. That none of us could.

The pain in Calina's eyes cracked—no longer just sorrow, but something harder. Sharper. The glimmer of a truth too long held back.

She wiped her face with her sleeve in one fast, angry motion, like she was done letting tears have a say in any of this. Then she nodded once, quick, decisive like slamming a door that would never open again.

"I understand why you did what you did," she said, voice tight, trembling. "But I will never agree with it."

Her eyes locked onto his, unflinching. "You don't get to be my hero anymore."

Gaaron flinched. It was subtle, just a small falter in his expression, but it cut deeper than a scream.

Calina wasn't done. "My whole life, all I wanted was to be like you. I'd sit by the window waiting for your letters, dreaming about swords and spells and taverns full of people whispering your name like a legend. You were this... this *shining thing* in the distance. Not just a dad, but a symbol. A hero."

She shook her head, jaw clenching as her voice sharpened. "But that was a story. One, I told myself, because the truth hurt too much. Because the truth was that you weren't coming home. That I wasn't enough to make you stay."

She stepped back from him then, not far, but enough. Enough to make her meaning clear. "The truth is, you were never a hero, Gaaron. Not to me. Not when it mattered."

The words hit like a hammer, and still, the bard didn't look away. He didn't argue or explain. He just sat there and took it.

"You're my father," Calina finished, softer now, but no less certain. "I don't even really know what that means anymore. This relationship, it's not what I spent so many years dreaming of, but it's not nothing. I guess we'll have to find a new way to define it, and we can do that together. It's just going to take time."

Gaaron reached out, fingers trembling like he didn't quite believe he had the right, but she didn't take his hand.

She didn't cry. Not exactly. But her chin quivered, and her eyes blinked too often, too fast, like she could force the emotion back inside if she kept moving.

Rurik stood nearby, arms crossed, shoulders hunched, bracing for an explosion that hadn't come yet. He stared into the fire pit like it held answers he couldn't understand anymore.

Tulip, for once, was quiet. She stood to the side, chewing the edge of a braid like a worried child. Her tail flicked once, then stilled.

Even Frosty had gone still. Claws halfway to a rock, nostrils flaring slightly, trying to smell the shape of grief.

Dayna turned her face away.

And I—I just stood there.

I wanted to speak. Gods, I wanted to say something, anything. To fill the space that stretched so achingly wide between father and daughter. To apologize. To shoulder it for him. For all of us.

Every nerve in my body screamed to take the blame. To confess. To shout that it was *my* fault—*I* was the reason he stayed too long, went too far, lost himself in the name of some impossible promise to me.

But guilt is a selfish thing when it tries to steal the spotlight from someone else's grief. So I swallowed it down, even though it choked me in the process.

The Genesis Crest lay cold against my chest, silent. Heavy. Not glowing and not whispering. Just... waiting.

And I understood, in that moment, more clearly than I ever had before: This was what it meant to carry it. Not the magic. Not the power. The *weight*. The responsibility of every person broken in its wake.

I couldn't take any more, not now, maybe not ever again. So, I took a page from Gaaron's book and walked away. Not all the way, not far, just to a place where I could be alone as I grappled with my emotions and tried hard not to feel any of them.

I found a quiet spot on a flat rock near the water, where the breeze painted shifting patterns across the surface. The light shimmered and scattered, like it couldn't decide what it wanted to be. Much like me.

I didn't know where the others had gone. Didn't *want* to know. Not right now. Not after everything Calina had laid bare.

They could keep their grief and awkward comfort

to themselves. I needed silence. Solitude. A single moment that didn't demand anything from me.

I reached up and pulled the crest from beneath my shirt, letting its full weight settle into my palm.

"You want me to carry all of this?" I whispered. "Fine."

The crest pulsed once, soft and indifferent—a shrug disguised as light.

"But you don't get to break anyone else." I stared at it, daring it to argue.

It didn't.

"Gaaron is done paying for this. Calina is done wondering. You've already marked me, so let's get something straight—" I tightened my grip around it, thumb brushing the carved spiral at its core. "I'm not the hapless fool you branded in a burst of magic and light. I'm the fighter who gets to decide how this ends."

I tucked the crest back into its place and stood, the moment closing around me like the surface of the Lazul—rippled, unsettled, but still intact.

Behind me, the world could have been burning, and I wouldn't have noticed. Whatever the others were doing—whatever was being said—I shut it out. Calina's confrontation had torn open something I wasn't ready to stitch back up. And maybe that was the point. Perhaps some wounds weren't meant to close neatly.

I didn't turn when I heard footsteps approach through the grass. Soft. Measured.

Dayna.

She didn't say anything, and neither did I. But she stopped beside me, close enough that I could hear her breath—steady, deliberate, like she was counting each inhale to keep herself grounded.

"I'm not okay," I said eventually, the words catching a little on the way out.

"I know," she replied.

We stood like that for a while. Not speaking. Not touching. Just two women who'd survived more than they ever asked to, holding the line in the ruins of everything that came before.

Finally, I turned to go, because the road ahead was still long. And no one—not even the crest—would walk it for us.

20

I returned to camp with Dayna at my side, both of us silent, pretending we hadn't just exposed parts of ourselves best left buried.

"Sit," she said gruffly, nudging me with her elbow. "Eat. Drink some tea. If you're dead set on playing martyr, you might as well do it with a full stomach."

I raised a brow. "Is that concern I hear?"

She gave me a shove—not hard, but not gentle either. I stumbled forward a few steps, glancing back just in time to catch the barest ghost of a smirk.

"I'm just trying to protect my investment," she muttered, crouching to tend the fire. "Don't flatter yourself."

"What investment?"

"Time."

I might've laughed if it didn't catch in my throat. Instead, I dropped onto a log near the pit and watched her stir something into a tin mug. Across the clearing, Frosty was frolicking at the edge of the Lazul like a toddler made of ice and elation, splashing up arcs of water as he chased his reflection.

For a moment, I let myself just sit. Watch. Breathe.

Tulip was with Calina beneath a scraggly pine, speaking softly and braiding wildflowers into her rose-pink hair—an effort to lift her mood, or maybe just keep her hands busy. Calina wasn't smiling, but she wasn't pushing her away either. Progress.

Rurik sat beside Gaaron, a battered old journal open between them. I recognized it instantly—Gaaron's own, once passed to Calina, now worn soft at the edges by Rurik's devotion.

"This saved me," Rurik said, tapping a page. "Gave me purpose when I didn't know who I was."

He held out a hand and conjured a flickering mote of fire—his old trick, the one he'd first used outside the tavern back in Briarhaven. It hovered, then swelled, growing brighter, hotter, wilder, until he launched it into the air with a dramatic flourish. It exploded overhead in a burst of gold and crimson, crackling like a firework.

Tulip clapped softly. Calina smiled—just barely.

Even Gaaron let out a warm, bard-like laugh. "Impressive," he said. "You've taken this farther than I had ever dared to dream. *Brava.*"

But it was a performance. I could see it. Gaaron's focus snuck back to Calina every few seconds when he thought no one was looking.

And I wondered, not for the first time, if we should've let him die when he asked. If the pain ahead was worse than death would have been. If the man he was now could carry the weight of everything he'd lost —and everything he'd broken.

Dayna's voice cut through the quiet like flint on steel. "We need to talk about what's next."

She wasn't loud, but she didn't have to be. Everyone looked up. Tulip stilled her hands where she'd been braiding a crown of clover for Calina. Rurik closed the journal he'd been showing Gaaron. Even Frosty stopped chasing his reflection and wandered closer, ears twitching like he wanted in on the plan.

"Maltherius won't stop," Dayna said. "He'll keep coming for Gaaron. For the crest. We all saw what happened the last time."

Gaaron nodded once. "If you won't kill me—and thank you for that—then we end this another way. We go back. We finish it."

The silence that followed wasn't indecision. It was an agreement steeped in dread.

Rurik cleared his throat and held up a folded, ink-smudged sheet, creased at the edges, stained with what looked suspiciously like a faint, dried thumbprint of blood.

"I've been going over Zephyriel's prophecies," he said, quiet but steady. "Trying to match what's already happened to what's still coming."

Calina crossed her arms. "And?"

"And..." He hesitated. "I think we're closer to the end than we realize."

He glanced down at the page, fingers tightening slightly. "The first line—the general prophecy, meant for all of us: *Two adventures both inexorably intertwined, both above your skill level... both quests you will ultimately conquer.*"

"That's Mystwood and Maltherius," I said before I could stop myself. "Assassinating the regent. Rescuing Gaaron."

"And we only managed the first one because Dayna beheaded the guy *after* Rurik brought the whole castle down on him, and he still somehow tried to crawl away." I glanced sideways. "Which is extra weird, considering you weren't even *in* the party yet when the prophecy was made."

Dayna shrugged, utterly unbothered. "Some people are just born essential."

"But we haven't conquered the second one yet," Calina added, her voice brittle. "We got him back... but he's not free. Not from the crest. Not from what it did to him."

Across the fire, Gaaron didn't argue. He just looked down at his hands.

Rurik gave a slow nod. "Right. That one's still in motion."

He flipped the page. "Next line: *'To emerge victorious, you will need to pay the ultimate cost. Sacrifice what matters most, and you will surely win.'*"

The air went still. The kind of still that makes you feel like the world itself is waiting to see what you'll say.

No one did.

Not right away.

The words settled over us like ash—soft, suffocating, impossible to ignore.

I didn't know what the prophecy meant. Not exactly. But I knew what it *sounded* like. And judging by the expressions around the fire, I wasn't the only one drawing conclusions.

Calina's arms had tightened around herself again, her jaw set like she was bracing for impact. I knew what she was thinking. *Gaaron.* Losing him again, for real this time. And maybe worse—losing herself in the process. Her whole life had been one long stretch of reaching for, resenting, and loving him despite everything. To sacrifice what mattered most? It could be him. It could be that last thread of hope.

Rurik's brow furrowed, fingers twitching at the edge of his notes. His gaze had gone distant, inward. Always the logician, trying to calculate what the "ultimate cost" might mean in measurable terms. But even he knew you couldn't quantify something like *loss*. I wondered if he was thinking of his magic. His mind. Or maybe... us.

Tulip sat completely still, except her tail twitched once behind her, then curled close. Her focus stayed fixed on the fire, but I could see it in the slope of her shoulders—that quiet acceptance. The kind people mistake for bravery. Or maybe it *was* bravery. She had already watched someone she loved die. She didn't fear the flames anymore. Perhaps she thought they'd come for her next.

Even Dayna didn't break the silence. Her hands were clenched at her sides, knuckles white. She didn't blink. Didn't shift. Just stared ahead, grasping the words aimed directly at her heart, she wasn't sure whether to dodge or take the hit.

And me? I didn't know what mattered most. Not

anymore. I'd spent so long trying *not* to care that I hadn't noticed when the things I couldn't live without started piling up like kindling. This ragtag party. Their stubborn loyalty. Dayna's scowl. Tulip's laugh. Calina's fire. Rurik's endless theories. Frosty's snoring.

Any one of them could be the cost.

And the worst part? I didn't know if I could stop it.

Or if the crest had already decided for me.

Rurik's voice dropped. "The next line is worse. *'The deaths will be swift and unforgiving, but they are needed for your party to persevere.'*"

No one moved.

No one breathed.

"Amariel," Tulip whispered.

She pressed a hand against her sternum, feeling the ache there. Her fingers curled lightly in the fabric of her tunic, searching for the edges of a hole that only faded with time measured in years. "She was the first."

The fire crackled. Frosty nudged closer to her side, nuzzling against her flank, unusually gentle. The kind of quiet that followed wasn't empty. It was full of grief, memory, and things none of us could say until now.

"She and I came as a set," Tulip said softly. "Maybe we were meant to leave as one, too."

She looked down at me, and the depth in her eyes

nearly buckled my knees. No fear. Just an unbearable clarity. She wasn't posturing. Wasn't angling for praise.

She'd made peace with it.

"If someone has to die next—if it has to be someone—I volunteer."

"No." The word tore out of me like it had claws. Immediate. Fierce.

Tulip blinked but didn't flinch.

"I'm not saying I want to," she murmured. "But I'm not afraid anymore. Not of what's coming. Not if it means the rest of you get through."

"Then be brave enough to live," I told her. My voice cracked halfway through, but I didn't care. "That's the harder thing."

Tulip's jaw tightened. She nodded, like someone accepting terms they didn't like, but understood anyway.

Rurik didn't rush us. He gave the silence a moment to settle, then turned the page slowly.

"There were individual prophecies, too," he said. "Tilda, yours was first."

He looked up. "Do you know what it might mean?"

I felt every eye drift to me.

My hand instinctively touched the Genesis Crest, cold through my shirt. I didn't speak right away.

Because how could I? I thought of what Zephyriel had said:

Two adventures... both conquered. Sacrifice what matters most. Swift deaths. Ultimate cost. Nearly everything you desire.

I didn't have a neat, single-line riddle like the others. Mine was the whole tangled mess. The path. The burden. The breaking point.

What mattered most? It could be Gaaron. The one I risked everything to save. It could be Dayna. The one I wasn't supposed to care about—but did, stupidly, fiercely, quietly. It could be the party. The little family we'd built out of pain and sarcasm and survival.

What mattered most wasn't a thing. It was *all of them.*

I closed my eyes and shook my head.

"No," I said. "I don't know what it means."

And that was the truest thing I'd said all day.

Rurik gave me a searching look, then moved on without pressing. "Tulip. Yours was: *'You would do well to remember that the most valuable riches are not made of gold but flesh and blood.'*"

Tulip nodded solemnly. "I think I finally understand."

She stared into the fire as she spoke. "My parents were always chasing something they couldn't hold.

Influence. Wealth. Expectations. They wanted me to be like that too, and I was, for a while."

Then she glanced around—first at Calina, then at Rurik, and finally at me.

"But now, I think... I've found something better."

Her voice was tender, but steady. "You. This. All of it."

No one corrected her.

Because she wasn't wrong.

Rurik continued, "Calina, yours said: *'Family is indeed a divine blessing, but it is not only the family to which we are born that deserves our love.'*"

Calina glanced toward Gaaron, then reached out and squeezed Tulip's hand.

"I thought it meant finding a way to forgive him," she said. "But it's more than that. It's you. All of you. The people I chose."

Rurik didn't meet anyone's eyes as he read his own. "*'You are only just becoming who you were meant to be. But your heart, not your mind, will get you to the place you need to find. Be open to these gifts of growth even if they go against logic.'*"

"On brand," I said. But my voice lacked bite.

"Yeah." Rurik gave a crooked smile. "The prophecy knew I needed to stop hiding behind equations and theories and start trusting... people. Magic. Purpose."

Rurik clenched the paper in his hands, hesitating.

"One more," he said. "Zephyriel gave it to who we thought was Amariel, but was actually Finnian in disguise."

The group froze, like we were bracing for a storm.

Rurik read aloud: "*'All your many tricks do not serve you well. You will not obtain what you desire until you learn to request it plainly and without artifice.'*"

I let out a slow breath. "Good luck with that."

Dayna didn't smile. "It's not for us to fix," she said. "But he still has a part to play. We should expect him to show up before the end."

Her voice was low, almost grudging, hating to admit he was even part of the story.

A heavy silence settled over us again.

This one felt different. Not just grief or worry, but the weight of inevitability. Accepting how the prophecy had laid out our path, and all that was left was to walk it.

We didn't have the appetite to finish breakfast. Whatever had been cooking over the fire sat untouched, now cold, forgotten.

Even Frosty, who had never once turned down food, ignored it in favor of trying to cheer up the girls with gentle nudges and chilly snuggles.

We sat like that for a while.

No more words.

Just the hush of the river. The ache of what we'd already lost. And the certainty of what we might lose next.

Eventually, I rose, brushing the dirt from my hands and knees. Every movement felt deliberate and final.

"We know what's coming," I said. "We don't know the exact details, but we know where it leads."

Rurik nodded. "Back to the Precipice."

I reached for the Genesis Crest—not to draw from it, not to whisper to it, but just to feel its weight. My burden. My bond. It had stopped glowing, but somehow that made it worse, like it was waiting for the right moment to wake up again. Like it already knew how this would end.

I took a few steps toward the edge of camp, expecting to hear others follow.

They didn't.

Instead, Gaaron's voice stopped me. Rough. Fragile. Real.

"Wait," he said. "Please."

I turned.

He was standing now, hand resting on a tree like he needed its strength to stay upright. His face was pale, drawn tight around the eyes, but his expression was clear.

"I know what we have to do," he said. "And I'm not asking to change it. I'll go. I'll face whatever's waiting for me."

He looked at Calina then. Not pleading. Just... hoping.

"But can we have today? Just one day. One normal, quiet, ridiculous day where I get to be myself. With her. With all of you. In case I never get the chance again."

Calina didn't speak.

She crossed the distance between them and slipped her hand into his without a word.

He let out a shaky breath, like the tension had been holding him up, and now he didn't need it anymore.

I looked around at the others—Rurik, Tulip, Dayna, even Frosty. No one moved to object. No one needed to.

Because Gaaron wasn't asking for much. Just a day. Just one more chance to live before we all went marching back toward death.

And gods help me, I couldn't deny him that. Not after everything.

I gave a slight nod. "One day."

21

The others drifted from the fire in slow pairs and quiet purpose, scattering across the camp like they didn't want to admit they were all doing the same thing—trying to make memories before we ran out of chances.

Frosty barreled toward the river with the force of a small avalanche, dragging half the camp's tension in his wake and tossing several ill-fated, frozen fish to the shore. Calina and Tulip followed quietly, Tulip's torso bent in low conversation. Rurik trailed them with his journal clutched to his chest like a shield.

But Dayna didn't move.

She sat back on the same log she'd used for breakfast, posture straight, expression unreadable. Her swords lay beside her, and with a slow exhale, she pulled out a whetstone and began to sharpen one, slow, deliberate, almost meditative.

It was a familiar rhythm—a comfort disguised as duty.

I lingered, not because I didn't want to follow the others, but because I couldn't—not yet. Instead, I crossed to her side and crouched, settling near the edge of the fire's warmth.

Dayna didn't look at me, but I saw the faintest hitch in her motion—just enough to say *I see you* without saying anything at all.

"You know," I said, watching her drag the stone down the blade, "you don't have to sharpen that today. You've got a whole twenty-four hours left to brood before we start dying again."

She didn't smile, but the corner of her mouth twitched. "You're assuming I know how to do anything else."

I waited a beat. Then, leaning forward, I quietly asked, "Are you staying because you have to... or because you want to?"

That stopped her cold.

She glanced down at the blade, then set it aside. Her shoulders stayed rigid, like she was still bracing for some unexpected impact.

"You've seen the crest. It's been in your hands, and

yet..." I added. "You could've walked away a dozen times."

"I know."

Silence stretched, long and brittle. Then, finally, she looked at me. Really looked.

"I haven't felt bound to anything in years," she said. "Not to a person. Not to a cause. Not even to myself. Just... surviving. One job to the next. One fight to the next."

Her eyes dropped to the grass. She plucked a blade of it between her fingers and rolled it absently, like it might anchor her to the moment.

"But watching them—watching you—it reminded me what it's like to care. Not out of obligation. Not because I was ordered to. Just because I actually do."

She paused, the words catching like they weren't used to being said aloud.

"Maybe I'm not done. Maybe I'm still becoming someone I could stand to be."

The ache in my chest was immediate—a fragile, breaking thing. I reached over and placed my hand on hers. And she didn't flinch. She just turned her palm upward and wove her fingers through mine.

We sat like that. No more questions. No more clever words. Just two people who had survived too much to pretend they didn't need someone beside them anymore.

I leaned into her shoulder, and she let me stay. I let myself believe—for just one day—that maybe this could be enough.

We didn't talk as the others fell into their quiet rituals of joy, but we didn't need to. Watching your people live, not fighting, not training, not arguing, just *being,* soothes a different kind of ache.

Rurik and Tulip had claimed a patch of sun-drenched grass near the riverbank. Tulip had knelt down and Rurik sat cross-legged. They faced each other with the intensity of a high-stakes negotiation.

"She's making him teach her magic," I murmured. "This'll end well."

Dayna snorted. "I give it five minutes before she sets her tail on fire."

"Three," I countered.

Negotiation complete, both rose and assumed their positions. Down by the water, Rurik gestured with wide, sweeping motions, likely over-explaining something that could've been summed up with *just wiggle your fingers and believe.* Tulip nodded earnestly and then stomped a hoof on his boot when he corrected her stance. He flailed backward, arms up, and fell on his rear end. She laughed—a big, braying sound that startled birds from the trees.

"You know," I said, watching them, "when we met her, I thought she'd be the first to bolt. She hated all of us."

"She still does," Dayna said dryly. "She's just emotionally codependent now."

I chuckled. But it caught in my throat when I saw how Rurik looked at her, as if she were made of stars, brute force, and things worth believing in. And the way she looked at him—awkward, awestruck, like she hadn't quite figured out how she'd ended up with someone who didn't flinch away from even her sharpest edges.

Tulip reached forward and tried the spell again.

This time, a soft glow bloomed in her palms. It was uneven, flickering, wildly unstable—but it was *magic*.

She shrieked in delight, then accidentally launched it skyward, where it exploded in a puff of pink sparks and a vaguely duck-shaped cloud.

I heard Rurik yell, "That was not part of the theory!" Tulip tackled him into the grass anyway, laughing so hard she wheezed.

Dayna's hand remained in mine. Not limp, not stiff—just there. Steady. Her thumb brushed small, slow circles across the back of my hand. Occasionally, her grip would tighten, just for a moment, like she remembered how fleeting this was, like she wasn't ready to let go.

Neither was I.

I glanced up to find her watching them too, not with her usual skepticism, but something gentler. Her mouth was tilted into something that almost looked like longing.

"They're good together," she murmured. "Odd as it is."

"Yeah," I agreed. "They're real. And somehow, real feels rarer than magic."

Dayna didn't reply right away. Her thumb resumed its slow rhythm against my skin. "That's what scared me the most," she said finally. "Not the crest. Not Maltherius. Just... this. Letting it matter."

I turned to look at her, but she didn't meet my eyes. "I wasn't sure I'd ever get back to a place where I could feel something like this again," she said. "Let alone *want* to."

I didn't say anything. I shifted closer, letting our shoulders press together, warm, solid, and steady. And for once, neither of us moved away.

warm and soft breeze drifted through the clearing, rustling the leaves in lazy whispers. The sun climbed higher, gilding the treetops and casting dapples of gold across the forest floor—like the world had decided, just for today, to be kind.

Dayna shifted beside me, adjusting her grip so our fingers were fully entwined. I let her.

Down by the river, Tulip flopped onto her back in the grass, horse legs kicked up rolling and twisting like she was claiming the whole meadow. Rurik lay beside her, hands behind his head, a smug grin on his face like he'd just rewritten the laws of magic and wanted full credit.

I thought that was the end of it.

But then Rurik sat up suddenly, brushed the grass from his tunic, and ambled toward Gaaron, who was seated beneath a tree, fiddling with snapped wood and frayed string.

I blinked. "Is he... rebuilding an instrument out of a mess kit?"

"Looks like it." Dayna nodded.

Gaaron's hands moved with practiced ease, but his eyes betrayed him. They were too focused, too careful, like he was holding something together that wanted to come apart.

Rurik hesitated nearby, then dropped into a cross-legged sprawl and pulled the leather-bound journal from his bag—the one that had once belonged to Gaaron. The one Calina had passed down. The one Rurik had filled with notes, sketches, and all the anxious, brilliant energy he never quite knew what to do with.

Gaaron looked up, surprised. "Didn't think anyone would read that."

"I didn't just read it." Rurik ran a hand over the worn leather. "It changed everything. Made me want to be more than just clever. Made me want to be *good*."

Gaaron swallowed. His fingers paused over the unfinished strings.

Then, quietly, he asked, "How do you do it?"

Rurik blinked. "Do what?"

"You're Calina's best friend. You're close. You know how to talk to her." Gaaron's voice was raw, uneven. "I want to reach her. I want to know who she is now. But I keep freezing. Saying the wrong thing. Or worse—nothing at all."

Rurik's face softened. He glanced down, thumb brushing the corner of the journal. "Start small," he said. "Ask who she is now. Not who she was. Not who you hoped she'd become. Just her."

I didn't realize I was holding my breath until Dayna released a slow one beside me.

"Good advice," she murmured.

"Rare sight," I agreed, quietly stunned.

Across the field, Calina was moving. But not toward her father. This time, she made a beeline straight for Tulip, who was still sprawled in the grass, now humming something suspiciously close to the duck-shaped spell explosion melody.

Dayna noticed too. "This should be good."

Tulip spotted her and bolted upright, brushing invisible grass from her tunic like she was about to undergo a formal inspection. Her ears twitched. Her tail rapidly brushed grass from her rump.

Calina stopped a foot away, arms crossed, chin lifted.

"I didn't always trust you," she said flatly.

Tulip blinked. "Um. Thanks?"

"But I like who Rurik is around you," Calina went on, unmoved. "You make him shine."

Tulip's jaw dropped. Her mouth opened. Closed. She looked like someone had just complimented her on her tactical instincts *and* her poetry analysis.

"And if you hurt him," Calina added, matter-of-fact, "I will end you. I may be small, but I fight dirty."

Tulip's mouth flapped open again—still nothing.

Then, finally, voice pitched a little high, just on the edge of a whinny, she stammered, "I... I wouldn't. I mean, I won't. Hurt him, that is. I care about him. A lot. I don't know what I'm doing, but I'm trying. I want to try."

Calina gave a single, satisfied nod. "Good."

Then she turned and walked away, heading back toward the river boulder with the kind of poise that said *this was a scheduled confrontation and now it is complete.*

Tulip sat frozen, ears still twitching. Then glanced over her shoulder toward Rurik like she needed confirmation that yes, she had just been emotionally gut-checked by the world's tiniest Starbrook.

Dayna chuckled. "She's not subtle."

"No," I said, smiling. "But she's not wrong, either."

I glanced back at Gaaron and Rurik. The bard was laughing at something now—probably a joke Rurik didn't mean to make. His posture had softened. So had Rurik's.

So had mine.

Because for the first time in a long time, it felt like maybe—not everything—but *something* might be okay.

"Look." Dayna tapped her thumb against my hand and nodded toward the trees.

Calina was walking again—this time toward Gaaron.

I tensed. My fingers curled tighter around Dayna's, and she squeezed back like she felt it too.

Gaaron had just finished restringing his makeshift lute and was testing it softly when Calina arrived. She didn't speak. Just nodded toward the woods.

He followed without hesitation.

They disappeared into the trees, slipping into a pocket of green-gold light where the canopy opened just enough to make the moss shine. I watched them go—not because I was worried, but because I wanted to see if they could get it right this time.

"She's giving him a shot," I whispered.

Dayna tilted her head. "He knows it matters."

"He's just afraid he'll mess it up."

"He might."

I didn't argue because he might. But he was trying. And so was she.

Calina and Gaaron stopped near a mossy ridge where the trees thinned and the sunlight poured through like liquid gold. They didn't speak at first. Gaaron settled on a log, resting his instrument across his knees, and Calina stood beside him with her arms crossed, unreadable.

He started to play. Just a simple melody—barely more than a hum—but it had the fragile softness of something made long ago and carried too far. The lullaby he'd written for her, probably before she ever heard it. Maybe before she was even born.

She didn't cry. But she sat. Quietly. Carefully.

And when he faltered, she asked—low, but clear, "Will you teach me?"

Gaaron blinked at her, stunned. Then he shifted the lute into her hands and guided her fingers across the strings, showing her where to press, where to lift. She tried it. It wasn't graceful, but it was sincere. And she didn't look away from him. Not once.

Watching from a distance, I bit the inside of my cheek to keep it together. The pain wasn't what made me ache—it was the effort because I wanted this for them. Not just peace. Not just forgiveness. *A chance.* One honest chance to know each other without all the years of distance weighing them down.

"I want them to find each other again," I whispered.

Dayna didn't respond right away. She leaned into me a little more, cheek resting lightly against my temple.

"You think they can?" she asked finally.

"I think they already are."

Because I could see it—in the way Gaaron gently tucked a pink curl behind Calina's ear. In the way, her hand lingered over the strings even after the last note faded. In the way, neither one of them said what they were thinking, but both stayed anyway.

They were trying.

And sometimes, trying was the whole figgin' miracle.

I turned my face slightly into Dayna's shoulder and let the feeling settle over me like a cloak. She didn't speak. Just rubbed her thumb over the back of my hand in those same soft, grounding circles she'd started hours ago. Still here. Still holding on.

By the time the sun dipped low behind the trees, everyone had returned to camp with the quiet energy that followed a good day, not loud, not boastful. Just present. Just *together*.

Dinner was simple but perfect. Gaaron and Calina had turned Frosty's unfortunate morning fish into something surprisingly edible. The stew tasted smoky and rich, with just enough freshly foraged wild onion to hide the guilt.

We sat close around the fire, bowls in our laps, spoons clicking against the sides. No one said they were hungry or scared, but I think we all knew. This was our last easy night.

Tulip gestured wildly as she recounted her magical duck-shaped explosion incident. "It was like—quack, boom, sparkle! You should've seen the bird! It had wings. *Wings*, Rurik!"

Rurik groaned, burying his face in one hand. "I specifically told you *not* to angle the spell skyward."

Tulip grinned. "I was being theatrical."

"You turned a duck into a cannonball."

"Art is subjective."

Even Dayna laughed, a rare, warm sound that rumbled through her chest and into mine.

Then Gaaron leaned forward and strummed a soft chord on his lute. The noise quieted, like the air itself was listening.

"Calina and I talked earlier," he said. "We thought we'd share something. An old song. One her mother used to sing."

Calina nodded, eyes swerving from person to person. "It's a song for those who fight with nothing but each other. We think you'll all already know it, so maybe we can sing together. Ready?"

She began alone.

"Where shadows fall and silence clings, We bind our hearts with broken strings. Through shattered light and paths unknown, We fight as one, or not at all."

Gaaron joined, his voice rough and golden like something half-forgotten but fiercely remembered.

"If we should fall, then fall we will— With blades unsheathed and spirits still. The wind may take what time forgets, But not the vows we won't regret."

The words found their way into my chest, like someone had carved them there long ago and was just now reminding me.

Tulip sang next—loud and off-key, but so *earnestly* that it made something catch in my throat.

Rurik tried to harmonize. Failed. Tried again. Failed louder.

Frosty warbled in what I could only describe as haunting counterpoint, like he was part tundra wolf, part cello.

And one by one, the rest of us joined in—not perfect, not rehearsed—but real.

"So light the torch and face the flame. We know our loss, we speak our name. Let fate strike true, let fear take wing— Together still, we rise and sing."

The final notes faded.

The stillness that followed wasn't empty. It was full of *everything.* Hope. Fear. Memory. Love.

And then—

SPLASH.

Frosty barreled in from the Lazul, hauling the *largest fish yet* like a goblin presenting a royal tribute. Water sprayed across the fire, hissing into steam. With a proud, dragonling roar, he dropped his prize at Tulip's hooves.

Tulip shrieked. The fish flopped once. Then again.

Then launched itself *at Rurik.*

Rurik screamed.

Dayna swore.

I laughed so hard I nearly toppled into the fire.

Frosty pranced in triumphant circles like he'd just saved us all from starvation *and* boredom.

It wasn't the right time. It wasn't the right place. But for one perfect moment?

Everything felt right anyway.

22

Later—long after the fire had sunk into embers, after the laughter ebbed and the music ran dry—we slept.

Well, most of us did.

I'd only just drifted under, after watching Dayna across the camp, wondering what it might feel like to fall asleep in her arms after so many years of going it alone, when something shifted. A missing noise. The sound of absence, sharp and wrong in the dark.

Heavy with dreams, I blinked and immediately registered the empty space near the fire. Gaaron's bedroll sat undisturbed.

But Gaaron was gone. I don't know how he had, once again, slipped away without my notice, but I knew why.

My hand flew to my chest, grasping for the artifact I'd once feared and now protected with my life. The Genesis Crest was still there, cold against my skin—still mine. I looked over to Dayna, heart already thudding. She lay curled in her cloak, swords near, but her breathing was deep and even. Asleep. Completely unaware.

My body moved before my brain could catch up, instincts honed from too many nighttime disappearances that ended in empty boots and never enough goodbyes. I slipped from the bedroll and crept through the grass barefoot, dagger in hand out of sheer habit, until I found him.

Gaaron stood at the river's edge, half-silhouetted in moonlight, still as stone, like he was waiting to be taken. Just like I'd found him the night before. And here I'd thought he'd finally come back to himself.

I was wrong. This man still wasn't the friend I remembered, at least not all the way. Maltherius still had far too great a hold.

Gaaron's back was to me, shoulders high with tension wound as tight as a drawn bowstring. His hand hung at his side, twitching rhythmically, like he was conducting some silent symphony. His lips moved—whispers, low and private. Words not meant for me. Words not meant for us. I didn't need to understand them. I knew a summoning when I heard one.

"Gaaron," I said quietly.

No answer.

I edged closer, heart hammering. "Whatever you're doing... stop."

Still nothing. The words kept coming. A prayer. A curse. Maybe both.

And then the wind died—like someone had exhaled and forgotten how to breathe back in. The soft ripples in the Lazul froze mid-wave. Even the trees held their branches in tension, unmoving. Above, the stars began to blink out, one by one, and a heavy wash of darkness crawled across the sky—not like a storm cloud, but something worse—something beneath the stars, pressing outward.

My skin prickled. My gut screamed. And I ran.

I didn't know what I was running from, not yet. But my feet moved on instinct alone.

And behind me... the sky screamed.

Not with sound I could describe. Just one I knew I'd never forget. Metal scraped over bone. Teeth dragged across stone. A thousand dead voices screaming through a single, narrow throat.

I crashed back into camp, half-collapsing at the fire ring, breath tearing from my lungs.

Dayna was already up—swords bared, eyes burning, stance feral. "What is it?" she hissed.

I couldn't answer.

Because the moon was gone, blotted out by wings.

Massive, rotting wings stretched across the valley, pulsing with infernal light. The screech came again. Louder. Closer. Then she dropped.

Cindara had come for us; this time, there was no abyss to jump into, no easy escape.

She landed in the riverbed like a collapsing cathedral, sending water crashing into the air. Tulip, caught mid-step, flailed back with a startled whinny. Her hooves slipped, legs sprawled wide like a newborn foal. But she recovered quickly, slamming her feet into the ground, rising tall and proud, steam curling from her flared nostrils.

Her fingers clenched the jeweled haft of her ridiculous, bedazzled battle axe with white-knuckled fury. No words. Not yet. Just fury. Raw. Ready.

The ground shook beneath us, hard enough to knock loose stones from their beds and send shudders up my spine. My teeth rattled with the force of it. Cindara reared her head back and let out another scream—this one deep and guttural, a sound that split the air like a blade. Her body shimmered with infernal runes, the sigils branded and fused into her flesh with necrotic magic. There were so many of them that a sickly miasma swirled around her clawed feet. After so long with Frosty, Cindara barely resembled a dragon anymore. She looked like the birth of a mountain jutting up from the ground.

The same malignant vapors curled off Cindara, practically pulling the color—no, life itself—from the vegetation. Trees shriveled and blackened, like spent matchsticks. Water blackened and bubbled and where the taint struck, dead fish bobbed to the surface. A hot, sickly breeze, smelling of the grave, flowed out from the gargantuan dragon.

And like he'd been conjured from my nightmares, came Maltherius.

His form didn't just arrive—it *coalesced*. One moment, nothing. The next, he was like an afterimage, as if someone had drawn a memory of malice in the air. A shadow made solid. The miasma flowing from Cindara surged into the outline of him, solidifying and refining him. Magic flashed and the image of him exploded into a solid form of the gaunt necromancer. Emerald eyes gleaming like cursed jewels, each housing a roaring column of fire behind them.

And Gaaron—oh, sweetest divinity—Gaaron stood there *smiling*. Like he'd just seen salvation. Like he'd seen a god. And for him? He had.

Maltherius landed beside the dragon, his robes swirling around him. His presence was wrong, too sharp and cold, like a knife's edge pressed behind your ear. Then came his voice. Not from just from his mouth. From all around and even *inside me*.

"You've carried it long enough, Tilda Quickthatch."

I staggered, hand flying to my chest, fingers closing around the Genesis Crest. Not in pain. Not from fear. Just... trying to keep myself together. Trying not to dissolve into the memory of what this thing had always been.

"You were never more than a vessel," his voice reverberated—words threading through bone and breath alike.

His burning green eyes—if you could call them that—fixed on me. Not on my face. Not even on my soul. On the crest.

"A convenient hiding place. It takes a rogue to guard against rogues."

He took a step forward, and my lungs stopped working. Because I felt it. The truth I'd buried for years. The choice I never made. The crest hadn't just fallen into my hands. It had chosen me.

And Maltherius... he'd always known. Had he planned for this from the start? Had he *wanted* me to take it—to run, to hide, to nurture its power in the dark until it was ready for him again?

And if that was true… then what had it become to me? A weapon? A binding? A piece of myself I didn't ask for but could never give back?

Behind me, the camp erupted into motion.

Rurik scrambled up, robes askew, blinking like he'd been dropkicked into consciousness. He patted around for his journal like it was a lifeline, gaze darting between dragon, sky, and nightmare.

Calina moved fast—always faster than anyone else. She hit the ground in one fluid motion, bow already in hand and quiver on back, crouched low and scanning for weaknesses like she might find one and target it out of sheer willpower. Outmatched didn't matter to her. She would shoot death in the knee just to see if it flinched.

Dayna didn't even need to move. She stood tall, swords loose at her sides, face hard.

"I told you," she snarled, voice just as sharp as her swords. "Should've killed him when we had the chance."

And then came Frosty.

He'd been curled beside Calina, snoring like a lullaby in a snowstorm. But the moment Cindara landed—when the air turned putrid—he froze.

His eyes went round. Too wide. Then he squealed, bolted straight behind Tulip, and buried his face behind her flank like he'd just watched his own mother crawl out of a grave.

"Again with this stupid dragon?" Tulip muttered, leveling her axe.

"Ancient undead," I said through clenched teeth. "She's very powerful and could kill us all without effort."

"I'd like to see her try," Tulip grunted through gritted teeth.

"No, no, you wouldn't. Tulip, just don't move. Don't breathe. Don't even blink aggressively."

Tulip blinked. Aggressively.

Thankfully, Cindara didn't notice. Unfortunately, it was because Maltherius wasn't done. And neither was Gaaron.

I turned—just in time to see him fall. Gaaron dropped to his knees with a bone-jarring thud, like a puppet whose strings had finally snapped. His hand flew to his head, clutching at his hair, fingers clawing as if he could dig the invading presence out by force.

"No," he rasped, voice hoarse and unraveling. "No, no, no. I said—I said—" His breath caught on the words. Broke apart. "I won't do that. I don't belong to you. I am my own man."

And then Maltherius laughed with all the cruel irony of untimely death. The trees, the wind, and the ground beneath us crackled with the noise. It came from the river, the bones in our bodies, and every dead thing that had ever heard a lie.

"Your own man," the dark sorcerer scoffed. "You've never been your own man. Even before I captured you."

Gaaron screamed. It was a sound that didn't belong to a person. It cracked the world open—raw, terrified, furious. And then he lunged at me.

One second, he was a man breaking down. The next, he was a missile of muscle and desperation, flying across the clearing and slamming into me with the force of a prophecy. We hit the ground hard. My shoulder cracked against a rock. My dagger spun into the shadows.

"Gaaron!" I shouted, but he didn't see me. His eyes were haunted, empty—someone else's horror living behind them. His hand shot out—not for my throat. For the crest.

I grabbed him, but it was too late. The chain snapped with a metallic *ping*, and a flash of pain bloomed at my collarbone, cold and sudden and wrong and bloody. He tore it from me. He held up the

Genesis Crest in his hand like it was salvation. A trophy. Or a venomous snake.

And then—something *changed.* His face faltered and his shoulders slumped. He cracked. A glimpse of our Gaaron shone through like fire behind stained glass. He looked at me, a weary smile playing at his mouth. "Sorry," he whispered. Then he reached down, with bloodied fingers, and swept up my dagger from the ground.

He didn't hesitate. Didn't aim it at me. Didn't aim it at Maltherius. With white-knuckled resolve, he turned it on himself.

"No!"

The blade came down hard. There was a sickening *squelch* followed by a *crunch*, sprays of blood, and his hand—*his hand*—hit the dirt like dead weight. Still clutching the crest.

He didn't scream or cry out. He just stared at the stump of his wrist, eyes glassy and far away, like he was looking at the final tally of an ancient debt.

And then... he exhaled. Long and low. Like it was finally over.

But that last breath must've been the only thing holding him up, because he collapsed into me, and I threw my arms under his shoulders, cushioning his fall as best I could. His bulk drove us both to the ground.

My hands slipped on his blood as I fumbled for his belt, and I felt it—warm, too warm—soaking through my tunic. I needed to stop the bleeding.

"Hey. Hey, stay with me," I whispered. "C'mon bard. You don't get to end your story like this."

His skin had already gone pale, the blood draining too fast. He needed a tourniquet or a heal—

"Rurik!" I shouted. "We need you—*now!*"

Footsteps thundered behind me. Lighter than Tulip's. Faster than Dayna's.

"Coming!" Rurik called, stumbling to my side with panic crackling from his fingertips. He skidded on the wet grass, dropping beside us in a tangle of limbs and glowing light.

"Clear space—I need space!" He smeared something from his pouch onto his palms, hands shaking, light already building between them in chaotic pulses of blue and white.

I pressed my hands to Gaaron's forehead and held him tighter, locking him against me as he sagged heavier.

Calina rushed forward, her arrows forgotten, her brow creased with worry. But Dayna caught her around her waist.

"Let me go!" Calina snapped.

Dayna didn't budge. "No." Her tone was calm. Flat. Not cold—*anchored.* "Watch."

Calina froze. We all did.

Maltherius had not moved. But something had changed. His expression had shifted. He showed no outward emotion, but his eyes blazed with sickly green, brighter than before, more colorful than any mortal magic had a right to be. Green sparks surged across the ground and up his robes to crackle along his arms, dancing along skeletal fingers.

Like Death beckoning, he raised his hand. Reaching for the crest.

It still sat in the severed hand beside Gaaron's crumpled body, fingers limp, knuckles crusted in blood. The hand twitched. And the crest rolled once. Just once. But it was enough. It landed an inch outside the severed palm.

And then it began to *hum*. It was not a noise I could hear with my ears—more like a vibration in my teeth and bones—the resonance of something ancient remembering it had a name. It pulsed once. A ring of golden light shimmered along its edge. Twice. The hum deepened, turning into something *felt* more than heard.

Then came a surge. The energy burst outward in a perfect sphere, sweeping the camp in a single, silent wave, like the moment between one heartbeat and the next.

Rurik froze mid-spell, arms outstretched like he was sculpting the air. Calina's shout caught in her throat, her lips parted but unmoving. Dayna—still gripping Calina by the waist—went statue-still, her expression unreadable except for the faint line of pain between her brows. Like she felt what Gaaron had done. Even Cindara was caught. The undead dragon hovered half-lifted into the air, wings flared in rage, mouth unhinged in a roar that would never reach us.

Only the sound of the Lazul remained. Even that was muted.

Maltherius stood frozen, fingers still curled, reaching for the crest. Even the sparks of his magic stood still. His expression said everything. Confusion. Panic. Fear.

And me? I could almost move. Just a little. A twitch. A breath. A thought turning over like a wheel stuck in the mud. I was stitched to the world by this moment, tethered to the air by grief, magic, and something else entirely.

The crest began to lift. Not fast. Not high. Just enough to rise above the blood-soaked terrain. Still dripping red from Gaaron's wound. It glowed. But not with light. With... was it memory?

It spun slowly, as if attached to an invisible thread. It glowed brighter, the kind of glow that wasn't illumination but presence. The kind of glow that meant something, even if you didn't know what just yet. It was like the rest of the world had dimmed and the crest took up more and more room. It was light for judgment, awake and aware.

But he crest wasn't taking sides. It was remembering itself. And maybe also deciding something.

I cradled Gaaron, warm blood soaking through my clothes, his weight still against me. I could barely breathe. But I could feel it watching. The crest hovered above us, spinning ever so slowly, dripping gold and red in equal measure. It didn't look like a relic anymore. It didn't look like a treasure. It looked like a question. Not a weapon. Not a salvation. A choice.

It pulsed again, steady as a heartbeat—its heartbeat—resonating across the clearing like it shook time and memory alike. Rurik remained frozen with his spell mid-cast, rings of healing light trapped in place like a halo caught in stasis. Calina still crouched mid-stride, half-lunging toward her father, fury and fear frozen in her eyes. Dayna's grip around her had tightened just slightly, like her body remembered what her mind couldn't command. Even Frosty had gone rigid behind Tulip, his tiny claws dug into her flank for safety, eyes giant and unblinking. Tulip, who had started to swing her axe, hovered mid-motion, muscles locked in place, defiant and unyielding.

Maltherius had miscalculated. The crest. Me. Us. He thought us all parts of the equation that led to his mastery of the crest.

But the Genesis Crest wasn't looking for masters. It was becoming. Not a god. Not a curse. Something else. Something older than the words we'd used to define it.

A shift in my mind brought me back to my own thoughts. I had felt the emotions of the others. Briefly. Like the barest of whispers. The crest. It was reaching inward. Into me. Into us. Reading our memories, our intentions, our pain. Not judging. Just recording. Just knowing.

It hovered higher now. No longer tethered to anyone or anything. Freed from every hand that sought to grasp it. No longer anyone's to possess. And then it stopped spinning. Like it had faced me. Perfect and poised. The golden glow sharpened to a fine edge, and in the space of that impossible silence, I knew one thing with complete clarity: whatever came next wouldn't be ours to prevent.

The Genesis Crest had made its choice. And now... It was time to see what that meant.

23

The world broke again.

No warning. No wind-up. Just a sound like glass, remembering it used to be sand, and deciding to fall apart midair.

The air split down the middle with a jagged shriek—a song ripped to shreds with discord. A pressure-crack imploded around us. One moment, we were suspended in the crest's golden hush. The next, time snapped back into place like a dropped plate. Gravity slammed into me. My lungs gasped for breath.

And the Genesis Crest dropped.

It landed in the blood-soaked grass beside Gaaron's severed hand with a soft, terrible thud, its glow snuffed like a candle pinched out by wet fingers. No flare. No magic. Just a sound that felt too real. Solid. Final. And somehow, that made it worse.

Gaaron groaned in my arms, the first real sound since the world had stopped. His body twitched faintly, heat still draining too fast.

"Rurik—" I croaked, throat raw, not even sure what I needed—just that I needed something.

But I didn't get the chance to finish the sentence. Because they arrived.

Five figures burst through a ragged hole in the air, trailing streaks of residual magic and shimmering after-shock. Four wore scout leathers, wings flared wide from the teleport burst. The fifth stepped forward like a man late to his own funeral.

Finnian Sly. Not disguised. Not cloaked. Not glamoured into civility. This was his true form.

A tanuki—broad-shouldered and fox-eyed, his fur rippled like shadowed velvet beneath a high-collared coat that shimmered faintly with leftover ember trails. Spell energy clung to him like static, twitching across his duster. His ears were pinned back. His muzzle was drawn tight. The sleek tail behind him flicked once. His hair, usually restrained, had been yanked loose by wind and stress. He looked more beast than diplomat —more god than either.

And his eyes? They scanned the camp like a book he already knew the ending to.

Blood. A castle-sized undead dragon looming behind us, wings as broad as the valley. A half-dead bard bleeding into my lap.

Rurik gasping beside me, one hand still lit with sputtering spell-light. Without waiting for instruction, Rurik stripped the shield from his back and pressed it into Gaaron's side—quick, sure, practiced. Not to fight. To protect. His healing spell was already in motion, but it would take time. Time we didn't have.

Calina crouched nearby—bow drawn, arrows nocked, her posture coiled like a spring. Breath shallow. Teeth bared. Daring someone to move.

Dayna stood with the stillness of a panther before the pounce. This moment had been coming for a long time.

And then there was everything else—the reality of it sinking in like ice in my bloodstream. Cindara towered over the battlefield like a mountain carved of grief and hatred. Her wings swayed behind her, massive, decayed, and still smoking from the perpetual miasma that seemed to follow her. And Maltherius... the necromancer closed his hand into a tight fist, his spell flickering out like campfire embers in the night. He hadn't spoken.

But he was watching, eyes narrowed.

Finnian's face didn't twitch. Didn't shift. It just set—like the last pieces of a puzzle had finally fallen into place. His eye locked onto mine, darted to Maltherius, Gaaron, and finally, back to me.

"Am I late?" he asked.

No one answered. But tension snapped through the clearing, thick as blood.

I moved instinctively, shifting Gaaron's weight into Rurik's care. My hands hovered, one protectively over the artifact, the other over the handle of my remaining dagger. The crest didn't stir. Didn't glow. It just lay there—cold, slick with blood, silent and still.

Maltherius, too, remained silent and still, eyes burning with emerald fire and hatred.

Behind Finnian, the wing scouts fanned out in careful formation, disciplined but clearly nervous. One of them glanced at Cindara and went pale, swallowing audibly. None dared to move or attack.

Finnian, of course, ignored the danger entirely as his attention pivoted to Dayna.

"Seems I was right to track you," he said. His tone wasn't cruel. It wasn't even cold. Just... inevitable. Like the words had already been spoken in another life, echoing back through this one.

"Others might've thought me mad, what with your

reputation for professionalism and ruthlessness. You probably didn't even think you would cross me. Oh, no, no, no, no. But I know my Tilly. I've never trained a better thief. If anyone could steal your resolve, my unruly daughter could. And since you hadn't brought me the crest, I just knew my little Tilly had stolen from me once again. So, I decided it was time to take matters, and the crest, into my own hands."

Dayna didn't flinch. Her swords remained at her sides, but I saw the shift in her stance. The coil. The turn. Not toward Maltherius. Toward the tanuki.

"You're not getting it," she said simply. Her voice was iron. Not raised. Not quivering. Just... certain.

Finnian tilted his head, tail flicking once behind him. "Really? Oh dear, why not?" he asked, almost lazily. "I mean, you don't even know what it is. What it's capable of. Perhaps you would like me to tell you?"

Dayna didn't blink. "In case you didn't hear me, you aren't getting it. I couldn't care less about your stories."

That got a small reaction—his lip twitching upward as the regular gleam in his eye turned to the sharp glint. Not a smile. Something colder. The kind of satisfaction a man gets right before revealing a winning hand or before he slides a knife between your ribs.

"Yes, yes," he murmured. "So you've said. It would seem my assessment wasn't far from the mark, was it? But you have to complete your task. That little bauble is mine."

Dayna scoffed. "I don't answer to you, and I don't owe you a *fushik* thing."

The silence that followed stretched out, thick with all the things they weren't saying. The tension between them didn't flare into violence. It didn't need to. It just hung in the air like old smoke. The thread between them was still intact despite everything. Not frayed and not cleanly severed. Just stretched to its breaking point.

Finnian's eyes glinted with something I didn't like. "Oh, no no no, my dear, that's where you're wrong," he said, his hand steepled in front of his chest. He stepped forward once. Not a threat. A *claim*. "You *do* owe me. Under the terms of our contract, you owe me a very special delivery. So unless you intend to hand it to me, no offense, Gaary, you've broken our contract."

Dayna's hand twitched on her hilt.

And Finnian—gods, he smiled, but not with kindness. His voice gentled like a blade in the night. "No, no," he said. "Come to think of it, there's rather a sort of symmetry to it all."

He turned his attention to me and the Genesis Crest lying dormant beside me. Then back to Dayna.

"Like a mismatched set of sorts. Little Tilly betrayed me, too, you know," he said, tone sliding toward playfulness. "Long, long ago. And I thought she'd do the right thing when it mattered. Much like I assumed of you from your reputation."

Then he stepped back, spreading his arms as if presenting a grand illusion. "Do any of you even know what it does? The Genesis Crest?" His eyes swept the clearing. "You throw yourselves at its feet. Kill for it. Bleed for it. But does anyone actually *know*?" His line of sight returned to me, cutting. "Would you like to?"

My throat locked. Behind me, Gaaron stirred faintly—still alive, still bleeding—but I couldn't look away.

Rurik knelt beside us, spell-light flaring, sweat spotting his brow as he focused on anchoring Gaaron to this world.

Dayna lifted her chin. "We don't need you to tell us what it does."

Finnian's tail flicked again. "No. You just don't *want* to hear. Because then you'd have to make a decision. And you're all so very, very bad at choosing."

His gaze swept through us all, assessing, or perhaps drawing out his dramatic monologue.

Finnian's smile faltered as his eyes tried to take in Maltherius and Cindara. Maltherius stared back at the tanuki, but Cindara was stock-still, her eyes still locked on the crest.

Finnian gestured between them both like a stage magician introducing his final act. "Well, here we are. The necromantic monster of legend. Dragon keeper, master of death. And of course, myself. The shapeshifting, fast-talking, quick-witted wonder, and father of legions. Two would-be gods. Two different brands of ruin. One relic. One broken bard. And one very small chance of survival."

His smile widened. All teeth. All threat. "So tell me, heroes—" He stepped forward, boots sinking into ash and blood-dampened grass. He didn't look at Gaaron. Didn't look at the crest. He looked beyond them. Up. Toward something only he could see. "—who's your *real* enemy?"

Finnian didn't wait for a reply. Instead, he addressed the clearing—his voice low, deliberate, and unnervingly calm. "The Genesis Crest was forged when the realms still touched. In fact, they barely existed at all," he said, almost reverently. "It wasn't a relic. It wasn't a crown. It wasn't even meant for us."

His eyes swept across us—Dayna, Calina, Rurik, Tulip, and me. The words weren't performative. They were surgical.

"It was born at the edge of everything. Fae, celestial, and mortal. Magic, music, and decay. It was a bridge to everything and never should've been broken."

From the edge of the riverbed, Maltherius scoffed. But Finnian didn't even turn.

"Of course, we broke it anyway. Like we always do. Like we always will." Now his gaze locked onto mine —direct, steady, and almost... gentle. "And now you're stuck holding it."

He stepped forward, and the weight of what he said next dropped like a stone into the silence.

"You don't understand what it is. None of you do. The crest isn't just a powerful artifact. It's an *impossibility*. It's perfectly flawed. It's the reverberation of the first spell—of the very Song of Creation. Older than any gods, stronger than every prophecy."

His voice sharpened. Not louder. Just deeper. More dangerous, bordering on fanatical. "This is creation itself made manifest. It can alter anything. Time. Space. Flesh. Memory. It is invention and inspiration, destruction and renewal. It rewrites existence itself."

His eyes came back to me, steady as ever. "And it's been waiting."

I didn't answer. Couldn't. The weight of it buzzed

under my skin—quiet now, but still there. Still listening.

Finnian's attention swiveled toward Maltherius.

"He commands death," he said, like reciting a fact from a tired ledger. Then back to me, voice sharp and precise. "But only because he's afraid of it."

That landed. I saw it in the flash of green lightning beneath Maltherius's skin. The twitch of his jaw. The way his flames flared too fast—like a lie catching fire.

Finnian kept going, voice soft but slicing. "That's not power. That's fear. That's pathetic."

And that was the last straw. Maltherius snarled, no longer a sorcerer in control—just a creature made of fury and ruin.

"I *endured!*" he roared, his voice cracking with heat and rot, layered with the howls of things that should never speak. "I *survived!* And while this filthy mongrel was nothing but an illusion in his ancestor's future aspirations, I found the crest. I secured it, studied it. And now, I plan to use it to fix this broken world."

Calina laughed bitterly at that. She stepped into the open, spine straight, bow lowered at her side—not from fear, but from clarity.

"Funny," she said. "How you say all that like it's impressive."

Maltherius ignored her, which was a big mistake. Because Calina wasn't finished. She turned to Finnian now, and the heat behind her eyes made the air tremble.

"And *you*! You already had the crest. You took it along with the rest of our gear when you locked us up in Mirathane. When you threw away the key and the context, you had it. You took it, and you gave it back. Since we technically already delivered it, I think that means any contract my dad and Tilda had no longer applies." The wind stilled. The air felt suddenly too quiet.

"How much could it even really have meant to you, if you already had it and you didn't even know what it was?" Calina finished, voice low but unwavering.

Finnian's expression didn't change—but something inside him did. I saw it. The glimpse of recognition. The ripple of regret he didn't have walls built to hide.

Even Maltherius paused to study him then, as if this was the real battle and he was just a spectator. And for a moment, the whole world held its breath.

"Tilda," he said, lowering his hands. "We've always been a team, you and I. We can both get what we want. " He didn't raise his voice. He didn't plead. He offered.

"Give it to me, and I'll take away all your pain. Like it never existed in the first place."

The words floated like drifting snow, soft and cold and sharp enough to cut. "I'll give you a life untouched by this madness. It could be *perfect*."

He took another step. "I can go all the way back, Tilly. I can make it so you never lost your parents. A life where you got to grow up whole, not scavenging or bleeding in gutters. The life I always wanted for you. No pain. No fear. No desperation. No daggers. No scars. Happy. Fulfilled. Loved."

I didn't scream, didn't cry, didn't laugh. But the hum in my chest returned. The crest—still slick with blood, still resting near Gaaron's severed hand—pulsed now. Faint, but steady. Like it agreed. A spark of golden light skimmed its edge, soft as breath.

And then...

It showed me.

It showed me a memory that never happened.

My mother stood behind the bar at the Mystic Mug, apron dusted with flour, rolling her eyes as I reached for yet another sugar biscuit from the jar. Her braid had streaks of gray in it now, but her smile hadn't aged a day. Her hands were busy—always busy—but warm, always warm.

My father leaned against the doorway, lute in hand, plucking out the same old tavern tune he used to hum under his breath. He winked when I passed. Told me I was late for supper.

I wasn't. I was never late in *this* life.

Even Durgan was there, shouting about a bent ladle like it was a personal offense from the gods. He swore he didn't miss adventuring, but he said it while checking the window for wandering monsters at least once an hour.

The house smelled like cinnamon and roasted nuts. The air was sweet and safe. The hearth warm and inviting.

Gaaron lounged near the stone well out front, his hands wrapped in soft leather cords, spinning stories for a ring of children who listened like he was the only truth in the world. Calina stood a few paces away, laughing at his antics—happy, whole, and radiant in a way she'd never been allowed to be. Brynlee stood between Gaaron and Calina, glowing in a way I'd never seen before. She tousled the hair of an elfin boy who sat at Gaaron's feet and I realized that was the son they'd never had.

Gaaron had both hands. He was whole. They all were. We were. Together. Safe. Alive. The kind of perfect that doesn't just fill a hole in your heart—it remakes you.

My throat clenched. My heart stuttered. My fingers itched with the ache of it, like I could reach out and make it real. And gods help me, for one fractured heartbeat—I wanted to.

My hand had drifted toward the crest again, hovering. Not touching. Not yet. But I could almost believe it. Almost. But that's the thing about almosts. They lie. And I've lived with enough lies to know precisely what they sound like.

I drew my hand back, slow and deliberate, pulse thundering in my ears. Finnian was still watching me. Waiting.

So I looked him in the eye—looked—and I said: "I already lost everything once." My voice cracked. I didn't hide it. "But I'm not trading that loss for a lie."

Finnian didn't speak. Didn't blink. He just stood there. And that was worse than anything he could've said. Because for once, even he didn't have an answer.

The silence that followed didn't last long. It never does when the truth's that sharp.

"Enough!" Maltherius bellowed. It wasn't a human sound. It wasn't even a living one, but that shout split the night like a ribcage cracking open beneath divine weight. His body flared—robes flaring as the magic that had built up in him surged forth. Green death like fire and lightning struck out at me.

No warning. No flourish. Not even enough time to blink. Just death—bare, direct, howling. I couldn't even shout out in reply. But Rurik could.

"No!" he roared in answer, throwing himself in front of me, both hands outstretched. His voice was spoken in almost a tribal melody of music. "This is not the end."

Simple woodwinds and drums infused his voice.

The necrotic magic struck the barrier with a wail like tortured souls. Rurik dropped to one knee, hands trembling, sweat pouring down his face as he forced more magic into the shield with raw will alone.

"Hold—hold—" he chanted, voice shaking, but mirroring his chant in music.

Calina, ever decisive, took action. She rolled to the side, gaining a better vantage and loosed an arrow— then another, and another in quick succession.

Twiff, twiff, twiff.

The first arrow skimmed by Maltherius's head, breaking his focus, as the second and third arrows came toward his heart. He threw his hand to the side, blocking the arrows, but knocking his spell just far enough off kilter that it skimmed sideways, carving a molten scar into the grass beside me.

Dayna stepped forward, swords drawn from their scabbards in an instant.

Her posture was loose, almost casual, but I knew that stance. She was inviting the next blow. Forcing the attack.

"Sloppy," she said, voice like smoke over glass. "You'd think after so long, you'd be a better shot."

Maltherius turned from glaring at Calina and his eyes narrowed.

And that's when I moved.

My fingers closed around the Genesis Crest, which lay in the trampled, bloodstained grass. Still warm. Still humming. Still waiting. I didn't trust it. I never had. But this wasn't about trust. This was about ownership.

And the truth was, this thing—this living knot of memory, magic, and myth—had made itself mine. Not by prophecy or destiny. By presence and pain.

It thrummed in my palm, like a heartbeat. A low, steady rhythm, just beneath my skin. Ancient. Patient. Alive.

The sky trembled above us. Clouds spiraled. Lightning cracked across the heavens in a jagged scream, lighting the riverbed in stark, blinding brilliance.

Once again, everyone froze. Rurik, kneeling, lips

parted mid-chant. Calina, bow lowered, another arrow nocked. Dayna, standing tall, blades out, still looking for the next attack. Tulip, shielding Frosty with her entire body. Cindara's wings stretched across the sky, noxious vapors still pooled around her.

And me. At the center. Blood on my hands. The crest in my grip.

With instant clarity, I knew. I had just used it. Not to destroy. Not to conquer. To pause. The crest had frozen time. For me. Because it didn't just want a wielder. It wanted me. It wanted to stay.

But I couldn't let that happen. Not the way it wanted.

I looked down at this artifact that had the audacity to pulse like a promise after showing me a life of lies. I knew what to say.

I met Maltherius's eyes one last time—those pits of green hatred and ghostlight. Then I looked at the crest.

"I'm not here to rule," I said, not loud, but confident. My grip tightened, the oblong diamond shape of the artifact warm against my palm. "I'm not here to rewrite the world so I come out on top."

The crest pulsed once—a low, mournful beat.

"I just want to make it right. Not for me. For everyone." Tears burned in my eyes, but I didn't look away.

"I'm not your vessel. I'm not your chosen. I'm not your queen. I'm Tilda Quickthatch. And I say—"

I turned to face them all. Rurik. Calina. Dayna. Tulip. Gaaron. Frosty. Even Finnian Sly and Maltherius.

"Let's finish this."

24

The world had quieted, but my mind hadn't. I could still hear Zephyriel's words echoing, soft and relentless: *Destroy what matters most.*

And I knew now what that meant.

It wasn't Gaaron. It wasn't me. It wasn't any of us.

It was the crest. This thing I'd carried like a curse. Feared like a god. Fought for like a fool. This thing that had whispered comfort and rewound the shape of my grief like it could offer a refund on pain.

It had to end, and I had to be the one to bring it to its inevitable conclusion.

So I moved. No command. No cry. Just a single, bone-deep certainty unspooling through my limbs.

I stepped forward, the Genesis Crest clenched tight in one hand, my dagger in the other. The hilt felt heavy with everything I still didn't understand—but solid. Real. Something I could trust, if only for what it couldn't do.

I raised it high.

And with every jagged shard of myself—every loss, every lie, every sacrifice we'd made to reach this point—I brought the blade down with a cry that scraped out of my chest like it had claws.

Steel met crest and passed right through. Like mist. Like memory. Like I hadn't mattered at all.

There was no shatter. No resistance. No satisfying break of sacred power. Just the soft thud of my dagger hitting the blood-wet dirt beside Gaaron's fallen hand.

I stood stunned.

The crest hovered above the impact site, untouched. Translucent. Its edges shimmered faintly, like it had slipped out of phase with the world. Spectral. Aloof. As if I hadn't wounded it—only insulted it.

"You're supposed to let me destroy you," I whispered, anger burning through the cracks. "You chose me."

No answer. No hum. Just the soft, slow pulse of something ancient and unreadable. Not rejecting me. But maybe... reconsidering.

Then he stepped forward.

Finnian Sly. Not the masked orphan keeper. Not the legendary thief. Just the tanuki—wrecked and wind-blown, with his ears half-folded back and his tail low behind him.

"Don't," he pleaded, voice frayed and broken, in a way I'd never heard before. "Please, Tilda. Don't destroy it."

I turned slowly, waiting for the trap. The twist. It didn't come.

He wasn't posturing. Wasn't manipulating. He looked more real now than he ever had.

"I know what it did. What it's still doing," he said, too fast, too raw. "But we can fix it. We can make it right. All this death—this pain—we don't have to carry it anymore."

He didn't sound like a liar or a would-be deity. He sounded like someone who had a shattered soul and was struggling to hold the last jagged pieces.

The crest pulsed again, an invitation. Its golden shimmer flickered beneath the surface like firelight under ice. Coaxing, gentle, it wanted to be held, heard. But it didn't reach for me.

It turned to him.

For the first time... it reacted to someone else's pain.

Finnian stepped closer, and something behind his eyes cracked open. *A memory.* It unfolded and poured into me, fast and full and unrelenting, like floodwaters crashing through the walls of my mind. I staggered beneath the weight of it—more than just Finnian's lies and stories, but the actual truth of it all.

And it wasn't mine. It was hers. The halfling princess. The girl he'd loved in secret, but with his entire being.

She wasn't prim, proper, or polished like the princesses in ballads. She had firelight eyes and crooked teeth. Hair too wild for court, a laugh too loud for the throne. The kind of girl who snuck out of castles just to steal a few minutes of fun amongst commoners. Who whispered through barred windows, taught him knife tricks with fruit rinds, sang lullabies with bawdy lyrics just to make him smile.

She'd been born to rule before Eldrin Grimlock put a crown of iron on her head, turning her into something breakable. Before she disappeared into politics, into illness, into death.

No wonder Finnian had needed Grimlock gone. No wonder he wanted the crest so badly. He didn't want power. He wanted her.

She danced through his memories like starlight

scattered on water—always in motion, always just ahead.

And I saw the moment she fell. I saw the way he didn't run. Didn't scream. Didn't shatter like I did when my world broke. He just... stopped.

Not right away. But the part of him that knew how to want anything else curled inward and died.

It was grief without spectacle. Love without closure. The kind that builds its home in your bones and never leaves. The kind that turns you into a person who sends thieves and mercenaries across continents because you've convinced yourself that if you just touch the right artifact, steal the right relic, rewrite the right piece of time... That you can fix it. And she'll be there.

It's why he sent Gaaron and me to recover the crest all those years ago, and it's why he sent Dayna now, why he burned every bridge save one—always, always —for her.

Because this wasn't about the artifact.

It was about a boy who wanted to give his love the happily-ever-after he didn't know how to stop craving. And maybe, gods help him, thought he still deserved.

I blinked once, and the world snapped back. Too bright. Too cruel. The princess was gone.

And the creature beside me—this tired thing wrapped in false glamour and grief—was still staring at me with the eyes of someone who had already lost everything... and was about to lose the only thing he had left to believe in.

And the crest had listened to him. Not to stop him or me. Which meant... it was trying to convince me. So it *could* be destroyed.

I looked down at it, still pulsing faintly. Still slick with blood and memory. Still waiting to be chosen by someone who'd choose it back. But not this time. Not me. Not again.

I drew in a breath that scraped my ribs and said, "No more illusions."

The crest pulsed once in protest.

"Time moves forward."

Another pulse. Sharper now.

"And so do I."

This time, it went still.

Finnian didn't argue. He didn't plead. He didn't beg. He just stood there, hollowed out by the memory he hadn't meant to share, his expression folding in on itself like a house gutted by a storm. His eyes stared off into the distance. Another land, another time.

And Maltherius's voice boomed across the expanse like a soul tearing free from a body that didn't want it back. His eyes ignited in green flame, magic coursing across his body. "Enough of this! The crest. Is. Mine!"

He reached a hand out, but rather than some blast of necrotic energies, Gaaron's body spasmed. His good hand jerked. His back bowed in agony. His eyes were wide, wild with panic, locked onto nothing and everything at once as something cold and foreign wrapped tight around his spine.

He rose.

"Gaaron," I breathed, stepping between them.

But it wasn't a choice anymore. Maltherius had found his lever. And he was pulling with everything he had.

Gaaron's hand lifted. Fingers twitching. Reaching. Toward me. Toward the crest. Toward death.

Tears spilled down his cheeks in thin, broken rivulets—grief etched into every line of his face like ink on a ruined letter. His lips moved without sound.

Don't. Sorry. Please.

But his body didn't stop.

Then Calina ran. She just moved with grace and purpose—a streak of pink fire across a battlefield of ash.

She reached him in three heartbeats and didn't hesitate, stepping into his space, wrapping one hand against his chest—flat and steady—and bracing the other behind his neck until their foreheads met. "Stop," she whispered.

And...

He did.

His head dropped to her shoulder. His breath shuddered out of him like a storm finally spent.

Calina didn't let go.

She stayed right there, one arm braced behind him, the other pressed to his heart.

"You're not his." Soft but fierce, her voice trembling with the weight of everything she'd refused to lose. "You never were."

She shifted her palm slightly against his chest, feeling for the beat beneath bone and blood and heartbreak.

"You didn't die. You were brought to the edge—dragged there, kicking and screaming. But you didn't fall. You came back."

Her voice slipped, but her grip didn't. She pressed her hand firmer. "You came back for me. For us. And you can come back from this, too."

His body shivered under her touch.

"I can feel your heart," she whispered again, softer now, her hand curling slightly over his heart. "It's right here. Still beating. Still yours. Not his."

He sobbed. A raw, open sound torn from somewhere deep inside.

And then the strings that had been holding him up snapped.

He folded into Calina like light folds into shadow—seamless, inevitable, home.

She kept him upright. Like a pillar of light and love. Like she'd built her whole self just to be the one he could collapse into.

And for one impossible moment, we won. Not the world. Not the war. Just him.

Then came the dragon's breath.

Green fire arced from Cindara's jaws like a curse-made liquid. It surged across the clearing, but Rurik had already risen to meet it. He stood, hands raised. There was no incantation. No flourish. Just light. A dome exploded outward, golden and holy, catching the fire mid-blast. The flames hissed and screamed, but the barrier held.

"I've got you," he said, voice reverberating oddly like two voices as one. "Just don't look back."

The ground trembled. Not from the dragon, but from the crest. Back in my hand. Still pulsing and still trying to save itself.

Energy wove itself around Maltherius, and color

seemed to drain from the world. He rose into the air, still below the massive dome Rurik had created. The necromancer shot a glance at his dragon familiar, most of her bulk outside the barrier. He hesitated only a moment before turning his flaming emerald eyes back to us. A strange word in an ancient tongue boomed out from him and echoed seemingly everywhere. The air thinned like it knew what was coming. From underground, skeletal hands shot forth, an army of dead soldiers rising to battle.

Tulip reared up, letting out a piercing battle neigh. She surged forward, pink axe blazing, hooves tearing up the scorched terrain. She charged headlong into the undead horde, her axe singing through skulls and spines in a blur of motion.

Dayna followed in her wake—blades lit with golden sigils, cutting through bone and armor like silk.

"Wound the dragon," she commanded, pointing Tulip to the parts of Cindara that sat exposed under the dome of magic protection. "Your orc won't be able to keep that shield up if she keeps up with that fire." Dayna split off from Tulip and started slicing her way through minions toward the floating necromancer.

I rose, the crest in one hand, my dagger in the other. Fire shimmered above the golden shield above me. Bloody mud below my feet. The storm drawing close. But I had already chosen.

Maltherius hovered like a storm loosed from its tether, lightning crawling across his skin, his eyes twin furnaces of emerald hate. His voice ricocheted across the clearing, laced with every ounce of cruelty he'd spent centuries perfecting.

"I have endured centuries, working in the shadows," he sneered, arms outstretched. "I've walked the boundary between life and death. And I have patiently waited for this moment. And I will not be denied by washed-up thieves and children."

"COME DOWN HERE AND SAY THAT!" Tulip roared, smashing her axe into Cindara's leg.

Dayna was right beside her, swords flashing through undead, teeth bared. Looking like a woman who seriously missed her wings.

Maltherius growled. "Your ignorance is the only reason for your bravado, child."

Calina stepped forward, voice calm, dangerous. "And your arrogance is the reason for your failure."

Maltherius faltered—just slightly. Enough to show he hadn't expected that tone, that certainty.

And I didn't wait.

"Rurik!" I shouted, lifting the crest above my head. "We can destroy it, I think! I just don't know how!"

Rurik didn't flinch. Didn't hesitate. His voice came back strong, clear, and terrible in its promise. "If we destroy the crest," he said, "it'll destroy him too. Him... and the dragon."

My breath caught.

The crest pulsed once, slow and warning. But I held tight.

Because now we knew. We could win this thing once and for all.

25

The crest pulsed hot in my grip in protest. No pain, not yet at least—but I could feel it trying. My burn flared beneath my tunic, that old mark twisting like it wanted out. Wanted to sever. Wanted me to let go. I didn't. Because we were already bonded, and it didn't want to get destroyed. Not like this. Not now.

Across the clearing, Maltherius descended. His body flickered, illuminating his skeleton under what was left of his flesh. The wind caught the edges of his robes while the rest of the world stood unnaturally still. All the years feeding on death and darker things had hollowed him into something awful and unrecognizable. His flesh stretched tight over his gaunt features. It wasn't clear if he'd been a human or elf or whatever else. His feet never touched the land. But his presence pressed down hard.

"Do you think yourself special because it chose you?"

My fingers twitched. My breath caught. The word *chose* echoed. If the crest had chosen me, then it was alive. At least a little. Like Zephyriel, when she'd momentarily taken control of her honored kobold servant through the tiara. That wasn't a spell. It had been will. Presence. Possession. Had the crest done something of the same to me?

Maltherius watched me touch my burn like a scholar watching a student connect the final dots in a lesson meant to destroy them.

"It didn't," he said softly. "*I* did."

My gut twisted.

"I needed someone weak and easy to manipulate. Someone naive enough to want the big score, but inexperienced enough to not want the fight. I watched Finnian and his children. So when I saw a silly little halfling with just enough heart to ruin herself and anyone who got too close, I said, that's the one for me."

I should've felt rage. Instead, I felt recognition. The first time I'd seen the crest—my first trip to the Precipice with Gaaron—I thought I'd been lucky.

Escaping with the artifact and slipping past death. I thought it was a victory. But now I saw it for what it was. Permission.

"It wasn't skills, or cunning, or even dumb luck that let you slip through my fingers," he continued, circling. "I let you take it. Remember how easy it was? No traps that weren't already disarmed, no patrols. It was just sitting there in a gift box. I had nothing living left to give the crest. It needed fuel. It needed time. And you..." He smiled like a knife unsheathing. "And you did everything I expected. For ten years, I've let it consume you so it could remain in this realm. I knew Finnian Sly would chase it—he was always going to. But I had you."

The burn. The light. The weight I'd carried ever since.

"Did I even have a choice?" I asked, voice low.

Maltherius tilted his head. "No. You were always playing my game. You just never knew the rules. Not until now."

He moved like smoke given intention, drifting closer. "You thought you were so clever, slipping away from my lair with the crest. You carried it across kingdoms. Hid it. Guarded it. Let it drink from your fear, your fury, your will. And in doing so..." He stopped. Looked directly at me. "You fed it."

My grip tightened. The crest grew hotter, the burn beneath my skin pulsing harder in protest.

"You strengthened it. You kept it alive. You call that survival." He leaned in, voice a hiss. "I call it obedience."

My breath stuttered.

"You think that burn makes you chosen? That it means you matter?" He raised one skeletal finger. "It's a tether. A leash. The crest needed a host. And you were... available. In fact, you came straight to me."

I didn't move. Couldn't. My body was stone, my heart a storm.

"I built you," he said. "You're the altar and the sacrifice, all in one tidy little package."

That's when Calina moved. She took a step forward, bow drawn, an arrow already nocked. She loosed it fast and true, straight for the hollow space behind Maltherius's ribs. It struck his aura and vanished. Not bounced. Not deflected. Just gone. Just like when I tried to stab the crest.

He turned toward her, unfazed. "Shh," he whispered, raising a skeletal finger. "It's not your turn, little one."

Calina's hands dropped, but her glare didn't fade.

As for me, I was breaking. I staggered, backing up a step. Then another. My vision blurred, and the ground seemed to tilt beneath my boots. My hand flew to the burn, not for comfort, but for confirmation. But it didn't scream. Didn't rage. It pulsed. Warm. Alive. Just... there.

I was the one who had slipped the crest from his lair. I was the one who carried it, lied for it, and lied about it. Was I chosen? Or just convenient? My heart thudded like a war drum, I no longer knew how to follow.

Maltherius raised his hand. Once again, a bolt of green fire surged toward me.

I watched it come at me. A final bolt of magic to strike me down and take back the curse he'd saddled me with. I didn't move. My muscles tensed as I waited for the blast to hit me.

And then, in a blur of motion, Dayna appeared in front of me. Even without wings, she was a body in flight. She shoved me back just as the spell hit.

And the world burned.

Dayna hit the ground with a force that made the air itself flinch. Her armor groaned under the impact, smoke curling from the scorched seam where the spell struck. Her limbs landed wrong, splayed like a broken doll tossed aside. My breath caught and shattered all at once as I stumbled toward her, heart already splintering.

We didn't have time.

Calina stood by Gaaron. He was pale, blood-damp, his arm ending in a bandaged stump. His wounds weren't fresh anymore, but they weren't healing either —not without help. Rurik had already given too much, and now we were asking him to give more.

The world held its breath.

Gaaron exhaled—not words, but music. A thread-bare melody rasped through his cracked lips, faint and tuneless but unmistakably a song. Not strong, but alive. Steady. Real.

And the crest stirred in my palm.

It flickered once, then again, syncing with Gaaron's breath like it recognized him. Like it remembered. The burn beneath my tunic settled, no longer raging or thrumming with refusal. Just... there. Not cold. Not gone. But calm.

I didn't understand it fully. But I felt it. Something had clicked into place.

Not the crest. *Me.*

I rose with purpose. The dagger still hung at my side, forgotten. The crest was hot and humming in my grip, but it no longer squirmed or bit. It felt anchored. Mine.

Maltherius hadn't noticed. He was too busy finishing his curse.

Green fire coiled around him, symbols blazing into the air like a god's handwriting. The wind screamed in reverse. The soil cracked wide beneath him, the Lazul River pulling apart at its edges. He wasn't casting a spell.

He was casting a sentence.

A final act meant to pull this place—and everyone in it—into a mass grave. Not because we posed a threat.

But because he was done with us.

Tulip stepped forward, slow and solid. Her hooves struck cracked stone and stayed there. She didn't draw her axe. Didn't raise her voice. She just stood between me and the growing chasm with the kind of weight that couldn't be shaken.

She glanced my way, then toward Maltherius.

"I'm really getting sick of this necromancer guy," she muttered. "Can we please just kill him already?"

No fire in her voice. No bravado.

Just conviction. Final. Certain. Terrifying in its simplicity.

Behind her, the trees bent inward, the river churned like it wanted to escape its banks, and the clearing fractured further—but still, we moved forward.

Rurik stepped to my side, golden sparks crackling

along his fingers, his shield spell wavering but intact. Big enough for protection, but small enough that Cindara couldn't fit entirely. Dayna hobbled into the circle, supported by Tulip's bulk and her own sheer refusal to be left behind. Calina braced Gaaron higher, his melody a thread still clinging to the world. And Frosty... that sweet little dragonling crept forward, his wide eyes locked on the undead colossus overhead.

Cindara stood like a statue of smoke and bone, jaw slack, wings twitching in uneven shudders. But now, really looking, I saw it—her body wasn't still out of patience. It was weakness.

She'd been faltering for a while: wings sagging, movements slow, her flame burned low. She could have ended us a hundred times over, but hadn't because she couldn't. Maltherius had powered her for too long without the crest. Dragons never stopped growing, and Cindara had become bloated on borrowed power —a force of ruin held together by his desperation alone. And now, the crest was no longer his.

Frosty must've felt it too. He crept beneath her massive foreleg and let out a sharp, high-pitched screech —a battle cry. He darted out again in a blur of scales and nerves, weaving just far enough to attract her. He wasn't trying to defeat her. He was trying to distract her.

And it worked. Cindara's head turned. One ponderous step followed, a groan in her ribs. Frosty darted left, then right. She followed—not much, but enough.

We didn't have a plan, but we had each other, and this time, it would be more than enough.

The wind howled louder, clawing through the clearing like it wanted to peel back time. Ash lifted in spirals. Cracks split the ground like ribs snapping under divine pressure. Maltherius's spell reached for the sky, and the sky screamed back.

But we kept moving forward.

Dayna, still scorched but standing, held upright by Tulip's steel will.

Rurik, hands glowing, eyes fierce with the last dregs of power he still hadn't spent.

Calina, jaw tight, arms braced beneath her father as his tune kept us steady.

Frosty, weaving beneath ancient bones, holding the eye of a god-dragon with nothing but courage and quick feet.

And me.

Dagger at my hip. Crest in my hand. The burn in my chest no longer fought me.

It thrummed with us, with Gaaron's song, in time

with my heartbeat, with all of us. We weren't the epilogue. We were the ending.

I turned toward Maltherius. He hovered above the cracked clearing, all fire, bone, and unspent wrath. His spell trembled at the edges, just like his dragon.

And I raised the crest.

"When it chose me," I said, voice steady and sure, "it chose all of us."

The artifact flared—not with fire, but with resonance. It echoed like a struck bell, filling the air with golden warmth.

Behind Maltherius, Cindara let out a sound I hadn't heard from her before—a shriek of fear. Her wings shuddered. One foreleg collapsed. Her mouth sagged open, trailing smoke as her eyes hazed.

She was breaking.

And so was he.

We weren't just the crest's past; we were its future, and it had made its choice.

Maltherius turned, confusion etched into the glow of his ruined face. Too late.

I stepped forward. "It's not yours anymore."

The crest glowed, the light swelling. Then it crackled. Then it hummed, power remembering its name.

And then everything went white.

26

The moment I spoke those words—*It's not yours anymore*—the thing in my hand pulsed so violently it nearly jumped from my grip. Light spilled from its fractured seams in jagged bursts, not golden now, but white, edged in green and violet, as if reality was remembering other versions of itself and bleeding them into the now.

The air warped around us. Heavy and fast. My skin tingled like pins and needles just under the surface. Time itself was glitching.

And then the river reversed. Starting at the edges, the trickle beside my boots began to pull *uphill*, threading backward with unnatural grace. The current peeled away from the shore. Frogs blinked and leapt backward. A leaf that had fallen during the fight now zipped back into its branch like a regret recalled.

I looked up, squinting against the radiance that overwhelmed my vision. The blinding brilliance transported me back to that moment with Amariel, when she'd taken Rurik and me to that in-between place. She had manipulated time then, rewinding it to save us from certain death. A chill ran through me despite the heat of the light.

Was the crest doing the same thing now? Not to protect us, but to preserve itself? To rewrite what was happening in a way that served its own purposes?

I didn't know, couldn't know, but still I had to try.

Cindara thrashed. The undead dragon roared in confusion, her wings flailing with broken rhythm. One eye still glowed—but the other *flickered*. A signal losing connection. Her ribcage spasmed with each pulse of the crest, as if every surge unraveled another thread that held her together.

The realization hit me then: the crest wasn't merely rebelling against Maltherius. It was rejecting all control. Something with such vast power was never meant to bend to anyone's will—not his, not even my own. An artifact of such magnitude was just cosmically wrong, a thing that should never have existed in the first place.

Maltherius faltered. The incantation he'd begun now sputtered from his mouth in half-sounds. The symbols spiraling around his form twisted and bled into themselves, failing to hold shape. His eyes darted from the crest to me and back. He didn't fully understand what was happening.

But I did.

The truth had finally hit bone. This artifact, parasite, relic was never meant to last this long. Not in one hand. Not in one plane. Not in one body. Not without a cost. A cost that all of us here had paid, over and over again.

This had to end. *We* had to end it.

I turned to the others. They were already circling back in.

Tulip, covered in ichor but standing tall, axe braced on her shoulder.

Dayna, breath ragged, one arm hanging a bit lower —but swords still in hand.

Calina, helping Gaaron stay upright, kept her bow by her side, arrow held to the grip by a finger. Ready to fire while supporting Gaaron's weight.

Rurik's face was pale green from exhaustion, but his eyes were glowing with that determined, divine fire that never quite left him.

And Frosty—his head low, wings half-spread,

ready to follow even if he didn't believe he was strong enough. All of them. Burned, battered, bruised. But unshaken.

"This thing—" I said, holding up the crest, its glow flaring like lightning in a snow globe. "It's taken too much." The words tasted final. *Right.* "We can't let it take anything else from us. We can destroy it. We have to, and we have to do it now."

No one argued. They just nodded.

That was the thing about this group. We didn't have speeches anymore. No final stands, no poetic declarations. Just scars, grit, and the unspoken truth that *none of us wanted to carry this into tomorrow.*

Dayna moved first, a half-step stumble to my right. She should've been down—burned, battered, barely standing—but she wore the damage like it meant something. Like it proved she belonged here more than any of us. Her face was all grit and quiet fury, and gods help me, it didn't make her look fragile. It made her *real.* Sharper. Unshakable. And at that moment, the truth hit hard and fast, with no mercy to it—I didn't just love her. I wanted to *be* her. Wanted to bottle up that impossible strength and carry it like a torch through every broken part of myself until maybe, just maybe, I was enough to deserve her.

Tulip took the left. Calina slid behind me, Gaaron

leaning into her but lifting his head, his mouth still murmuring that soft, broken tune. Rurik stepped forward last, lips forming words in three languages—orcish, celestial, and common—all laced with the same intention. *Together.*

We didn't know what we were doing. Not exactly. There was no scroll for this. No temple rite or ancient verse buried in a ruin that would tell us how to destroy something forged before time had manners. All we had was a pulsing artifact, a fractured circle, and a choice. But maybe that was enough.

Rurik stepped forward. Not past me. Not ahead. Just enough to meet the space between us all. The light in his hands flickered—first blue, then white, then that soft, low gold that always reminded me of sunrise on old pages. His eyes fluttered closed, and I felt the moment his magic shifted—not outward, but inward. He wasn't calculating. He wasn't channeling.

He was remembering.

"She's here," he said, almost to himself. "Not in the spell. In the beat between."

There was no logic in it. No arcane formula. Just trust—just heart.

"It doesn't have to make sense," he whispered. "It just has to feel true."

He pressed one palm to his chest, fingers curled

over his heart, and the golden light swelled—gentle, not demanding, the kind of light that didn't burn but beckoned. It spread down his arms, lacing through his fingers, wrapping him in threads of warmth and memory.

"Let this be your last light," he said softly. "Through me."

The energy reached the air around the crest, and the crest responded—not like before, not wild, not defiant. It shimmered, like a breath held and finally released.

Rurik opened his eyes. They were wet with unshed grief, but his voice didn't shake.

"She's with us," he said again, and this time, it didn't sound like hope.

It sounded like faith.

I didn't ask who. I didn't need to. He took his place in the circle, still glowing softly.

And then Tulip stepped forward. No fanfare. Just a deep breath and the heavy thunk of her axe as she drove it into the ground beside her hooves. The land answered her. It groaned—a low, grounding vibration that I felt in my knees before I heard it in my ears.

Tulip closed her eyes and pressed both palms to the hilt of her embedded weapon. Her hooves shifted slightly, adjusting their grip on the dirt like roots choosing where to hold.

"Gold won't save us now," she murmured. "But people might. The ones we fight for. The ones we bleed for. That's the only wealth that matters." Then, steady as ever. "I am stone. I am family. I hold this world steady."

The glow that rose from her wasn't light—at least, not like Rurik's. This was green, dull, threaded with iron and wood. It pressed down, not up, spreading through the cracks beneath us like a promise made of pressure. A net of grounded force that caught the spell's chaos and held it fast, like pinning a butterfly in place before it could remember how to fly.

The river, still trying to reverse, *slowed.* The pulled air settled. The crest's vibration narrowed, the wild arcs collapsing into a tighter, steadier rhythm.

And I breathed again. Just once. But it was enough to believe this might work.

Dayna hadn't moved until now. She'd stood at the edge of the circle, watching, assessing—silent in that way she always was when something was about to go very right or very wrong. Then, finally, she stepped forward. Her boots scraped the ground. Her eyes glinted with resignation.

She pulled a slender dagger from her belt—one I

hadn't seen her use in battle. It was short and curved, the blade dark and slightly iridescent, etched in runes I recognized from old warnings in older books. Infernal. Without a word, she drew it across her palm.

The blood came bright and quick, spilling into the runes etched in the metal, and from there... into the air. The magic responded immediately. Lines of red-hot script—ancient, angular, and *wrong*—appeared along the edge of the crest. Symbols that shouldn't exist outside a contract. Glyphs that once bound creatures of ruin.

"I swore I'd never use this again," she murmured, voice low, almost lost in the hum. "But for you?" She looked at us—at me. "I'd damn myself twice."

I had no time to process the weight of her confession—the magic was already responding, the moment rushing forward. The crest's energy pulsed around us, demanding my complete attention.

She knelt, placing her bleeding hand on the edge of the circle closest to the crest. The runes pulsed, sizzled, and locked. The previously chaotic currents looping inside the artifact jolted into place, a closed circuit finally grounded. The crest surged. For a moment, the pulses were clearer, tighter, and ordered. It wasn't stable, but it was closer.

I glanced back.

Gaaron stirred. He was still held up by Calina, pale and waxen-looking, his song catching on every breath. But something had changed. His lips were moving. And then I heard it. A note. Just one. Low. Hollow. Familiar in the worst way. It was the same note Maltherius had used to summon him. To control him. To puppet him through whatever spell bound his body to the necromancer's will.

But this? This wasn't Maltherius's voice. It was Gaaron's. His tone cracked halfway through. The pitch bent under the weight of what he'd endured. But he kept going. He hummed again, clearer now, as if that note belonged to him again.

And then, barely above a whisper. "I survived him," he rasped, breath thin, "Now I undo him."

The crest flared again—briefly, but unmistakably. A harmonic thread shimmered across its surface, responding not to power but liberation.

Calina moved before the moment could pass. She dropped to her knees between Gaaron and me, one hand on each of us like she could hold the whole fraying world together with her grip alone. Her fingers trembled, but her voice did not.

"You're both mine," she said, soft but certain. "Not because of fate. Not because of blood."

She leaned over Gaaron first, brushing his damp

hair from his brow with aching tenderness. "I love you, Dad. Always. Still."

Then she turned to me, her hand tightening on my shoulder. "And you," she said, meeting my eyes with that same fierce calm, "I chose you. And I won't let go."

The light around us pulsed once. She didn't need to be chosen by destiny to make it happen. She'd already chosen us.

It wasn't a promise. It was a command. A pulse of pink light—soft, warm, human—spread from her skin and wrapped around the crest's central node like a ribbon of breath. For a heartbeat, the artifact's frantic energy dimmed. Quieter. As if it, too, remembered what it meant to be held.

The light was beautiful. For a moment—just one—everything held. The energy looping through the Genesis Crest flowed in rhythm with us. It was not perfect, not clean, but aligned: Rurik's radiance, Tulip's grounding, Dayna's blood, Gaaron's music, and Calina's love. Even the air paused. The storm above seemed to hold its breath.

But beauty doesn't mean stability. Not when the thing at the center wasn't built to be undone. The crest pulsed once, twice, then shuddered—a fissure of green split through the golden thread.

I stepped forward, something sharp and specific locking into place beneath my ribs like a gear finally catching.

"*Nearly all you desire shall be yours in due time.*" The prophecy fell from my lips. I didn't even mean to say it—it just came, steady and sure, like the truth had finally decided to speak for itself.

I reached out, threading my magic into the fragile weave we'd built together. This wasn't like before. No jagged flashes of tomorrow. No hollow ache of might-be. Just presence. Power. Mine.

Because I'd already found what I was looking for.

Not revenge. Not redemption.

Them.

Dayna, scorched and breathing. Calina and Gaaron pressed shoulder to shoulder like two halves of something that refused to break. Rurik, glowing from within. Tulip, steady as a mountain. Frosty, brave as anything. My people.

My family.

My place.

I already had everything I'd ever wanted.

Now I just had to fight my hardest to keep it.

"You don't get to break everything," I snarled, pressing energy into the crest until it vibrated under my skin. "Not this world. Not these people. Not when I've finally found something worth protecting."

For a moment, the crest was silenced. Its chaotic patterns stuttered and faltered, considering her words. Then it convulsed violently, fighting back with renewed fury. Even still, we weren't enough.

Maltherius's voice cracked across the valley, piercing and raw, a furious rattle from a throat that refused to rot. Above us, he lifted higher, arms wide, magic spiraling down from the storm like veins of lightning drawn toward hunger.

The crest—still in the center of our circle—began to drift. Not fall. Not jump. Pull. He was reclaiming it. Reeling it back like a fisherman yanking a hook out of a wound he never cared to close.

His words carried to us, but the language was ancient and foreign.

The crest fought us now, its energy jittering erratically, snapping between pulses. Calina winced. Rurik gasped, dropping to one knee as the divine threads buckled under pressure. Dayna swore and shoved her palm harder into the dirt, reopening the cut. The spell was fraying.

And I staggered—one foot forward, then the other. My hand still held the dagger. My fingers still burned from the crest's heat. I stepped past the circle, toward the chaos. Toward the breaking point.

"No," I said. It came out hoarse.

Maltherius didn't stop. The crest shuddered toward him, trailing strands of light like unraveling silk.

"We're more than enough to defeat you," I said louder, voice climbing past the pain, the fear, the grief that lived in my throat like it had paid rent.

His voice cracked through effort. "You don't even understand what you're holding!"

I raised my voice until it broke. "No. But I understand what love can do."

The light pulsed again, once, bright. And... Maltherius flinched.

The crest wouldn't break. It should have. We had given everything: blood, light, music, faith. I could feel the weight of each thread holding it in place—Calina's pulse on my shoulder, Rurik's breath beside me, Dayna's blood still sizzling in the dirt, Gaaron's hum fading into silence. But the crest just... flickered. Its light shivered between forms, unstable, not resisting exactly, but searching like it was still waiting for someone to finish the story.

And I understood. It wasn't just bound to me. It never had been.

I turned slowly. My eyes found the one person who hadn't joined the circle who stood at the edge, silent and staring, like he wasn't sure if the world would let him walk back into it. Finnian Sly.

He hadn't moved since his memory had played out to me. He looked smaller now—no longer the master thief, tactician, or ruthless general—just a creature lost in the echoes of his mistakes. And I didn't want to ask. But I had to.

My voice cracked open when I spoke. No steel. No snark. Just a threadbare breath across scorched lungs. "It chose you, too. It went with you. Willingly. You are a part of this, whether or not you want to be."

He flinched.

"Please," I said, quieter. "Help us."

The words hung there, raw and unsheltered. For a second, I thought he wouldn't answer. Then he exhaled. It came out in a broken gasp, like something inside him had been held underwater for years and finally surfaced.

"I was cruel," he said, voice shaking. "Because I was afraid."

His eyes lifted to mine, bloodshot and burning with more than magic. "I thought strength meant shutting you out. That if I let myself care again—if I let myself need—I'd never survive that war a second time."

He took a step forward. "I was wrong." Another step. "I always loved you, Tilda."

His voice cracked again. He didn't stop. "You were my daughter in all but name."

The mask was gone. Every lie he'd worn like armor —cracked and discarded. Tears were in his eyes now, cutting through the grime and power. He crossed into the circle. No magic. No drama. Just truth.

Finnian took my hand. There was no ceremony in it. Just an old tanuki, a middle-aged halfling, and the ruins of what once passed for a future. His grip was firm, but not possessive. He didn't lead. He didn't follow. He stood beside me.

And the crest responded. The glow pulsed once, twice, then shattered into threads of light that raced across its surface like veins surfacing on too-thin skin. The sound it made wasn't a hum anymore. It was a scream.

Spiderweb cracks etched through the artifact, white-hot and pulsating, light leaking out with each frantic burst. I felt the thing fighting even now, trying to find a loophole, a back door, a willing vessel. But we'd closed the circle. We were all here—even him.

A pulse burst outward as the first crack reached the crest's core. The air howled. And far above, Cindara collapsed. She was mid-roar, wings arched in fury, when her body convulsed. One wing snapped backward. Then the other. She didn't fall. She disintegrated. The great, undead dragon came apart midair in a burst of black ash and glowing bone fragments, her frame torn loose from the magic that had animated it for far too long. Her breath vanished. Her flame died. Her roar became wind.

Maltherius saw it. He felt it. And he screamed. A primal roar of rage and grief. It broke on his tongue. The wind swallowed it. His body flared—green fire, black smoke, bone—but no form could hold. He reached toward the crest with a desperate, final lunge —and then dissolved. There was no flash. No great burst of magic. Just a slow, gray unraveling. Dust rising in the wind like ash from a fire that had long gone cold.

Maltherius was unmade. And with him gone, the crest sang. A single note. Harmonious. Familiar. Not one of domination or corruption, but of release. It rang through the circle like a bell tolling for memory itself, vibrating deep in the chest and marrow. And then it exploded.

Light surged through the circle. Pure, blinding, beautiful. It hit us all at once, knocking me backward into the dirt. Calina cried out. Dayna cursed. Tulip fell to one knee. Rurik's light flared so bright I couldn't look at him. Even Finnian dropped to the ground beside me, hand still clenched in mine. But none of us were burned. None of us was broken. Just thrown.

When I opened my eyes again, the sky was clear. The crest was gone. Transformed into dust and starlight. Gone. Finally gone.

Smoke curled low across the riverbank, thin and harmless now. The world looked faded around the edges, like it had exhaled too hard and hadn't quite found its shape again.

Everyone was down. Tulip sprawled on her side, snoring faintly through a smear of soot. Rurik lay flat on his back, arms out, like he was listening to the ground breathe. Calina knelt with her forehead against Gaaron's shoulder, both of them shivering in that post-magic way. Dayna had collapsed where she stood, swords still clutched tight in her hands, even unconscious.

And me? I sat up slowly. Every bone in my body screamed—but my scar didn't burn. For the first time in ten years... it was just a mark. A memory. I touched it lightly and let out a breath.

Then I turned. Finnian was still kneeling beside me, head bowed, hands limp in his lap like he didn't quite know what to do with them. The mask was still gone. All that was left was the creature behind it.

"You did good," I said, voice gravel-soft.

He looked at me. And shook his head.

"No," he said. "*You* did."

And just like that, it was over.

27

The silence after the crest shattered didn't feel like victory.

It felt like vertigo—like the world had been spinning along and suddenly stopped, too fast, too final. My ears still rang with the echo of that impossible note that tore through us and left nothing behind but breathless stillness.

We were alive. Somehow. But not whole.

The smoke hadn't even cleared when Finnian dropped to his knees. With a sharp gesture, he dismissed his four wing scouts—the ones I'd lost track of during the chaos. They'd hovered at the edge of battle, never truly engaging unless he was in danger. And now, with nothing left to guard, they dissolved into the wind like they'd never been there at all.

I didn't notice right away. Not with Rurik gasping beside me. Not with Calina still clutching Gaaron, as if she loosened her grip, he might vanish. Not with Frosty curled tight in the crook of my arm, his wings trembling, his small body radiating heat like he'd burned himself out from the inside.

But then I heard it.

Soft. Cracked. Barely audible through the settling dust.

"Kill me."

My body locked. I turned, and everything inside me went still.

Finnian was folded in on himself, hands limp in his lap, eyes hollow and wet. Not angry. Not even shattered in the way I'd come to expect. Just... emptied. Like he'd finally poured out the last of whatever had kept him upright this long.

My feet moved before my mind did. I knelt beside him, knees stinging from ash and grit. "What did you say?"

His voice didn't rise. If anything, it dimmed.

"Kill me," he whispered again.

He didn't look at me. Instead, his focus hovered just past my shoulder, like he was already slipping, already partway gone.

"I thought I could hold on," he murmured. "If I

just kept moving. Kept planning. Kept building something sharp enough... I'd find a way."

His fingers twitched, like they expected to close around something that wasn't there.

"The crest was the last thread. My last anchor."

He looked at me then, and sweet stars, did it hurt.

"I didn't care about power." He drew in a ragged breath. "It was her. She was everything."

I didn't need to ask who.

"My princess," he breathed. "Gone. And I thought... if I could just rewind it. Just one thread. One reversal. I could have her again."

He pulled something from his robes—a small metal token. Round. Worn. Meaningless to anyone else. But he held it like it was a heartbeat.

"She gave me this," he said. "Found it in a palace bin. Told me value was whatever we chose it to be. And I believed her."

His thumb traced its edge.

"I wasn't trying to control the world," he said. "I just wanted one more morning with her. One more cup of tea. One laugh. One moment where I didn't fail."

He bowed his head. "When she was gone, I told myself there must be a way back. Some loophole. Some divine crack in the weave."

And then his eyes lifted. Found me.

"And then I saw you."

The words didn't land like a blessing. They landed like blame.

"You looked like her. Not exactly. But enough. The tilt of your jaw. The way you moved like nothing could catch you unless you wanted it to."

He shook his head, more at himself than me.

"You weren't her. But you were the closest thing I'd seen in a decade. And you were good. Gods, you were good. I thought if I could get the Genesis Crest into your hands... you'd do the rest. Crack the vault. Outrun the gods. Make the impossible happen. And when you did..."

His voice cracked.

"I'd have her again. My princess. My future. Everything I was owed."

He didn't weep. He just looked at me with something ancient and broken.

"You weren't my daughter," he said. "You were my last chance. My only hope is that the story could still go right."

And then he offered me the token. No flourish. No speech. Just held it out.

"Give it to someone worth loving."

I didn't speak. Couldn't. Just curled my fingers

around it like it might vanish if I didn't.

The silence between us stretched, taut as a violin string. I didn't know what to say to him—what *could* you say to the man who'd used you as a last hope, not out of malice, but desperation?

But I didn't have to answer. Rurik did.

He stepped forward and stood beside Finnian. "You were never a villain."

Finnian flinched like it physically hurt.

"You were a man with a badly broken heart," Rurik continued, "doing whatever you could to hold on to the pieces."

Finnian's throat worked. His hands trembled in his lap. "That doesn't make it right."

"No," Rurik agreed. "But it makes it real." He placed a hand over Finnian's, steady and warm. "Even with everything I can do now, with all the divine power surging through me, there are some things that can't be healed. Some wounds that don't want to close."

Finnian didn't respond. But his breath hitched, and his shoulders sank like something heavy had finally been acknowledged.

Rurik reached for his flame.

"No," I said suddenly. My voice cracked with panic. "Don't. Please. Not like this."

He looked at me with a strange mix of sorrow and satisfaction. "I have to," he said gently.

"But he's still—" I didn't know how to finish. *Alive? Mine? Forgivable?*

Rurik didn't make me. He stepped closer, the glow of his fingers steady and small, like a single candle clinging to breath.

"This is his choice," he said softly. "It was always going to be."

Then he glanced down at Finnian, who hadn't moved, hadn't flinched. Who only sat there, steady and ready.

"You remember his prophecy?" Rurik asked. "*You will not obtain what you desire until you learn to request it plainly and without artifice.*"

I stared.

"He's asking now," Rurik said. "Plainly. Clearly. Not for power. Not for rewrites. For release."

And Finnian finally looked up at me—nothing hidden, nothing masked.

"I'm not strong enough to carry this any further," he said. "But you are."

I didn't answer. I couldn't. I just nodded, slowly, heart shattering one piece at a time.

And Rurik... Rurik knelt.

Not with ceremony. With reverence.

He didn't reach into a satchel. He didn't summon celestial fire. He lifted one hand—the same one that had once barely summoned sparks when the world said he wasn't enough—and lit it.

A single flame. Small. Steady. The first cantrip he'd ever mastered.

He cupped it like it was sacred.

"It was the only spell I had," he murmured. "Until Amariel gave me everything."

His voice caught, just for a second.

"But this? This one was mine."

He leaned forward and pressed the flame gently to Finnian's chest, just over his heart.

"Let this be a light that frees you," Rurik whispered. "And carries you forward."

The flame didn't burn. It didn't consume. It sank into Finnian's chest like breath. Gold. Then amber. Then white.

A final blessing. A quiet goodbye. And maybe, just maybe, a start.

Finnian gasped softly—but not in pain. His hand found mine again, steady now. His other rested over the token. His eyes, when they met mine, were wet but clear.

"I love you, Tilly," he said. "Make your pa proud."

Then he looked at the others—at Tulip, Calina,

and Dayna, even Frosty perched like a tiny statue on a rock with glistening eyes.

"You'll see," he whispered. "It's not the end."

And then, as the light rose through him, breaking him apart one thread at a time, he smiled.

There were no screams, no ashes, just soft particles of light drifting upward on a wind none of us felt. His silhouette held a second longer, like the world wasn't quite ready to let go. Then it scattered—dust, light, memory. He was gone.

None of us spoke.

Tulip moved first. She unsnapped one of her shoulder plates and slid it from her arm with careful fingers. The metal clattered low as she set it down at the circle's center, where the last light had faded. Then her forearm guard followed. She didn't kneel. Didn't bow. Just let her offering rest in the stillness.

Dayna came next. She moved more slowly, favoring her left side. No ceremony, just purpose. Her fingers found the rust-colored sash wrapped around her midsection—the one that marked her as a member of the wing scouts—and untied it. The fabric unfurled like a story released. She folded it with care and set it down beside Tulip's armor.

"He wasn't all bad," she muttered. No one disagreed.

Rurik knelt last. He pressed a palm to the ground, divine light still trembling faintly through his fingertips, and drew a simple sigil in the dirt: a crescent cupping a rising sun.

"He found his way," Rurik said softly. "That's all any of us can hope for."

The wind picked up—just enough to lift a few glittering motes of ash from the ground—and none of us moved to stop them. We let them go. Let him go. Let it matter.

Calina helped Gaaron sit upright, her hands bracing him gently as he reached for the battered instrument slung across his back. His fingers shook as he unfastened the last strap and pulled it into his lap, as if it weighed more than he did.

He struck a note. Then another. Uncertain. Wobbly.

Then came the third.

It held.

He hummed with it—a threadbare melody, thin and cracked like parchment left in the rain. But it held.

A lullaby.

It was the song he used to hum for Brynlee. The one I'd heard dozens of times drifting from the back room of the Mystic Mug while she restocked or refolded napkins or made faces at customers through the crack in the door.

That soft, simple tune I'd always rolled my eyes at —but secretly loved.

It belonged here.

And it reminded me that she'd been with us, too.

Holding space in our hearts while we bled and clawed and clung to whatever hope we could find. Her love, steady and real, had carried him—and through him, all of us.

A tear slid down my cheek.

And I let it fall.

Gaaron's fingers moved more surely now, coaxing harmony out of an instrument that shouldn't have survived the battle. One he shouldn't have been able to play with only a single hand. But maybe that was the point. None of us should've survived either. And yet here we were—tattered, scorched, shaking—but still making music.

A beat passed. Then two.

He stopped strumming just long enough to look up at me with those half-lidded eyes that never quite lost their bardic mischief.

"It's all right again," he said, voice raw but filled with something almost like wonder. "I can finally hear the music."

He blinked. "And for once, it doesn't sound like a bag of cats being slammed against a wall."

The sound that escaped my throat was half-laugh, half-sob.

Calina choked out a noise, burying her face in his hair as she shook with laughter-or maybe relief.

Tulip cracked a grin. Dayna rolled her eyes. Rurik chuckled under his breath like the sun had risen just a little earlier than expected.

And Frosty? Frosty climbed into my lap, curled himself into a tight little ball, and let out a satisfied sigh like he'd been waiting for this moment of calm.

The music continued—soft now, familiar, full of love instead of loss. A memory not trapped, not painful. Just true.

I didn't realize I'd stood until my knees straightened and the quiet wrapped around me like a coat too light for the cold. The music faded behind me—not gone, just dimmer now, like it had done its job and was content to linger. My boots crunched softly over ash and leaf litter as I crossed to the center of the circle, the place where Finnian had stood. Where he'd burned bright and then vanished like smoke into the wind.

I reached into my pocket. The token was still there. Still warm, like it remembered the shape of his hand more than mine. I turned it over slowly in my fingers—

just a small, worn metal disc. Dented. Unremarkable. Except that it wasn't. Not really.

Not to him.

She'd given it to him once. A princess surrounded by splendor, plucking a scrap from the trash and turning it sacred with a smile. He'd held it through everything and carried it like a prayer stitched into his chest.

And maybe he hadn't known how to say goodbye.

But maybe he didn't have to.

I looked up at the stars, the drifting motes of light still swirling where he'd gone, and felt something shift inside me.

This wasn't mine to keep.

I stood again and stepped carefully into the circle's center, back to where Rurik's sigil glowed faintly in the dirt. I knelt, heart thudding, and held the token between my palms for one last moment.

"You always said it was worthless," I murmured. "But you knew better, didn't you?"

I smiled, soft and uneven. "Maybe she's waiting for you now. Maybe you can finally give it back to her. Or you can share it."

A tear slid down my cheek. I didn't wipe it away.

I placed Finnian's talisman in the center of the sigil, nestled where his spirit had gone. It shimmered faintly in the starlight, like it remembered her voice. Like it could still echo back. And echo it did... a final vestige... Not from her but from *him*. An atonement.

> *Wind blows from my home*
> *Carrying with it, the snow.*
> *Flakes fall around me.*
> *Safe, I gather them to me.*
> *To protect them from the heat.*

Then I sat back beside the others and watched the sky.

And for the first time since we left Briarhaven, I felt something that hadn't stirred in me in a very, very long time.

Peace.

The quiet didn't press in this time. It wrapped around us, gentle and complete, like the final note of a song that knew not to overstay its welcome. Around me, no one spoke. Tulip and Dayna leaned into one another, armor loosened, heads bowed. Calina had tucked herself against Gaaron, one arm across his shoulders while the other reached for mine. Rurik sat like a monk in prayer, calm despite the weariness I knew was burning him from the inside out. And Frosty... Frosty was curled in my lap again, warm and impossibly soft, humming faintly like the world hadn't just cracked open and stitched itself shut again.

And above us—the stars.

They burned brighter than they had any right to. They'd seen what we did and were already setting it into a constellation. A halfling with a dagger. A dragonling humming lullabies. A broken bard finding his way home. They weren't just lights in the sky tonight.

They were witnesses.

I looked up and let my heartbeat slow. Let the air fill my lungs without the weight of battle on every breath. Let myself believe, just for a moment, that we had made something out of all this mess. Something worth surviving.

"We did it," I whispered. Maybe to them. Maybe to myself.

No one answered.

They didn't need to.

"We really did it."

28

It was over. Somehow, impossibly, we'd completed our quest.

We'd survived. Well, *mostly*.

I still wasn't sure how to breathe around it. My body kept waiting for the next ambush, the next betrayal, the next impossible thing that needed doing.

But there wasn't one.

All that awaited our tired, triumphant party was the long road home. And so that's what I did my best to focus on—the here and now, not the done and dusted. I quieted my thoughts and listened to the uneven clomp of boots, hooves, and feet against dirt and scattered stones, the creak of old straps, the whispers of shifting weight, and the heavy silence of just sheer survival.

Beside me, Dayna marched steadily, almost mechanically, her presence a calm gravity I didn't dare disturb. Ahead, Calina and Tulip walked woodenly as Frosty gamboled like a much-too-large puppy, sending up clouds of dust and snow with every enthusiastic bounce.

I should have felt relieved. Triumphant, even. I knew how hard-won our battle had been, and I was so very proud of us. And yet...

Even now, my heart remained a mess of tangled vines, threatening to choke out any emotion that dared to reach for the sun.

Whenever I closed my eyes, even just to blink, Finnian's furry, masked face flashed before me. Sometimes I was greeted by the wry, infuriating smirk he wore when plotting something ridiculous; sometimes the raw, broken creature who'd knelt in the dust and begged me to end it. No matter his mask, he was always there, waiting to greet me.

I still couldn't believe he was really gone. In truth, he'd been the one constant in my life, even when I spent more than a decade avoiding him. And all this time, he hadn't been the monster I'd assumed, nor was he the savior he once saw himself as. At the end of his journey, the tanuki master thief had just been a person.

He'd been someone who'd hurt deeply, loved fully, and clung to hope in the worst way imaginable.

Respect, anger, gratitude, grief... They all knotted together inside me in a way no sword or spell could ever cut free.

Finnian Sly had shaped me. I couldn't deny it, even if I wanted to. His betrayals, lessons, and stubborn belief that survival was an art worth mastering were stitched into the very fabric of me. I didn't much care for that, but I also couldn't change it. But maybe I didn't have to forgive him to honor the pieces of good he'd left behind.

I exhaled slowly, the chill of early morning catching on the edge of my breath.

"Thinking dangerous thoughts again?" Dayna murmured.

I tipped her a sideways glance. "Always."

Her mouth twitched into something that almost but didn't quite constitute a smile. I relished the sight all the same.

We walked in companionable silence for a few minutes, the dusty golden fields stretching wide on either side. We were veering away from the river now, and it felt odd to leave it behind as we headed for the mountains that marked the way home. The sun hovered low, smearing soft orange light across the cracked dirt.

Finally, Dayna spoke. "You know, when I was younger... I thought I could fix it if I fought hard enough and smart enough. All of it."

I tilted my head, curious. What was she going to say to me? And why now?

She shrugged, eyes distant. "The world. The corruption. The men who thought cruelty was currency." A humorless chuckle slipped out. "Turns out, you can kill a hundred monsters, but there will always be more waiting in line."

"That's cheery," I said dryly. I couldn't tell whether this was meant to comfort me about Finnian or to communicate something important about us.

"Yeah, well." Dayna's mouth turned down. "I gave up trying. Figured I'd do the job, take the coin, keep my head down. Maybe I wasn't fixing the world, but at least I wasn't pretending anymore."

My brow furrowed. "But now?"

"Now," she said, nudging me lightly with her wrapped hand, "I think I was wrong twice. You don't fix the world by being better than everyone else. You fix it by being better *with* everyone else. One act at a time."

I chewed on that for a long moment. Small acts. Small kindnesses. Small rebellions against despair.

Hope, not heroism.

That was the answer, but why was she giving it to me? Why now?

"Okay," I said slowly. "But that definitely sounds like something you read carved into a prison wall next to a tally of how many guards someone shanked."

Dayna's grin finally spread across her face. "If it was, I never noticed. Guess the kids taught me something, after all."

I bumped her back with my shoulder. "Scary thought." I didn't quite understand what she was telling me, but I was happy all the same. She was sharing the things that mattered, the lessons.

Ahead, Tulip threw a stick into the field. Frosty bounded after it with a trilling noise that could only be described as draconic glee. Calina laughing, said something to Tulip, who laughed in turn.

I slowed, letting my gaze linger.

Tulip and Calina had been at each other's throats once. Brash pride clashing with aching loneliness. And now they moved in sync, like a party, like a family, like *friends*. Neither had changed. Calina still stalked around like a lioness ready to pounce, and Tulip still barreled through the world like a sparkling battering ram, but somehow they had found a way to fit together. Huh, I hadn't seen that one coming.

Frosty galloped back, proudly presenting not the stick but an entire armful of wildflowers snagged from a ditch. Tulip accepted them with great ceremony, bowing low while Calina giggled so hard she nearly fell over.

A lump formed in my throat, unexpected and stupid.

Not long ago, they'd asked if Frosty would ever grow as big as Cindara had. The answer was no. He'd live a full life, a natural one—small by dragon standards, but whole. Cindara had never been given that chance. She'd been twisted into something monstrous by a master who must've seen her as a weapon, not a creature. Not a soul.

But there was Frosty, living his life fully, a scrappy little dragon flouncing through a patch of weeds like they were treasure, free, ridiculous, alive. For a moment, I pitied the dragon that nearly ended us.

In the end, she hadn't killed us, and I wasn't about to take that continued life for granted. Not for Frosty, not for any of us.

I turned slightly, catching Rurik and Gaaron trailing behind. Gaaron still looked like he'd clawed his way out of a grave—thin, pale, missing a hand—but he was upright, his steps steady if slow. Which was an improvement over Rurik having to carry him on his back. And *no one* was going to make the mistake of asking Tulip to carry him. And Rurik... Rurik had a book open, scribbling notes with one hand while occasionally steadying Gaaron with the other.

"—and if you look here at how the healing spell works to close the wound," the half-orc wizard explained, "there should be a way to adapt it to actually regrowing a severed... Hmm, but the bone issue is still there. I think I read something in your early work about a phantom hand of sorts—"

Gaaron made a soft sound of skepticism.

Rurik grinned. "Right, that wouldn't hold flesh. But you know, you survived years of Maltherius. I'm sure you can handle a couple experiments to get your hand back."

Gaaron's mouth twitched. "You sound... determined. I might even say, bold. But definitely at least a bit concerning."

"Somebody has to figure out how to fix what got broken. It might as well be me."

I swallowed hard at that. Yes, Rurik, why not you? Why not now? The kid was awkward and strange, but he'd always known exactly who he was, even when others had told him he was wrong. He'd still managed to find a way back to himself, a way to not only be seen, but celebrated. I could learn a lot from Rurik. In fact, I already had.

He called toward Dayna, his toothy grin sharpening. "I could fix your eye, too, if you'd let me."

Dayna didn't even break stride. "You put one hand near my face, kid, and I'll nail your spellbook shut with your teeth."

Rurik paled slightly, wisely falling silent. A moment later he raised a hand to stroke his healed tusk, caressing it as if to promise he wouldn't let the mean old mercenary hurt it again.

I hid a smirk and glanced between them. Might and magic. One was never guaranteed to beat the other, especially not when Dayna was involved.

Her hand found mine again, the gesture casual but grounding. I squeezed back, heart doing a ridiculous little skip.

The trail curved gently through the lowlands, the river's shimmer now fully out of sight, its music faded into memory. The hush it left behind felt heavy—the world was holding its breath, waiting to see who we'd be without a quest to complete or a battle to fight.

We walked on, not speaking and not needing to.

Ahead, Frosty rustled through a patch of dry grass and came up with a mouthful of burrs and something that might've once been a rabbit. Tulip and Calina dissolved into giggles and coos as they deburred the poor dragon.

Rurik muttered something about "needing more time to think" and snapped his book shut. Gaaron hummed low under his breath, something tuneless but real. Still tired, still healing—but here.

I let the sound of it all wash over me.

Boots. Breath. Laughter. The soft creak of leather, the rhythm of living.

Not surviving. Not escaping.

Living.

Oh, sweet divinity, I still had so much more of that to do.

We walked for days after that.

Through scrubland and shadow, over windswept grasslands and aching stone. We avoided all major towns and villages, sticking to the wild and each other. The monotony wore at us until all that was left was breath, blister, and the quiet, stubborn promise of forward.

No more battles. No more monsters. No distractions. And no stops at the abandoned town in the mountain pass.

Just the long ache of living—of returning—one step at a time.

And then, finally, as the last rise gave way to open sky, I saw it.

Briarhaven.

The rooftops leaned like old friends waiting to welcome us back. Chimney smoke curled lazily into the early afternoon air. No doubt Bramble Thistledown's baking. As the sun poured over the town, chasing the shadows away, it felt like we'd stepped into our own little fairytale hamlet. It felt like I had lived a thousand lives since I'd seen it last. And it had never looked so good before.

"We made it," Calina said, nudging Tulip with her shoulder.

Tulip grabbed her and pulled her into a hug. "We're almost home!"

Frosty shrieked and flapped a few feet into the air, tumbling sideways into a patch of brittle weeds. He emerged proudly with a stick, another burr stuck to his snout like a badge of honor.

Rurik didn't look up. He was still lost in thought and half muttered words formed in his mouth as he considered some magical conundrum. Somewhere in the strangeness of his mind. For him, that had always been home.

But Gaaron had stopped moving entirely. His eyes locked on the town, jaw tightening. His breath hitched once, then again, and then he spoke on the exhale. "Brynlee."

All he said was her name. That's all he had to say. His voice cracked down the middle. Tears welled up in his eyes, silent and unshaken. He didn't wipe them away, didn't try to hide.

I swallowed hard again. We'd completed our adventure. We'd won. So why did I constantly have to fight back tears?

Ahh, dear, sweet Brynlee.

I'd be glad to see her, too. Of course I would. She was part of my past, part of the old story, and she'd still be a part of my future, too. But I didn't ache for her the way he did now, the way I had once before.

Because I already had what I needed. I had her right beside me, hand tightly holding onto mine. *Dayna.*

She wasn't looking at the town.

Her gaze was fixed on a field just off the road— wild sunflowers, tall and tangled, their faces tipped to the sun like they knew how to survive anything.

"They were always my favorite," she said, quiet but clear.

I blinked up at her. "Sunflowers?"

She nodded. "They always turned their faces to the sun. No matter how heavy the storms."

I hesitated, then stepped into the grass and hacked one off with my dagger. The stem gave with a crunch and slapped wetly against my pant leg. I came back holding it like a crooked offering.

"Here," I said.

Dayna took it gently. Her fingers brushed mine. She smiled, soft and unguarded, like something inside her had finally let go.

"This is one of the only things I've ever been sad to see killed," she whispered.

"The flower?"

"No." Her eye swept the field. "The part of me that believed in things like this."

I swallowed against the lump rising in my throat. "Then I'll bring you more," I said. "Every storm. Every season. You'll always have flowers."

Her hand found mine. Strong. Sure. No walls left between us.

We stood together at the town's edge, while Tulip and Calina joked with each other, Frosty flopped, and

Gaaron cried in anticipation of his reunion with the woman he loved.

And I... I just held on.

To Dayna. To this moment. To the ridiculous, stubborn fact that we'd made it.

We started down the path to the bridge.

Suddenly, unexpectedly, I stopped.

It wasn't dramatic. No gasp or stagger or big revelation. Just one foot caught on a stone's edge and dragged mid-step, the way it never should have for a rogue of my fluid and dexterous nature. I stumbled, barely recovered, and stood frozen, staring at the rooftops waiting ahead—familiar, battered, impossibly real.

Briarhaven.

It felt like a dream, what I'd hoped for so long to return to.

And I couldn't move.

Not forward. Not yet.

Because this wasn't just a return, it wasn't slipping into a familiar inn with my hood pulled low. It wasn't a whispered identity at a tavern door or a safehouse, stolen bed, or even a rented moment of stillness on someone else's map.

This was home.

Not a mission. Not a cover story. Not a place to disappear.

A place to exist. A place that was mine.

For the first time in my life, I had a home. And that thought gripped me by the heart and wouldn't let go.

I wasn't Tilda the rogue, the thief, the liar. I wasn't the coward who lost Calina's dad or Brynlee's love. I wasn't the villain I thought myself all those years ago. I wasn't a hero, either.

I was just... *me.*

And that felt—oh, sweet divinity, it felt like someone had set off an avalanche behind my ribs. I realized I was clutching Dayna's hand hard enough to leave a mark.

"Quickthatch?" she asked, voice low. Steady. "Talk to me."

"I can't just walk in," I said, too sharply. My voice cracked like dry wood. "I can't just pretend it's normal. That I can go down there and be whatever this is now."

Tulip, still breathless from her victory whooping, turned. "Uh, Tilda. Why did you stop? Are you okay?"

Rurik glanced up from his spellbook, silent but with a perplexed expression.

Calina slowed, brow furrowing, lips pursing as if preparing to ask a question.

Gaaron wiped his face with his sleeve, blinking like he'd just realized I wasn't beside them anymore.

I stood there like a broken hinge, holding the pieces of myself in both hands, afraid to push them forward.

"It's not a disguise anymore," I said, quieter now. "It's not a job. It's not borrowed. It's me. I don't know how to be me without something to fight."

There was a pause.

Then Dayna said simply, "You already are. *We* already are."

I turned toward her. She wasn't smiling. She wasn't even trying to fix me. Just there, firm and real and impossibly still.

"This place doesn't need you to fight it," she said. "It just needs you to show up."

I breathed in—slow, ragged.

Calina took a tentative step back toward us, eyes bright with worry. "You don't have to prove anything anymore. We've already done it. We're already heroes."

"You get to be who you are," Tulip said, gently, but firmly. "Not who everyone else expects you to be."

Rurik tucked the weathered journal into his satchel, and said, "You're allowed to be whoever you want to be, Tilda, even if that's not the same person you were before. You're allowed to be happy, even if you don't yet know how."

Gaaron, soft-spoken and still shell-shocked, offered a quiet nod. "You brought us home. All of us. This is your home, too."

The wind stirred the sunflowers.

Dayna squeezed my hand. Just once.

And the knot in my chest began to loosen.

The masks were gone.

This was real.

Terrifying. Beautiful.

Mine.

I looked at the crooked rooftops, the plastered walls, and the well-trod planks of the bridge.

And then I took the next step forward.

29

The path into Briarhaven wasn't marked by grand gates or polished stone. Just that small, familiar footbridge that rose over the stream and the lopsided sprawl of homes that looked like they were huddling together against the next hard winter.

It was perfect.

We trudged into the village, kicking up little puffs of dust with every step, our ragged shadows stretching long across the square. It was the second half of the day, which meant most villagers were busy with work or otherwise engaged in their routine activities.

Even still, we'd hardly made it two steps into town when a bright figure came sprinting toward us out of nowhere. Of course, it was Brynlee. She came running down the main path, skirts flying, hair unbound, barefoot and reckless as a summer storm.

I stared for a second, stunned. How had she known? Some whisper of magic, or maybe just the impossible gravity of love pulling her to the right place at the right time.

Calina let out a half-sob, half-laugh and surged forward to greet her mother.

Brynlee crashed into her like a wave hitting a cliff, gathering her daughter into her arms with so much force that it knocked the breath from both of them.

"Oh, my star, my little star." Brynlee peppered Calina's hair and cheeks with frantic kisses, barely pausing for breath. "I've missed you—I've missed you so much—"

Calina wriggled, laughing and half-crying, trying to free herself. "Mom! I'm not a baby anymore!"

"You'll always be my baby," Brynlee insisted, hugging her again before letting her go.

Calina pulled back, cheeks flushed, grinning despite herself—and that was when Brynlee finally looked up.

She went completely still. Her gaze locked on Gaaron, standing a few feet behind us, pale and worn and trembling from the weight of everything that had been and everything he still carried.

The whole square seemed to hush, the wind itself holding its breath.

Brynlee took one step forward. Then another.

Gaaron's voice cracked the silence, low and raw.

"I stayed alive for this moment," he said. "It wasn't always easy, but it was always, always worth it."

Brynlee let out a garbled sound—a gasp, a sob, a laugh—and then she ran the last few steps into his arms.

He caught her like he'd never let her go again.

They held each other so tightly, I wasn't sure where one ended and the other began.

"Your hand," she mumbled tearfully, and I couldn't tell whether she was crying more from joy or pity. "You only have one now. Your music. How will you play?"

Gaaron pulled back just enough to rest his forehead against hers. "This?" He raised the stump of his wrist and flashed a debonair smile. "It's nothing more than a flesh wound. My spirit is finally whole again, and my heart is overflowing with love. That's all I need to make music. Besides, the orc kid says he can fix it for me, so don't worry. It's not at all important."

Brynlee laughed through her tears, nodding wordlessly, one hand tangling in front of his tunic, as if she had let go, the world would break again.

Behind me, Dayna shifted, her arm brushing mine, a silent reminder that sometimes the world *didn't* break. Sometimes it bent. Sometimes it healed.

They stayed locked together for a long moment—Gaaron and Brynlee—until Gaaron finally eased back, brushing a stray curl from her tear-streaked cheek like he couldn't believe she was real.

"We made such a wonderful kid," he murmured. "Such a stubborn, brave, brilliant kid. We made her, and you raised her. I love her. I love you. I love that we're all together again. At last."

Brynlee laughed softly. "Oh, Gaary. She's so much like you, you know."

Gaaron blinked.

Brynlee cupped his face in both hands. "Not just the adventurer's spirit. Not just the stubbornness. She's got your heart. Your way of seeing the good, even when the world tries to grind it out of you."

Gaaron made a helpless, broken sound.

Brynlee grinned and pulled Calina into another hug, tighter this time, and for once, Calina didn't squirm away. She just held on.

Gaaron stepped closer, uncertain at first, his hand hovering like he wasn't sure he had the right anymore.

Calina turned without hesitation and reached for him too, tugging him into the circle of her arms.

And just like that, they were all three tangled together—past, present, future—breathing the same ragged air, anchored to each other like the world might tilt again at any moment, and they had no intention of being torn apart.

"I love you," Calina said, voice muffled against Brynlee's shoulder. "I love both of you. I'm so happy we're together again."

Gaaron drew a raddled breath against her hair. Brynlee tightened her grip so hard Calina squeaked, but didn't pull away.

"I always knew you could do it, Calina. I always knew you'd succeed at adventuring. I'm so, so proud of you." Brynlee pulled back just enough to look at them both. Her cheeks were flushed, her eyes shining with emotion that didn't even try to hide. "I can't believe you found your dad and brought him home to us. You really are a hero, my sweet, little girl."

Calina scoffed and jabbed a finger lightly into her mother's chest. "Me? No way. You're the greatest hero I'll ever know."

Brynlee laughed through her tears—a rough, cracked sound—and shook her head helplessly. "What? How am I the hero? I didn't go off to fight monsters or rescue bards. You did all that."

"No," Calina said, smiling through her tears. "But

you stayed. You fought real life. You fought for me. Every single day."

She pulled both parents in again, fiercely, stubbornly, like she could weld them together with the sheer force of her will.

And for a heartbeat longer, none of them let go.

Dayna nudged my side lightly, and when I glanced at her, I noticed something suspiciously shiny in her one good eye. Not that I was going to call her out on it. Unlike Gaaron, I didn't think I could survive very well without both my hands.

I turned to find Brynlee watching me now, still holding Calina close like we might vanish again if she let go. Her eyes sparkled, the beginnings of a smirk tugging at one corner of her mouth. Then she noticed Dayna's hand in mine. More specifically, the bracelet encircling Dayna's wrist—delicate, valuable, unmistakable. The same gift Brynlee had given me at the start, the one I passed to Dayna as the end drew near.

We'd passed it back and forth in quiet moments throughout the journey, never talking about it, always slipping it onto the wrist of the one doing the holding. It felt like a promise, or maybe a question we were still too scared to ask out loud.

Brynlee tilted her head, eyebrows lifting in faux-academic curiosity. "That looks suspiciously like a gift I once gave a very stubborn halfling."

Dayna raised an eyebrow at me. "Is that so?"

Brynlee's gaze flicked between us, and then she grinned. "Well, it looks even better on you."

The heat rose to my ears so fast that it was a miracle I didn't burst into flames on the spot. Dayna smirked and gave my fingers a deliberate squeeze. Absolutely *no shame whatsoever*.

"You know," Brynlee said, laughing, "I always did have excellent taste. It seems Tilda does, too. I whole-heartedly approve."

"Thank you, Your Majesty. I'll add that to my glowing list of accidental achievements," I managed to quip despite the intense embarrassment that had taken hold.

Brynlee laughed again, and the sound lifted something heavy from my chest that I hadn't even realized I was still carrying.

For a long time, I'd thought maybe I loved her. How could I not? Sweet Brynlee, with her easy smile and patient heart, her way of making even a half-feral rogue like me feel like maybe I wasn't beyond saving.

But standing there now, watching her radiant with happiness, reunited with the love she'd refused to let go even when it seemed he had abandoned her, I realized what I'd really been chasing.

It wasn't romance. It wasn't even rescue.

It was *connection.* Something real. Something that lasted. And my closest friend in town had been the easiest target for all that misplaced longing.

I'd wanted to belong.

And here, hand-in-hand with Dayna, I finally understood the difference between reaching for something safe and *finding something true.*

I squeezed Dayna's hand back, my throat tight in the best, stupidest way.

Brylee's smile softened. She tugged Calina closer, like she couldn't bear even an inch of space between them.

"Keep the bracelet," she said. "As a gift. It's nothing next to what you all have given me."

I blinked. "Bryn—"

"You brought him back," she said, voice thick with feeling. "You brought her back safe. You gave me back my family." She brushed a kiss against Calina's forehead. "And you gave me the sweetest words a mother could ever hear."

Her smile trembled, but didn't break.

"I'm not sure there's a gift in the world big enough to repay that."

I opened my mouth to say something clever or sarcastic or, failing that, just vaguely not-embarrassing.

Nothing came out.

Because there wasn't anything clever enough for this. Just an intense, messy gratitude blooming hot behind my ribs, too big and wild to put into words.

So I did what any self-respecting gal would do: I grinned like a fool, squeezed Dayna's hand again for good measure, and vowed silently to make sure none of them ever regretted letting me be part of this ridiculous, beautiful life.

For a moment, everything was still—just the fragile, golden aftermath of reunion.

Then the thunder of hooves shattered it.

I spun, instincts kicking in faster than reason, one hand flying to where my dagger used to live.

A whole swarm of centaurs galloped into the square, hooves kicking up fountains of dust, banners trailing from their spears, ribbons streaming from their hair.

At the head of it all, radiant and utterly unstoppable, Tulip's mother, the mare mayor.

She drew up in front of us with a theatrical rear and a flourish of her braided mane, scattering petals and dust in every direction.

"MY PONY!" she bellowed, voice carrying to the

farthest rooftops. "MY BEAUTIFUL, TRIUMPHANT PONY RETURNS!"

Tulip visibly flinched, her ears burning so red they could've outshone the sun.

"Hi, Mom," she muttered, trying to shrink into the cobblestones.

Tulip's father trotted a step behind his wife, wearing an expression approximately three degrees past resigned. Their servant Jonquil flanked the mayor's other side, apparently this was a good enough reason to leave the host's stand at the Stable unmanned, at least for a little while.

Before Tulip could bolt, her mother leaned down and cupped Tulip's face in both hands, inspecting her like a prize melon at the market.

"Intact!" she cried. "Victory shines upon you, my sweet filly! We must hold a celebration! A *grand festival* at the Stable! A feast for the ages! Musicians! Storytellers! Cakes taller than the temple spires!"

The words tumbled over themselves, building into an unstoppable tidal wave of enthusiasm.

Tulip's face had gone from red to nearly purple.

Out of the corner of my eye, I caught Frosty, who had never met this particular brand of chaos before, screeching in terror and launching himself into the air, wings flailing.

He scrambled upward like a panicked cat, claws scratching along the side of a building until he managed to wedge himself, trembling, atop a crooked roofbeam.

Calina groaned and immediately scrambled after him, climbing the trellis like she'd done it a hundred times, muttering curses the whole way.

The villagers who'd gathered to watch the spectacle parted hastily to let her through, half-amused, half-terrified.

Meanwhile, Tulip's mother continued her monologue, oblivious to the airborne dragon emergency that was happening twenty feet away.

"We shall commission new banners!" she declared. "We shall invite the bards from Mirathane! We shall—"

Tulip finally held up both hands, palms out. "Mom. Whoa."

Her mother blinked, disoriented like someone yanked off a charging horse mid-stride.

Tulip took a breath. Squared her shoulders. She looked smaller standing there, but somehow steadier too.

My heart ached as I watched. Not because Tulip faltered, but because I remembered the words Tulip had once confided at a campfire, voice low and bitter:

They don't care about me. Only what I represent. Only how shiny I look when the spotlight's on.

Maybe absence had made the heart grow fonder. Or perhaps this was just another excuse to throw a party and bask in borrowed glory.

Either way... Tulip deserved better.

Tulip *was* better.

"I'm happy to celebrate," Tulip said, voice careful. "But it's not just about me. It never was. We all came back. Together."

Her mother's mouth opened, then closed again, confusion twinkling across her stunningly gorgeous, immaculately made-up face.

Tulip forged ahead, cheeks burning, eyes bright. "I want the party to be for *everyone*."

Her father, bless him, gave a quiet, approving snort behind her.

"And maybe..." Tulip lowered her eyes to the ground before lifting them to meet her mother again. "Maybe we could hold it at the Mystic Mug instead? There's less chance of... You know..." she waved vaguely at the horse manure smell wafting over the square, "festive aromas."

The mayor hesitated, visibly struggling with the death of her grand equestrian procession fantasy.

But after a long, weighty pause, she gave a regal nod.

"If that is your wish, my pony," she said, dramatically clasping Tulip's hands. "Then so it shall be."

Tulip blew out a shaky breath, relief and disbelief warring on her face.

Before she could escape, though, Jonquil cleared his throat pointedly.

"Aren't you going to introduce your... companions?" he prompted with a little too much innocence. I was pretty sure this was one of the first times I'd ever heard him speak Common instead of the huffs and chuffs that made up the strange and confusing Centaurian tongue.

Tulip's eyes widened in abject horror.

"Oh, right," she croaked. "Um. Mom... this is Rurik. My, uh... boyfriend."

The square fell silent.

Even Frosty, perched awkwardly on the rooftop with Calina halfway up the side of the building, seemed to freeze.

Rurik, gods bless him, stepped forward with a bright, earnest smile—and promptly doomed himself. "My condolences," he boomed, bowing deeply, "for Amariel's passing."

Tulip's mother gasped so sharply I thought she might inhale half the square.

"What?!" she cried, clutching her chest with one hand like she'd been physically stabbed.

Tulip whirled toward Rurik, expression somewhere between horror and betrayal.

"Suh-suh-sorry. I thought she knew!" Rurik cried out, wild-eyed.

"How could she have possibly known? It happened when we were away," Tulip moaned, cradling her forehead in despair.

I stepped forward, raising both hands. It meant letting go of Dayna's hand, which I didn't love, but I knew I could take it back again after the situation was diffused correctly.

"Could everyone just relax?" I said quickly. "Amariel loved her peace and quiet, so let's honor her memory by talking about this calmly. It's true. She's passed on, back to the celestial realm. But—" I caught Tulip's mother's flaring nostrils and pressed on— "But while she's no longer with us, she continues to affect us all here. Through the people she helped. Through the legacy she left behind. Especially through Rurik, actually."

Tulip's mother swayed in place for a moment. Then, slowly, she straightened, head held high.

"Then we shall mourn her properly," she declared, voice shaking only a little. "We shall honor her spirit with celebration. With joy. She would not want grief to steal the homecoming she made possible. Besides, she was really, very old. It's not that much of a surprise."

Tulip's hand slipped into Rurik's, her fingers curling tightly around his.

And somehow, impossibly, the moment's chaos settled into something almost... solemn. Despite his awkward social graces, Rurik had inadvertently done himself a favor by revealing Amariel's departure from the mortal realm. He'd taken the heat off his newly revealed relationship with Tulip, which meant he'd have time to better strategize his next encounter with the haughty centaurs, another chance to convince them he belonged... or at least that he wasn't going anywhere.

Everything seemed to hang suspended for a moment—the storm of hooves, the swirl of dust, the laughter and tears, and the thousand things left unsaid.

Two families, pieced back together.

Brynlee, Gaaron, and Calina, had engaged in an embrace years overdue.

Tulip, red-faced but smiling, standing under the watchful, adoring chaos of a mother who cared more for the story than the soul—and still, somehow, cared.

And somewhere between all that noise and celebration, something quieter bloomed.

Dayna's hand reclaimed mine.

No grand speeches. No sweeping declarations. Just the simple, stubborn fact of her being there. Of us being *here*.

It was enough—more than enough.

I glanced sideways and caught Rurik glancing around the square, trying to hide it.

His eyes scanned every face, every doorway, every knot of gathered villagers.

But there was no sign of his family.

I saw the flicker of hope fade around the edges of his expression, even if he tried to mask it with a tilt of his chin and a quick, studious glance back to the journal he'd pulled out again.

Up near the trellis, Calina clambered back down, arms full of squirming, wide-eyed Frosty.

The little dragon flapped his wings frantically as she stumbled into the square, laughing.

Tulip's mother gasped, hand clutched to her ample bosom.

"By the stars above!" she cried. "What *is* that majestic creature?"

Calina struggled to control Frosty, who kept trying to twist around and preen for the growing audience.

"A baby frost dragon," Calina chirped, adjusting her grip as Frosty's tail knocked over a flower pot.

Tulip's mother's mouth fell open, then snapped shut into a sharp, calculating smile.

"How rare!" she exclaimed, eyes practically glowing with mercantile delight. "How *valuable!* We must have him at the celebration! Just imagine the attention! The prestige!"

Frosty honked proudly and accidentally slapped her with his tail.

Tulip covered her mouth to muffle a laugh. Calina wasn't as successful.

Through it all, Rurik stood a little apart from the clamor, hands tightening and loosening against the journal, trying not to look too obviously at the empty road.

No parents rushing forward.

No cheers.

Just the absence where someone should have been.

I crossed to him quietly, touching his arm. "They just didn't know you were coming yet," I said. "That's all."

He nodded, too fast.

I waited until he looked up at me, those bright, brilliant eyes full of everything he didn't dare say. "And even if they don't come running," I added softly, fiercely, "you're enough all on your own, kid."

His breath caught.

"You're the best of us," I said. "We couldn't have done this without you. Without your magic. Without your heart."

His throat bobbed once. Twice. Then he squared his shoulders and nodded.

Having escaped Calina's arms again, Frosty swooped low over our heads with an indignant squawk, scattering petals, dust, and something that might have once been someone's laundry.

Rurik laughed at that, and so did I.

Across the square, Tulip's mother was already planning to outfit Frosty with a floral garland and parade him through the Mug like a conquering hero.

Dayna shook her head beside me, amused and exasperated in equal measure.

"You're not half bad at this whole mentoring thing, Quickthatch," she murmured.

"Don't let it get around," I muttered back. "I've got a reputation to uphold."

30

The music reached us before the tavern did—bold and brassy, spilling through the winding streets of Briarhaven like it couldn't be bothered to stay inside. Laughter chased after it, bright and reckless, mingling with the smells of smoke, roasted meat, and a night too full of joy to be contained by walls.

We'd taken a few hours to rest and freshen up while Tulip's mother and my old friend Durgan busily worked to prepare our homecoming festivities. And now we rounded the last corner through town and came upon the Mystic Mug, blazing like a beacon.

Lanterns swung drunkenly from every rafter. Streamers tangled in chaotic bursts overhead, half falling down already but somehow making the whole thing feel more alive. The crowd was everywhere, pressed into the street, leaning out windows, perched on crates, hooting, clapping, and stomping in time with the music.

The centaurs clustered outside in rings, hooves tapping to the beat, laughter booming in rhythm with the drums. I hadn't seen so many of them gathered in Briarhaven since the Centennial Centaurian Festival the week before we all left, before everything broke.

This was like that, only wilder. Louder. Joyful in a way that hurt, because it was real.

Our whole ragtag little party paused just shy of the tavern steps, momentarily caught in the flood of golden light. Rurik and Tulip walked ahead, heads bent close in easy affection. Gaaron and Calina strolled beside Brynlee, locked in animated conversation about something musical I didn't understand but loved hearing anyway. They all looked tired, rumpled, alive.

And me? I was walking hand-in-hand with Dayna as she clung to the sunflower I'd gifted her just outside town.

I kept sneaking glances at her, which was idiotic, but I'd earned that right. I wanted her to see this town as I saw it now—messy and magical and so very worth staying for. I wanted her to feel what I felt when I entered this light. Like maybe home wasn't a place you fled from or fought for. Maybe it was a place you chose. Maybe it was a person. Maybe even me.

Above the door, the old Mystic Mug sign swung lazily in the breeze, its corners battered from too many storms and too many thrown mugs. Durgan had hung it from the haft of his old battle maul—the one that used to shatter bones and now held up joy instead. He hadn't lifted that maul again. Not even when I asked him to, he'd chosen this life: love, stability, Pat, and the stubborn, beautiful business of staying.

And for the first time, I finally got it.

My chest ached in that stupid, swelling way it always did when something mattered too much. I looked at Dayna again.

She caught me. One eyebrow arched. "Sentimental?"

"Always," I muttered, then elbowed her lightly. "Slap the sign. It's tradition."

She looked up at the hanging plank, then at the maul holding it. Something like respect flickered across her face. Instead of reaching up, she turned to me with a grin far too smug for my own good. Then she picked me up.

"Hey!" I squawked as my boots left the ground. "Put me down, you unrepentant showoff!"

"Not until you do your part," she said, utterly unbothered.

Laughing, heart thudding too bright and too fast, I slapped both palms against the sign like I was high-fiving the whole town for surviving, just like we had.

A cheer erupted from inside, wild and muffled. Dayna set me down with exaggerated care, though her hands lingered a beat longer than they needed to.

"Consider it properly blessed," she said.

"You're ridiculous," I mumbled, cheeks aching from grinning.

"You're welcome," she replied, and sauntered inside like she already belonged.

As a rule, in all proper villages, magical or not, gossip moves faster than a hummingbird can blink, so news of our return and various bits and bobs of our adventure arrived before we did.

The cheer that went up when we stepped through the door was deafening. The whole blessed town was there. Voices shouted our names from every corner. Tankards thudded on tables. Someone started playing a fanfare on a kazoo, wildly off-key and completely perfect.

"Our guests of honor at last!" Durgan roared from behind the bar, slapping a keg so hard the tap popped loose and sprayed the nearest elf with foam. "Our conquering heroes return!"

It was chaos in the best possible way: blurry with motion, glowing with magic, warm with welcome. I tried to take it all in, to spot familiar faces in the crush, but I barely took two steps inside before—

"*Tilda! Rurik! Calina!*" a voice thundered, as a golden blur hurtled toward us like a runaway wagon.

Before I could brace, I was intercepted by eight and a half feet of overexcited half-giant, cheeks flushed, curls bouncing like he'd styled them for this exact moment.

Pat.

I blinked up at him, up being the only possible direction when faced with Pat in height.

"Uh, what?" I managed.

"I see my work has kept you alive," he bellowed, vibrating with giddiness. "You all look mostly intact. But I have to ask, did I hear properly that one of the daggers I made for you took off Gaaron's hand? I can only assume you need better lockpicks."

He looked so happy he might burst.

"What?" I gasped with feigned indignity. "Gaaron did that to himself."

"Yeah, but he's also right," Dayna said in that

deadpan way of hers. "You need better lockpicks. Metal is too pliable."

Calina, ever the escape artist, had already skipped off into the crowd, trailing laughter like fairy lights.

Rurik stepped in beside me, calm and steady, the battered metal shield cradled under one arm. He offered Pat a quiet smile, the kind that held weight.

"The shield helped," Rurik said, fingers tracing the dents and battle damage.

Pat beamed so hard I swear the rafters glowed.

But then Rurik shifted his shield forward, offering it with both hands. Steady. Deliberate. It had often been forgotten during our journey, but Rurik had brought it tonight to return it to the man who had forged it for him.

"This—" he said, "—this meant more than you knew."

Pat blinked. Confused, maybe. But listening.

"I know why you gave it to me," Rurik continued, voice pitched just loud enough to carry over the din without demanding silence. "Because you know what it's like. Being half one thing, half another. And you wanted to protect the part of me you thought would break first."

Pat opened his mouth, then shut it again, clearly unsure of what he could possibly say to all this. He was probably still inwardly obsessing over his steel-tip arrow prototypes and their current lack of feedback.

Rurik smiled again, broader now. Fierce in a way that lit up the room.

"But I'm not half anything," he said. "I'm one hundred percent me. And that's stronger than any shield you could make."

He placed the shield in Pat's massive hands like he was returning a sacred relic, then turned and strode into the crowd, no hesitation or doubt.

A little breathless, I watched as he slipped his arm around Tulip's waist and pressed a quick, laughing kiss to her temple like it was just another part of his day. Like he belonged.

Pat stared after him, shield clutched to his chest, mouth slightly open.

"Well," he said at last, voice quiet with wonder. "Clearly, he's gone through something and come out better for it. No idea what the particulars are. Probably don't want to know, either."

"Safer that way," I agreed cheerfully.

Pat grunted, staring at the shield like it might start talking if he stared hard enough.

Then he brightened. "Still gonna want to hear the story. How everything held up, performed, issues, improvements. I'm also interested in your friend's swords there."

"Of course you are," I muttered, and shouldered my way into the glowing chaos of the Mug, pulling Dayna and her flower after me.

Cheers erupted like fireworks. Someone knocked over a chair. Frosty dive-bombed from the ceiling rafters with a delighted screech that sent half the tavern ducking for cover.

Outside, hooves stamped the ground in celebratory rhythm—Centaur applause.

Tulip's mother, resplendent in a new floral sash that matched absolutely nothing, clambered atop an overturned crate and flung her arms wide to a crowd of onlookers.

"Behold!" she cried, one hand sweeping grandly toward her daughter. "Our brave Tulip! Slayer of shadows! Defender of light!"

Tulip groaned, covering her face with both hands. "She's been rehearsing, I just know it."

"And this!" her mother shouted, pivoting to point both arms at Frosty, who had perched awkwardly on a windowsill like an anxious gargoyle. "The rarest of beasts! The heroic drakelet! Gifted by fate itself!"

Frosty blinked and sneezed, launching a shower of frost that turned the edge of a curtain to an icicle.

"He's so proud of himself," Calina murmured, after popping up behind me, her voice fond.

Then, across the room, Brynlee stepped out from behind the bar, holding something gently in her arms. A mandola. Old, polished wood. Familiar as breath.

Gaaron's eyes widened. For a heartbeat, he looked like he might cry.

"I kept it here," Brynlee said softly, almost apologetically. "Just in case you ever came back. Or—" her voice faltered as she glanced toward her beloved, "—just in case someone else wanted to play."

She didn't say the rest out loud: *In case he didn't. In case he couldn't.*

One of Gaaron's hands was gone now, taken not by Maltherius, but by his own will. He'd stolen my dagger and severed it himself in the moment he chose us over the necromancer's command. That hand had once coaxed lullabies from strings, had danced with melody. But in the end, he'd offered it up without hesitation.

And for a bard, that was no small thing.

Ten years, he'd been imprisoned—robbed of song, of freedom, of the simple act of strumming comfort into the silence.

Then came the curse. Maltherius's control twisted

his mind until the music inside him quieted. He couldn't hear it. Couldn't feel it.

And now?

Now he stood near the bar, tankard tucked against his ribs in his remaining hand, face unreadable but too still to be at peace. Even free, even whole in spirit, the music remained out of reach.

He was a bard without a song—a musician with no way to play.

Unless...

Calina nudged Rurik gently. Her voice was soft, but sure. "You've been studying this for weeks. It doesn't have to be perfect. Maybe it just has to be now."

Rurik froze like she'd smacked him between the eyes with a spellbook.

Tulip stepped in, bumping his arm with a warm grin. "We all know you can do it."

Rurik looked down, brow furrowed. "I haven't tested it. The theory's solid, but—"

Gaaron turned toward them with an amused tilt of his head. "I've played with worse odds."

Rurik swallowed. "Are you sure?"

"I chopped off my own bloody hand," Gaaron said dryly. "I think I can survive a magical prosthetic."

That earned a ripple of laughter, nervous and fond.

The tavern quieted just enough to let the moment breathe.

Rurik stepped forward, exhaling slowly and steadily as he lifted his hands. Words spilled from his lips—quiet, precise, careful. Arcane energy shimmered into being, swirling around Gaaron's wrist like mist catching the moonlight.

Light gathered, cool and blue, weaving itself into a translucent shape. A hand. Ghostly. Luminous. Waiting.

Gaaron stared at it. Then, slowly, flexed the phantom fingers, testing their shape, their balance, their reach.

And then he reached for the mandola.

Brynlee passed it to him like it was sacred. Gaaron cradled it in both hands—one flesh, one fluttering spell—and held it close for a beat, as if steadying something inside himself.

Then he played.

The first few notes were hesitant. Uneven. The ghost hand twitched, adjusting with each new string. But the sound was there. Real. Whole.

And then it bloomed.

A melody spiraled upward, soft and plucky at first, then gaining strength—growing rich and layered and utterly alive. The ghost hand moved fluidly now, guided not by nerves but by will, by memory, by music.

He played like someone remembering how to breathe.

Not perfect. Not polished. But full of heart. And that made it whole.

Durgan appeared beside me, scratching his beard. Then he gave his ear a slow, deliberate tug.

I blinked, surprised—and then grinned—our old signal.

"Come on," he said, jerking his chin toward the back corner. "Back room."

He led me past jostling villagers, through laughter and noise and a haze of warm candlelight, until we found a quiet pocket behind the barrels of ale and mead.

"Wasn't sure you'd come back," he said.

"Wasn't sure of that myself," I admitted.

He nodded once, eyes kind. "You alright?"

I hesitated. Thought about it. About everything.

And then I nodded. "Yeah. I think I am."

He studied me a beat longer, then grunted his approval.

"The past can haunt us, Tilda," he said. "But it can't possess us. Not unless we let it. I'm glad you finally exorcised yours."

I nodded and exhaled slowly, keeping my eyes fixed on the many baubles that adorned my old friend's bushy red beard. There was a new bead nestled into its coarse strands. Was that one for me?

I was just about to ask when the dwarf elbowed me lightly and jerked a thumb toward the bar. "Don't get comfy. You're on the morning shift tomorrow."

As we returned to the front, the laughter and conversation around the Mug swelled, wrapping around me like an old, familiar cloak. I drifted back toward the hearth where Gaaron and Calina were still holding court with Brynlee perched beside them, soaking up every word like sunlight.

"And then," Calina was saying, her hands animated, "Finnian Sly, master thief and underworld mastermind, himself showed up, flanked by wing scouts, like some sort of vultures."

"And Maltherius was, of course, just ahead of him," Gaaron added, voice grim but steady. "Dragging that poor broken dragon with him."

Brynlee's hand flew to her mouth.

"We didn't run," Calina said proudly. "We stood together even when it was awful. Even when..." Her voice caught. "Even when Dad had to—"

She faltered, and Gaaron gently reached across

with his shimmering ghost hand, curling spectral fingers around hers.

"I chose," he said simply. "And I'd choose it again."

Brynlee's face crumpled and smoothed all at once, pride and pain warring across her features like weather on stone.

"And now Rurik's already crafted that magical hand for him," Calina said, a little breathless with hope. "He's even researching how to make it permanent. Maybe better than new. With runes and everything."

Gaaron chuckled, the sound soft and real. "Wouldn't be the worst souvenir."

They smiled at each other—a little awkward and a little offbeat—but finding their harmony, one note at a time.

Across the room, Tulip clinked her mug against Rurik's, laughing as he nearly dropped it trying to keep hold of her hand.

"It's nice," she said loudly enough that half the tavern could hear, "seeing everyone together. Centaur, halfling, elf, human, *everyone.*"

There were a few awkward coughs from the older villagers—a few sidelong glances from the centaurs huddled near the windows.

Tulip raised her mug higher, daring anyone to

argue. "It's going to stay that way," she said firmly. "Starting with the Stable."

Rurik grinned at her like she hung the stars herself.

Somewhere, I hoped Amariel was watching. She'd be proud of her charge, proud of all of us.

"And speaking of the Stable," Tulip added, winking at him, "first official date's already booked."

More cheers. Some ribald whistles from the centaur contingent.

Tulip's mother chose that moment to reclaim the spotlight.

She stomped both front hooves sharply, sending a thunderclap of sound through the tavern.

The conversation stumbled to a halt.

She tossed her mane dramatically and bellowed, "In honor of our victorious youth, it is my profound pleasure to announce the founding of the *Briarhaven Adventurer Academy!*"

A ripple of surprise, followed by confused clapping, spread across the room.

"To further the glorious tutelage of my darling Tulip," her mother continued grandly, "and, coincidentally, to qualify for a generous royal tax break!"

Standing stoically behind her, Jonquil gave a slight cough that suspiciously resembled a laugh.

"And!" she added, sweeping an arm toward me

with a flourish that nearly knocked over a candle, "to ensure only the finest instruction, Tilda Quickthatch shall be its headmistress!"

I almost inhaled my drink.

Dayna, standing suspiciously close, pounded me on the back with far more amusement than medical concern.

The Mug erupted into a wild, uneven roar of approval.

Even Frosty, perched on a rafter, flapped his wings and sent a puff of glittery frost raining over a startled gnome below.

I turned to Dayna, still coughing. *"What just happened?"*

She smirked, that familiar glint of danger and affection lighting up her face.

"You got voluntold," she said. "Congratulations, Headmistress."

Nope. Still didn't make sense.

Why in all of Verandel would anyone want *me* to run an academy?

I was a halfling who sometimes forgot to tie her boots the same way twice. I was good at taverns. Good at knives. Good at surviving.

I wasn't good at standing in front of a room pretending I knew what I was doing.

I gripped the edge of a table, hoping it might anchor me to the floor. I tried to nod. Tried to smile. Mostly succeeded in looking like I'd swallowed a fork sideways.

And then—mercifully—chaos arrived right on cue.

A crash. A thud. A distinctly comical honk.

Heads whipped around just in time to see Frosty teetering atop the bar, front paws braced on either side of a tankard as he buried his snout in it and started lapping with the gusto of a dragon who'd just discovered fermentation.

"Is that—" Dayna started.

"Frosty discovered the mead!" Calina called out, fully horrified and proud.

Before anyone could stop him, Frosty lifted his head with a mighty, frothy belch that echoed off the beams.

There was a moment of stunned silence.

Then—*hiccup*. A crystal shard zipped across the room and embedded itself in the rafter.

I yelped and ducked as another icy dart whizzed past my ear.

A third missed the barrel of spirits by a whisker.

"Frosty, no!" Tulip cried, lunging toward him.

Too late. Another hiccup. Another honk. A flurry

of glittering icicles exploded from the dragonling's snout, sending the tavern into gleeful disarray.

Villagers scattered. Centaurs reared. Someone shouted for shields, and Pat eagerly produced the one Rurik had just given back.

With a theatrical wail, Tulip's mother flung herself behind a table. "Protect the academy headmistress!"

I ducked under a flying shard, heart still thumping, and locked eyes with Frosty, now hiccuping snow flurries and looking deeply pleased with himself.

"You are cut off, mister," I snapped.

Frosty slumped sideways on the bar, exhaling a puff of cold that knocked over two mugs and froze a tray of sweetbreads solid.

Dayna caught my arm as I stumbled back, laughing harder than I meant to—part nerves, part sheer absurdity.

Her grip steadied me. Her voice, low and close against my ear, cut through the din like a lifeline.

"This whole headmistress thing. You're allowed to panic about it," she said gently. "Just not alone."

I opened my mouth to argue—to deflect, dodge, spin some line about how I was fine, thank you very much—but she didn't give me the chance.

Dayna grabbed me by my shirt collar and spun me around so fast I nearly tripped over my boots. She leaned in, close enough that her breath stirred the hair against my temple, and said very firmly, "Be quiet."

And then she kissed me. Not cautiously. Not like a question. But like a declaration.

Her hands slid into my hair, grounding me with quiet ferocity, and her mouth met mine like she knew exactly what she was doing—like she'd waited long enough, and so had I.

The noise around us didn't stop—Frosty hiccuped, a chair overturned, someone shouted something about runaway cheese—but it all faded into the background, hazy and distant, like we'd stepped outside time for a minute or two just to exist here. Together.

Her lips were warm, confident, a little chapped from wind and weather. I curled into her like she was gravity, like she was shelter, like I hadn't known how badly I needed this until she gave it to me.

There was nothing tentative in the way she kissed me.

She wasn't testing the waters—she was naming the storm. And for once, I didn't flinch.

I melted.

I let her in. I let it happen.

Because, dear sweet divinity, I was allowed to be happy.

When we finally broke apart, I was breathless in the best way—like I'd just remembered how lungs worked, like the world had clicked into place around this quiet truth.

Dayna was still close. Still steady. Still mine.

Frosty was hiccuping upside down in a barrel of mead, Farmer Dewglen was chasing a glowing wheel of cheese across the floor, and Brynlee was laughing so hard she had tears streaming down her cheeks.

But me?

I was still kissing her.

Even if our mouths had parted, I was still kissing her—with the shape of my heart, with the steadiness of my feet, with the choice I'd finally made.

And at last it felt like freedom.

I leaned back just enough to see her face, still flushed with mischief and meaning. "So... the academy," I said, breath catching on the words. "Do you really think we should do this?"

Dayna didn't hesitate. "Only if we do it together," she said. "Only if we make it ours."

She exhaled, long and slow, giving me a moment to take in what she had just said before speaking again. "My wings are gone," she said softly. "Time to put down roots."

She met my gaze. Steady. Unflinching. No masks,

no edge. Just her. "We could shape the next generation. Raise them to be better. Real heroes."

Not the kind we'd had. The kind who'd know how to *stay*. To protect instead of destroy.

"There's just one problem." She tilted her head, smirking. "For this to work, we'll need students. Got any orphans stashed somewhere?"

Actually, I did.

I did have orphans stashed somewhere.

A whole gang of them. Back in Mirathane. Sticky-fingered, wide-eyed little nightmares that Finnian had half-raised between cons and card games, like his version of doing penance.

They weren't perfect. But gods help me—they were mine now.

I swallowed hard as the thought tightened in my chest.

Finnian.

He was gone, but this part of him didn't have to be. The best of him. The part that believed broken things could still be sharpened into something better.

Somebody needed to look out for them. Might as well be me.

I turned to Dayna, my voice quiet but solid. "I'm going to get them. The Mirathane kids. Finnian's crew."

She arched an eyebrow. "The pickpocket squad?"

"The future first class of Briarhaven Adventurer Academy," I said, trying not to laugh.

Dayna gave a low, approving hum. "Going to be a hell of a graduation ceremony."

"They'll probably steal the stage," I muttered.

We stood there for a moment, just watching the chaos unfurl around us—a seemingly sentient cheese wheel glowing faintly as it spun in lazy circles on the floor, Frosty now passed out with a mead barrel clutched between his claws, Calina braiding flowers into Tulip's tail as Rurik looked on like she was creating high art.

I leaned into Dayna's side. She didn't move away.

Around us, the people we'd nearly died for—and with—were laughing, dancing, living.

My found family. My ridiculous, brave, broken, beautiful family.

The masks were gone. The lies were buried. The past was quiet.

And the future?

For once, it felt like mine.

The End

When a lonely forest gnome makes a desperate wish to the goddess for someone who truly understands her, she doesn't expect to wake up with a telepathic wheel of cheddar rolling around her pantry.

Now magically tethered to a snarky dairy product with more charisma than she'll ever have, she's been drafted into the ancient art of Wishcraft—tasked with uncovering the secret desires of her neighbors and somehow making them come true.

Between divine pop-up windows, cryptic magical quests, and a cheese companion who clearly thinks *he* should be in charge, she's starting to suspect that being seen was only the beginning of her problems.

The Wheel Deal is the first book in **The**

Wheyfinder's Guide to Wishcraft, a whimsical new Cozy Fantasy LitRPG series from Luna Ryder packed with magical errands, found-family feels, and one extremely opinionated wheel of cheese.

Make sure you're signed up for Luna's newsletter, so you don't miss the release announcement.

When real life feels a bit too crazy, you can always find comfort in the fantasy realm!

Yup, this feels like the exact right time to send you the first of my monthly slice-of-life stories starring Durgan Stoutbarrel, dwarven tavern owner and everybody's favorite guy.

I hope you'll enjoy learning more about his backstory and witnessing the meet cute with his half-giant husband Pat.

I'll write a new story about Durgan each month and deliver it exclusively to my newsletter subscribers. It's my version of giving you a warm, mead-drenched hug. *Awwww.*

You can sign up at www.LunaRAuthor.com/ subscribe to start reading the first delicious slice-of-life instantly. Enjoy!

WANT EVEN MORE?

If you loved this book and want to go deeper into the world of Verandel (or just collect shiny things), here are two ways to keep the adventure going...

SHOP THE LEGENDARY LOOT

Signed books. Special editions. D&D campaign adventures. Swag fit for a Chosen One (or a tavern wench with good taste).

Find it all at my official shop:
www.LunaRyderBooks.com

JOIN THE SECRET SCROLLS SOCIETY

Want to:

- Read new books *as I write them*
- Unlock exclusive lore and magical backstory
- Vote on plot developments and future projects
- Possibly become a character in a future book?

Then my Patreon is the place for you:
www.patreon.com/LunaRauthor

Your support helps me keep telling stories that are gloriously weird, queer, and chaotic... and I'd love to have you along for the ride.

Thanks for reading. Stay strange. Stay brave. Stay bard to the bone.

— Luna

ACKNOWLEDGMENTS

When you reach the end of a trilogy, you realize two things.

One: Writing books is a weird, exhausting, exhilarating magic trick.

And two: it takes a whole dang village to keep pulling rabbits out of your hat.

So here's to the ones who made this book, and this ending, possible...

To my kiddo (whose preferred name is now Vincent), thank you for being a daily reminder that it's never too late for a new start, or to discover who you were always meant to be. Watching you become more *you* each day is one of my life's greatest joys and inspirations. These books echo you in every chapter, in every character who dares to defy the world's expectations and define themselves on their own terms.

To Dayna, who not only beta-read the heck out of this story, but also *is* this story in so many ways. We wrote side by side, swapped plot twists over meals at my favorite restaurant, and she cheered me on every time I threatened to kill someone off. (Spoiler alert: she never told me no.) Dayna lent me her name, spirit, and beautifully ruthless instincts—and Tilda's ending wouldn't have worked without her. She's not just *my* Dayna. She's *our* Dayna now.

To Crystal, editor of my soul, slayer of ellipses, and sometime therapist when the words refused to behave. And to SJ Gautreaux, whose bold, high-concept covers gave these books their striking visual identity and whose original title helped shape the soul of the entire trilogy. Your art didn't just decorate the story. It inspired it.

To Luca Strati and Lucy Loo, the illustrators who truly brought the characters to life. I kept your drawings beside me daily while writing, and it felt like my party was right there with me, looking over my shoulder, eager to see how things turned out. I like to think they approved.

To my incredible ARC team: those beautiful gremlins who scream in caps lock and quote me to myself like I'm not just winging it 90 percent of the time. And to the Kickstarter backers who quite literally funded the dream. You gave me the power to finish this story exactly how it needed to end. You are forever part of this world.

To my dogs: Sky Princess, my mainstay muse and four-legged therapist, and her backup bark brigade, who offered moral support and just enough tail thwaps to keep me on schedule. And to the cats, who knocked over just enough stuff to keep me limber and blocked my keyboard whenever I forgot to rest. You're jerks. I love you.

To every reader who stuck it out, especially those who started with *When Life Gives You Legends* and are now blinking in disbelief at the end of *Bard to the Bone*. You didn't just read this story. You lived it with me. Thank you.

And finally, if you ever feel like the world is too dark, too twisted, too far gone... show up anyway. Justice is real. Hope is stubborn. And you're allowed to win, even when you've been broken.

Weird little heroes can save the world, too. Just ask Tilda.